———————— ★ ————————

She dismounted quickly, tied the pony to the bush and pushed aside the lower branches to see what damage the girl had sustained.

When she saw, she stood frozen for perhaps half a minute. For another half minute she concentrated on what she was seeing, in case someone came by and disturbed the scene after she left. The gaping wound in the throat, ear to ear as before. The denim jacket pulled halfway down her back, imprisoning her arms. The putty-colored jodhpurs down to her booted calves. She was a child, not even as old as Charisma, and she was dead.

———————— ★ ————————

Also available from Worldwide Mystery by
JO BANNISTER

A BLEEDING OF INNOCENTS

Forthcoming from Worldwide Mystery by
JO BANNISTER

NO BIRDS SING

Jo Bannister
Charisma

WORLDWIDE®

TORONTO • NEW YORK • LONDON
AMSTERDAM • PARIS • SYDNEY • HAMBURG
STOCKHOLM • ATHENS • TOKYO • MILAN
MADRID • WARSAW • BUDAPEST • AUCKLAND

CHARISMA

A Worldwide Mystery/October 1997

First published by St. Martin's Press, Incorporated.

ISBN 0-373-26253-1

Printed in U.S.A.

Charisma

I

ONE

THE MASTS ROSE out of the shadows of Broad Wharf like the upperworks of a schooner, higher than the surrounding warehouses. The dock bustled with more activity than it had seen in fifty years: the throb of generators, the rumble of tractors, heavy boots splashing through a layer of greasy dirt, men's voices affronting the Sunday morning with orders and curses in a variety of gruff accents.

Like the skin of a great whale, grey and wrinkled with age, the canvas lay along the ground. Cables led from the baling rings to the mastheads and down to three small ancient tractors. Lighter ropes, still as much as a man could handle, led from the shoulders of the tent to a row of giant pegs driven into the wharf.

At a bellow from the ganger the men stood back. They knew the routine and also the risks: a snapping cable would whip back with enough force to disembowel a man. Snorting like plough-horses the tractors took the strain. By degrees the ropes tightened. The blocks creaked, the masts groaned; the great rings stirred against the timber. The canvas began to rise.

People all around paused to watch. People whose journeys had taken them near the canal stopped their cars; some took photographs.

Before the canvas was up and the cables secured men were waiting on the shoulder ropes. There wasn't much wind but the thing was as high as a tithe-barn: it caught whatever air was moving and bellied out, testing the strength and the skill of its handlers. Men fought the weight of it to fasten the guys, then again to tighten them until all

the free play that let it flap and beat like a bad-tempered
seagull was controlled. Finally it looked like a tent.

A big tent.

Among those watching on the wharf were an old man
walking a Jack Russell terrier and a young man on a motorbike. 'Circus coming to town?' asked the old man.

'Too right,' growled the young one.

The old man beamed. 'I haven't been to the circus since
I were—' He waved a hand not much higher than the dog's
head to indicate extreme youth. 'I wonder if they'll have
performing bears. Do you think they'll have performing
bears?'

'They sure as hell have one,' grunted the young man
sourly. He kicked his machine into deep throaty life, turned
his back on the spectacle and rode off into the May morning.

It was only when the old man and the dog ambled over
to ask the roustabouts if they really had a performing bear,
and if they did cheap tickets for pensioners, that he found
out it wasn't a circus at all but a gospel mission being
conducted by the famous Welsh revivalist Rev Michael
Davey.

FRANK SHAPIRO sat at his desk, surrounded by paperwork,
surrounded by cups containing half an inch of cold coffee
each, listening to lugubrious bells chime from the smoke-
black tower of St Jude's Waterside, knowing that most of
his friends and colleagues were at home with their families:
playing with their children, grooming their cats, looking for
the missing wheel off their golf trolleys.

Yet a surprised observer would have recognized that
curve of the lips between the strong nose and the double
chin as a smile of pure contentment. Detective Chief Inspector Shapiro didn't mind spending Sunday morning in
the office speeding the progress of burglars, muggers and
street-corner cannabis dealers through the machinery of the

law. He was counting his blessings. CID was about the only department of Castlemere police which hadn't been turned upside-down by the imminent arrival of God's right hand disguised as a Welshman in a white suit.

Uniform were laying plans for crowd control—Ha! thought Shapiro. In Castlemere? They really thought they were going to have to deal with throngs of Castlemere faithful fighting their way into a gospel mission? Traffic branch had little maps up on the wall showing how they could reroute different quantities of pilgrims at different times of day so as to avoid bringing the town to a standstill. Even the traffic wardens were in on the act, detailed to direct visitors to the designated car-parks; though Shapiro had heard, and had no difficulty believing, they had also ordered extra pads of tickets in happy anticipation.

But CID were not involved. He was aware that there would be incidents: if anything like a crowd assembled there would be dippers to work it. Since the average turn-out for a religious meeting in Castlemere was four old ladies, two old men and Mavis Spurge who wanted to be a nun, Shapiro was disinclined to cancel all leave on the strength of it. He confidently expected the Michael Davey Gospel Crusade would be one of the great non-events of all time, was actively looking forward to seeing egg on the faces of colleagues who had no choice but to treat it as a major happening.

Because the hype preceding the arrival of the Big Top—if they called it that; perhaps they called it a Succoth, Shapiro thought with a malicious grin—could hardly have been greater if Rev Davey had organized the Second Coming for nine o'clock on the first night and the Third Coming for nine o'clock the night after. For a month no billboard, no building-site hoarding, no gable-end in town had been safe from the posters. They showed a broad-shouldered, middle-aged man with a shock of white hair and expensive teeth, wearing a white suit. The backdrop was a city nightscape with the street-lights contrived to give him a halo. The first time he saw that poster Shapiro thought it crude, vulgar and sensationalist. If anything, he liked it less now.

So he sat alone in his upstairs office, savouring the eerie quiet of a town-centre Sunday, and thanked his lucky stars that all he had to deal with were thugs, thieves and the occasional murderer, and crusading preachers were somebody else's problem.

DISAPPOINTED, THE MAN with the Jack Russell turned away from the great tent now straining its ropes on Broad Wharf and ambled along the tow-path towards Cornmarket.

In the heyday of the canals narrowboats coming in from the north joined the Castlemere system east of town to avoid the congestion in Mere Basin. Traffic jams were nothing new here. Those who thought the occasional spats between pleasure-boaters and anglers lowered the tone of the place should have been around when bargees were cutting one another's ropes and nobbling one another's horses in the race for cargoes.

When the railway came the station was built on open land along the northern spur to facilitate the transfer of freight. It was then the most dynamic part of Castlemere, with frenetic trading in corn and other goods. But after the canals waned most trains went through Castlemere without stopping, and when the railways declined in their turn the big lorries by-passed the town altogether. Cornmarket that began as wasteland and reigned for a time as the *de facto* heart of burgeoning industrial Castlemere returned quietly to neglect. In the 1960s a passenger halt was built nearer the town centre. Freight yards where old rolling-stock went to die and a cracked, abandoned wharf almost a mile long were all that remained of the glory days.

But every cloud has a silver lining. A derelict wharf is the ideal place to exercise a Jack Russell terrier: there's almost nothing still intact for them to damage. The man, whose name was Herbert Pendle, and the dog, whose name was Mary, walked beside the canal with the big old buildings of Castlemere shrinking slowly behind them and the empty space of Cornmarket opening ahead.

Herbert was brooding on the callous way he'd been misled. He'd been looking forward to seeing a performing bear. Herbert had no time for the modern notion that bears belong in mountain forests not circus rings. It was his experience that people like what they're familiar with and he saw no reason why bears should feel differently.

When Mary let out a low growl his first thought was that she was agreeing with him. If the proper place for bears was mountains, he pondered, what was the proper place for Jack Russells? Was there a chapter of Animal Liberationists meeting in a Castlemere cellar right now planning to set Mary free? Mary's idea of a walk on the wild side was coming in wet and finding her towel in the laundry.

But the little dog growled again, tugged at her lead and wouldn't walk on when Herbert did. She was on the edge of the tow-path staring at the water, and her hackles were up.

HALF AN HOUR earlier the clatter of china from the hall would have drawn an urgent enquiry from Liz Graham. Now she only gritted her teeth and carried on decanting a tea-chest into the kitchen cupboards. She had passed beyond panic, beyond concern for earthly things like how much of her mother's dinner service lay in sherds on the parquet flooring. She'd chosen to move to Castlemere in the furtherance of her career, now she had to deal with the consequences. She winced. With a dustpan and brush, by the sound of it.

The thing that amazed her was how smoothly it had gone so far. She and Brian had talked for four days, then decided to do it. His enquiries about vacancies for art teachers in Castlemere met with three expressions of interest and, before the month was out, a firm offer. Their house sold quickly despite the recession, and while they were awaiting completion they found this place: a nineteenth-century farmhouse with a two-acre paddock and a stable. The house needed some work but nothing they couldn't tackle themselves. Or rather, nothing Liz couldn't tackle. Brian Graham the art teacher underwent a crisis of confidence when faced with a brush more than an inch across.

Liz could pin-point the precise moment at which organized endeavour turned to chaos. It was when Donovan came to help. It was a kind thought, he meant well, but he wasn't very careful. He stacked the crates in teetering towers in the sitting-room and dropped the chandelier in the bath.

Telling herself it was all insured, even against cack-handed Irishmen, she wondered if it was because he wasn't used to houses. Verticle walls, high ceilings, floors that stayed still and enough space to swing an obliging cat probably confused him. Donovan lived on a narrowboat on the canal, he ducked going through doors.

The telephone rang. She couldn't remember where it was, tracked the sound to the dining-room, opened the door just in time to see Donovan answer it. Irritated, she stuck her hand out.

He shook his head. 'It's for me.'

'What?!'

'Shapiro. I told him I'd be here.'

The voice growled at them out of the phone. 'Detective Chief Inspector Shapiro, Sergeant Donovan. My apologies to Inspector Graham, but would you tell her I need you both back here—I've got a body in the canal.'

TWO

'WHO IS SHE?'

Death the Leveller had worked his magic again. She hadn't been in the water long enough for her flesh to begin dissolving and her features to blur beyond recognition. But the manner of her dying had stripped away clues by which she might have been identified.

Immersion in the Brown Windsor soup that was Castle Canal had ruined her clothes so that they told little about her. All Liz could say for sure was that she'd been wearing a short black skirt, a white blouse and a short red PVC jacket. Presumably she'd been wearing shoes too but they were missing, rolled off her feet by the patient gentle movement of the water or lost in the struggle.

For there had been a struggle, if only a brief one. A button was torn off her blouse violently enough to rip the flimsy fabric. Liz hardly expected more. There's a limit to how long anyone goes on struggling with her throat cut back to the spine.

She'd have been wearing make-up too, in all probability, that would have helped form an impression of the sort of person she was, the sort of life she led. But it had washed off. Under the weedy scum that had settled across her face like a veil when they pulled her out her skin was the bluish-white of skimmed milk. Sometimes the victims of violence die with pain and terror etched indelibly on their faces, but this girl had no discernible expression. Long dark curly hair clung to her shoulders in rat-tails, but whether it was the ruins of an expensive cut or just how it grew was hard to judge. Death the Leveller had reduced her to something anonymous.

A few hours ago, at the most a couple of days, she'd been a living girl, warm and quick, aged probably between fifteen and eighteen years. Like most teenage girls she would have alternated bursts of mercurial activity with spells of lethargy. Her family—she must have had some family though no one had reported her missing—would have despaired of ever holding a sensible conversation with her; they would have worried about her schoolwork and her friends, how she spent her allowance and how she'd ever make her way in the world when all that seemed to interest her were pop music and boys.

And now she was gone, switched off like a radio that was making too much noise, and the people who cared would be denied the privilege of worrying about her ever again. If they were strong and lucky they would grieve until the grief turned to sorrow; if not, the same slash of blade that ended her life would destroy them too, drowned not in blood but in bitterness.

'She called herself Charisma. I don't know her real name.'

Liz had forgotten she'd asked. She eyed Donovan blankly. 'You knew her?'

He shrugged. The dark clothes he favoured emphasized the narrowness so that he looked like a black heron shrugging. 'Everyone on the canal knew her. This was her beat. She was a tom.'

Startled, Liz looked again at the white face, at the young figure still padded out with puppy-fat. She wasn't wearing tights. Liz had thought nothing of it: it was spring, she was young. But perhaps the real reason was the professional girl's awareness that time is money. 'She's a child!'

'Yeah.'

She hadn't known Donovan very long; there was a lot about him she hadn't worked out. Certainly she knew better than to expect outpourings of sentiment. But this was a young girl and things had gone terribly wrong with her life long before she was murdered. Even Donovan's stony indifference might have cracked for that.

Irritated, Liz said, 'If she'd been peddling her wares in my street long enough for me to know her name, I think I might have done something about it.'

Donovan bristled. 'I did do something about it. I took her home. Jubilee Terrace. Her dad was dead drunk in the living-room and there was no food in the house. So I took her to the women's refuge on Cambridge Road. Next night she was back on the tow-path. I didn't see how locking her up with the rest of the toms would further her moral welfare so I let her get on with it. You can only do so much to save people from themselves, you know?'

'And that was it, was it?' Liz's voice was barbed with scorn. 'Your contribution? A ride to the women's refuge. And she still managed to go wrong after that? You can't help some people, can you?'

Donovan's eyes glittered and a muscle ticked high up in his cheek. 'I never wanted to be a social worker. Ma'am.' He added courtesies to his speech the way other men add curses, tersely, through tight lips. Anger always thickened his accent.

It had taken Shapiro a little time to come up with a satisfactory method of dealing with their squabbles but now he had adhered to it rigorously. He ignored them. At first he'd been afraid that two people who struck sparks off one another so readily couldn't do good work together. But there was no real animosity between Inspector Graham and her sergeant, they just saw things differently. It made for argumentative tea-breaks but there were advantages too. They covered different ground, were at home in different worlds; smelled out different kinds of rat. Beneath the scratchy surface lay a healthy mutual respect.

Pointedly turning his back on them Shapiro asked the pathologist, 'Was she raped?'

Dr Crowe was a large, genial young man with large, soft,

oddly gentle hands and rather long ginger hair that flopped in his eyes. He shook his head non-committally. 'That's one for the autopsy. There are no overt signs of violence— well,' he gave a rueful grin, 'apart from the obvious—but she's been in the water a while. I'll have a better idea when I've had her on the slab.'

Shapiro winced. Even for a man in Crowe's trade it was a brutal way of putting it. 'How long was she in the water?'

Again the pensive shake of the head. 'That's hard to say too. Sometime last night? But she was dead before she went in.'

Shapiro looked again at her throat. There was no blood, just the gaping wound. 'I thought she probably was.'

'I mean, she'd been dead a while when she went into the water. She was killed, she lay for some time—long enough for the lividity to be well established—on her side, then she was put in the canal.'

Shapiro's eyes slipped out of focus as he pictured it. His voice was quiet and slow. People sometimes thought, see-ing him ruminate, that his mind was slow too. Nobody who'd worked with him thought that. 'So why didn't he get rid of her right away? Perhaps he didn't kill her near the canal. Perhaps he killed her miles away, waited till it was dark then brought her here.

'So what was wrong with leaving her where she was? If she was safe there for several hours, why not for longer? Maybe it was somewhere he has a very specific association with: somewhere that if she was found we'd come straight to him.'

He was considering the philosophy rather than the facts of the murder, not for the moment concerned with strict accuracy so much as the feel of what had happened: the choreography. He had found there was a certain logic even in murder. If the account was not logical, probably the thing didn't happen that way.

'So let's say he met her on Friday night—it had to be

Friday if she was going to lie more than a few hours where
she died, none of this would take place by daylight. Maybe
they talked, maybe went somewhere to make love, then he
killed her. Then he hid her and waited. It was too risky to
move her at once. There may have been people about: it
was Friday night, maybe not long after closing time. So
either he left her where she was, temporarily, always meaning to dispose of her properly when it was safe. Or he
panicked, bundled her out of sight and took to his heels,
but later he got worrying that he should have made a better
job of it.'

'But did he? Make a better job, I mean.' Liz had lost
interest in needling Donovan when Shapiro began to talk.
She wasn't unduly modest about her professional ability but
she recognized that while he had taught her most of what
she knew he hadn't taught her all *he* knew. Any time Frank
Shapiro cared to talk she was ready to listen.

But not uncritically. 'What I mean is, when he put her
out of sight immediately after the crime she wasn't found.
When he put her in the canal she was.'

'Hiding her bought him time to get organized. To get
himself an alibi, perhaps. Once he'd done that he wanted
her off his hands.'

'It was a hell of a risk. You're saying he killed her on
Friday night, hid her and so far nobody knew anything
about it. Then last night he took her from her hiding-place
and put her in the canal. Why? It doubled his chances of
being caught. He'd need an absolutely compelling reason
to go back to her. He mustn't have had any choice.

'What if he killed her at his own house? She was a teenage prostitute living with her dad: they went to the man's
place for privacy. That means he probably lives alone.
That's where he killed her, and that's why he had to move
her, whatever the risk.'

'You don't think she was killed here then?' said Donovan, expressionless as the dead girl.

Shapiro looked at him, his eyes clearing. 'I doubt it. If she was he'd have put her in the canal right away. On the other hand, maybe she wasn't killed that far away. This was her beat, and...' He looked up the tow-path towards the distant shunting yard, down the canal to the crowded buildings of the town centre. 'It's the sort of place where people do get their throats cut,' he finished lamely.

'This may look like nowhere to you,' Donovan said forcibly, 'but there are people around, even after dark. Half a dozen of these boats are lived on. Somebody'd have seen something. If they didn't see him do it they'd have seen him walk away with blood all over him. Cut somebody's throat like that and the stuff goes everywhere.'

Dr Crowe put in his ten-penn'orth. 'Can't say for sure, but the easiest way to inflict a wound that deep and that wide would be from behind.' He demonstrated, slashing one of the big soft hands across Liz's throat. 'In which case the blood would have gone everywhere except over the killer.'

Donovan was unconvinced. 'He still had to move her. All the front of her would be covered in blood, there'd be a pool of it on the ground.' One eyebrow climbed interrogatively.

'The lads are looking,' said Shapiro, who'd reached the scene first and so organized the search. 'Nothing yet.'

'If she was killed here there'd be blood on the ground and blood on whatever he covered her with. He must have covered her or she'd have been found. She wasn't killed here. She was killed somewhere else and brought here after dark. If he drove out to Cornmarket he'd be far enough from the moorings that nobody'd hear anything, not the car and not the splash.'

Shapiro looked up and down the wharf, assessing the distances. They were a hundred metres from the nearest houseboat, half a mile from Doggett's Lock where the northern spur branched off. 'You mean she didn't necessarily go in where she came out?'

Donovan's face held a waterman's scorn. 'She'd move about a bit in twelve hours. It's not like a river where everything goes downstream but things don't stay put either. There's a lot of traffic through here, pleasure boats and the like, especially Sunday mornings. It all moves the water round, and anything in it. She could have gone in anywhere along here. But if I wanted rid of a body I'd be looking for privacy, and the quietest bit of Cornmarket is out by the junction.'

'All right,' agreed Shapiro, 'go and look. See if there are any fresh tyre marks or signs of something being dragged.' When Donovan had loped off he said to Liz, 'I suppose you know why he wants her to have been killed somewhere else.'

Liz shook her head.

Shapiro nodded at the houseboats. 'The green one is Donovan's. If she was killed here, he was probably within earshot at the time.'

They talked to the man who found the body but learned nothing more. By then Donovan had returned, looking discouraged.

'Nothing. It doesn't look like anybody's been there for days. No signs of a car; no signs of something being pushed over the edge.'

The pathologist and the photographer having finished, the crew of the waiting ambulance wrapped the body carefully and took it away. It occurred to Liz that it could have been a long time since men treated that young girl's body with respect.

'Right,' said Shapiro, briskly, when she'd gone. Like all of them he found it easier to breathe when the reason for his presence no longer physically dominated the scene. 'Donovan, try the other way, see if you can spot anything. Uniform have already looked but you're familiar with the place, you might see something they've missed. If we can find where she went in it'll be a start. Before you go, which was her house in Jubilee Terrace?'

'The second from this end. You can't miss it, it's the one with no paint.'

'I suppose,' said Liz resignedly when Shapiro said nothing more, 'that the happy task of telling a drunkard that his teenage prostitute daughter's had her throat cut falls to me.'

THREE

THE HOUSE was one laggard step ahead of a public nuisance order. Bits fell off it in high winds. The chimney canted charmlessly and could have burned the house down had anyone been rash enough to light a fire in the grate. You could smell the rot in the windowsills; broken glass in the door had been patched with a bit of cardboard box advertising a defunct brand of dog-food.

Castlemere Borough Council had a file on Philip Pierce thick enough to obstruct a main drain and heavy enough, if dropped from sufficient height, to crush the life out of a good sized rat. (Computerization came late to the Borough Council and was substantially pre-dated by its difficulties with Pierce.) The house had been his grandfather's, his uncle's and an older cousin's before it passed to him, there being no other members of the family it could devolve upon. The settlement of the cousin's estate was the last time rates were paid on it. From time to time Pierce went to prison, quite amiably, considering it a reasonable alternative. He spent a little longer inside for not paying his council tax, a fact he put down to inflation.

He had long ago had everything which could be cut off (in a civilized country) cut off: the gas, electricity and telephone. He hardly missed them. A gas cylinder supplied a bare minimum of heat and cooking, candles enough light for a man who didn't read on principle, and since there wasn't a bookie left in Castlemere who would take his bets except for cash the phone was only an irritation. He lived simply and alcoholicly on what was left of his Social Security after a begrudged portion had been extracted to pay official debts. On a list of nominees for a Citizen of the

Year Award he'd have figured rather lower than Nero and
Sweeney Todd.

All of which, somehow, made it more difficult to tell
him what had happened.

Most people are essentially the same in all the ways that
matter: no amount of money protects them from the pain
of a lost child, no depth of poverty steels them against it.
But Liz had no idea what to expect from a man so beyond
the pale of ordinary human decency that he preferred prison
to paying bills and let his teenage daughter go street-
walking rather than work himself.

The doorbell didn't work either. There was a knocker
hanging by one rusty screw: she tried that then, dissatisfied
with the result, rapped on the door with her knuckles. When
nothing happened she rapped on the window. At length she
heard shuffling in the hall and the door opened.

Philip Pierce emerged blinking, like a bear leaving its
den in the spring. In his hand there was a carving-knife.
Down the front of his old grey sweat-shirt were rusty-red
stains.

For ten seconds they eyed one another in silence. Liz's
mind split like a sunbeam meeting a prism: one half raced,
the other froze. Finally she found a voice. 'There's no need
for the knife, Mr Pierce.'

He looked at it. He looked at her. His face creased in a
slow frown. 'How do you cut a loaf then, missus—with a
spoon?'

Behind her Shapiro gave a little gruff chuckle. He nodded at the rusty stain on Pierce's front. 'Baked beans?'

'You try opening them with a chisel. They go everywhere.' The man gave a sudden raucous laugh and tossed
the pelt of black hair—the same curly black hair as the
dead girl's—out of his eyes. 'What the hell, if they was
less trouble you wouldn't enjoy them as much.' He looked
at Liz again and leered. The smell of stale cider hit her in

the face. 'What's the matter, missus? Did you think I'd killed the cat?'

Shapiro took over. 'We'd like to talk to you inside, Mr Pierce. We're police officers. I'm afraid we have some bad news for you.'

Inside, surrounded by incredible squalor, they told him. Shapiro talked and Liz watched Pierce's reactions. He didn't see it coming the way most people do. He sat on the broken couch hardly seeming to listen, inaccessible behind an expression compounded of boredom and insolence. He thought he knew what they were going to say. He thought they'd picked the girl up for soliciting. That would be bad news right enough; but if there was a fine she could pay it without recourse to him.

Shapiro said, quiet clearly and gently, 'She's dead, Mr Pierce. Charisma—that's your daughter, isn't it? She's dead. Friday night we think. She was found in the canal this morning.'

Something terrible was happening to Pierce's face behind its veil of sullen indifference. It was breaking up, slowly crumbling, like jelly left too long in a hot kitchen or a sand-castle before the rising tide. The eyes had rounded to a shocked vastness, yawning black holes that all his imme-diate universe was collapsing into. The sardonic twist of the full lips had softened to a tremble; a tiny gap between them formed a kind of question mark.

Sitting alone in the middle of the couch, fists bunched loosely either side of him with the fingers turned up like something that had died, he began to cry. Without reserve or dignity, great racking sobs that twisted his mouth into ugly shapes came out of his throat and tears spilled on to his unshaven cheeks.

Taken aback, Liz watched him through a veil woven of pity and distaste, helplessly. She didn't understand his re-action or know how to respond to it. This was a man who let, even sent, his young daughter out to sell her body.

Whose efforts to make a home for her wouldn't have convinced the RSPCA he was a fit person to keep a rabbit. Every time Charisma had closed the front door he must have known there was a good chance he wouldn't see her again. Her profession was not only the oldest in the book, it was also the most dangerous. She was a young girl and she went with men she didn't know in the dark corners of the Castlemere waterfront. Pierce couldn't be surprised at what had happened to her. If he cared, why hadn't he cared enough to prevent it?

Shapiro claimed no special insight into the human condition but he'd been in this business longer than Liz and had seen more of both its villains and its victims. He had learned to be less judgemental: however appallingly Pierce had behaved, right now he was a bereaved father. He asked Liz to find some tea.

There was none, or anything else she could make a comforting hot drink of. Finally she poured Pierce a glass of water and took him that. She had to wash the glass first.

By then Pierce had got some kind of grip on himself, enough to start answering questions as long as they were simple and repeated as necessary.

Charisma was his daughter. Her real name was Charlene: she thought the amended version was better for business. She was sixteen years old. He last remembered seeing her on Friday afternoon before she went out. She left him a fiver to buy beer and chips. He hadn't left the house since.

His eyes, red-rimmed, crept up Shapiro's waistcoat slowly, as if afraid what they might find. His voice wasn't much more than a whisper. 'Did she fall in the canal?'

Shapiro shook his head sombrely. 'No. She was murdered.'

Pierce drew a deep, ragged, shuddering breath. 'Someone pushed her in? Why? Why?'

Shapiro didn't, at least for the moment, go into the manner of her death. 'We'll find out.' The tone was reassuring but it was not an idle promise. He was not a hard man. His career had been an uphill struggle against people who thought him too soft to be a detective. But what he lacked in machismo he made up in sheer professional ability.

Liz had known policemen who considered the death of a prostitute an occupational hazard. Shapiro took a different view. A girl had been killed, murdered, in his town and that offended him. What the girl was mattered less than what the man was: a murderer at liberty in Castlemere. Shapiro wanted him as much as he would have wanted any other murderer. He meant it: if it was humanly possible he would find out why Charlene Pierce died.

She suspected Brian might have to finish unpacking the china when he arrived with the furniture tomorrow.

THE TOWPATH was to Donovan what the street in front of his semi is to the average householder. He drove along it twice a day, parked his bike on it every night. When he couldn't sleep he walked for miles along it, watching the moon in the canal, smelling the sweet ripeness of the water. If he went westward he passed through Broad Wharf where the evangelist's tent was pitched and under an arch of warehousing into Mere Basin, geographical and spiritual heart of Castlemere. If he walked east the tow-path followed the edge of Cornmarket until it turned north. To continue eastward into the quiet countryside of the Castlemere Levels he crossed the spur at Doggett's Lock, walking across the lock gate, a feat most ramblers considered dangerous even in daylight since the Castlemere Canal Restoration Society took away the handrail in order to get a new one cast.

But familiar as he was with it—with its kerbstones worn smooth by generations of mooring ropes, with its cobbled surface designed for boat-horses rather than motorbikes, with its iron furniture of rings and bollards that here were the decent shades between black and rust and in Mere Basin had been painted by the council in primary colours like garden gnomes—he had never looked at it this closely, this intently. He'd never noticed the dates cut into some of the stones that made Castlemere Canal among the earliest in the country. He'd never noticed the perfect fit of the masonry. If they did it now, he supposed, they'd use concrete and all the water would leak away in ten years.

Moving this slowly, scanning every inch, he was easy prey for the man with the Jack Russell. Herbert Pendle fell into step with him as he walked, and as he walked he complained. 'You told me it was a circus. You told me they had a performing bear.'

'I lied,' said Donovan.

Herbert sniffed. 'I suppose you think that's funny—telling lies to old men. We had some respect when I were your age. If I were ten years younger I'd teach you a bit of respect.'

Donovan broke his scrutiny of the ground long enough to look at him: not in anger, perhaps with exasperation. He said nothing. But Herbert, who had already framed his next remark about the war and the various things he didn't fight it for, among them the employment by the British police of Irish hooligans unable to keep a civil tongue in their heads, suddenly saw the bleakness in the young man's eyes and changed his mind, and said to the dog instead: 'Come on, Mary, it's time we was home.'

Donovan watched him go, his dark face creased in a frown. He got no pleasure from upsetting old men. Still less did he want to scare them—for he'd seen that look before in the eyes of people who'd started to say something to him and then changed their minds. He didn't know why. He didn't mean to intimidate people. He wasn't a violent man. He was a public servant. It troubled him that ordinary decent people sometimes looked at him and were afraid. He wondered what it was that they saw.

For a moment he thought of calling an apology after the

old man. Then the urge, which was uncharacteristic, passed and he returned instead to his inspection of the wharf.

Finally he found what he was looking for: a place where the slick of grime had been smeared at the edge as if something heavy had been put down there and then pushed into the water. There was no obvious explanation: no rungs down to the water that could have been used by someone getting into a boat, no bollard where a shaggy mooring rope could have rubbed the spot. Not even the sort of little boy who played round the Castlemere wharves would have sat in the dirt and the damp dangling his feet over the edge.

Donovan straightened and looked around him. He was midway between a day-boat and a little cabin cruiser, neither of them occupied by night, and the quiet splash of a body being let into the water by an arm or leg wouldn't have travelled much further than that. Not as far as fifty metres, say, to the first of the narrow-boats which was permanently occupied.

Donovan didn't call them houseboats: that suggested the fat families of Birmingham shopkeepers sunning themselves on deck-chairs while firmly attached to the bank. All the narrowboats in the small residential community along the tow-path occasionally disconnected their power supply, took in their ropes and set off for a cruise round the inland waterways.

Including the one tied up beyond the cabin cruiser, her steady green and black reflection in the water a tribute to Shapiro's first instinct which was to stop all movement on the canal until he was sure there was no more evidence to disturb. Not that *Tara* would have been going anywhere today. Her owner was working.

He stood beside the canal, his eyes narrowed as if to cut out the daylight, desperately thinking back to last night. He'd heard nothing. He'd been on board, he'd been reading till the early hours; the boat had been quiet, the wharf had been quiet; he'd been only fifty metres away. And he'd heard nothing. A killer had consigned the body of a girl to the water so close he might have felt the ripples of it, and he'd known nothing.

His only comfort was what the pathologist had said, that she was already long dead. He might have seen, even caught, her killer. He could not have saved her life.

It made no difference that he had been close enough to see or hear something and had not. If she'd gone into the water close to the *James Brindley* he wouldn't have blamed Martin and Lucy Cole for not knowing: he'd have understood that they had things to do with their evenings. If her killer had tramped across the deck of the *Warwick Castle* with her in his arms no one would have expected Clay Pottinger to notice: Pottinger was famous for sleeping through anything, including his own parties.

The fact that Donovan was a policeman was irrelevant. It didn't make his hearing sharper or imbue him with a sixth sense, something like a smoke alarm that went off in the presence of crime. It just meant he'd kick himself harder for missing the action, and that when he stopped there'd be somebody happy to carry on.

With only a little sigh he turned away from the boats and looked at the wharf. It was about ten metres wide at this point, lined with warehousing. The building on the right was a garden supplies centre, that on the left a timber yard. Both had their frontages on Brick Lane and now that goods arrived by road rather than by water the rear access to the canal was rarely used. They kept their dustbins in the alley between them, and often there was a skip there too or a pile of scrap wood.

An uncomfortable thought occurred to him. He began walking towards the alley just to reassure himself it was unfounded; but before he got there he knew in his heart that it was worse than he'd feared. Charisma hadn't just gone into the canal within earshot of where he'd slept, she'd spent the day between her death and her committal to the waters here too. He called over some of the searching constables to guard the marks on the quay and those he expected to find among the stacks of timber. Also he thought they'd be useful for the heavy work.

In the event it didn't take much effort. He knew what he was looking for and went straight to it: a sheet of faded tarpaulin, long past keeping the rain out but still good enough to hide something, which was bundled up and stuffed under an overhang of planks. Handling it carefully, though he doubted the bleached canvas could yield a useful fingerprint, he pulled it into the open and unfolded it gingerly.

At the first sign of blood he stopped. 'Get Mr Shapiro back here.' There was blood on the ground too. So this was where she died.

From the alley between the buildings to the mark on the edge of the canal was a direct line. Donovan walked it, a little to one side, looking for a footprint or other sign. He found nothing more. But when he straightened up and looked past the timber yard to the great canvas on Broad Wharf, he saw something that jolted him to his heels. Only for a moment, then the man was gone.

He might have been mistaken. There was nothing remarkable about him, a lean man of average height with dark hair starting to recede now he was into middle-age. Any gang of labourers would have contained two or three such, similarly attired in faded jeans and black singlet, similarly occupied in fetching and carrying. He was carrying stacking chairs from one of the vehicles into the tent.

There was no reason Donovan should have given him a second glance. Except that Donovan knew him. Was sure he knew him, would have known him if twice the thirteen years since he last saw him had passed.

'Brady!' Shock rooted him to the ground. Even with the constables' eyes curious upon him it was a moment before he could shake himself and start breathing again. Then he shook his head once, decisively. 'Coincidence? In a pig's ear.'

FOUR

'WHO IS HE?'

Like the constables, Liz was curious. Though she hadn't known Donovan long she'd worked with him in circumstances which had put a strain on them both and thought she had probably seen the best and the worst of him. He was dour and uncompromising, ruthless in pursuit of what he wanted. He was also a talented detective, dogged and perceptive. She had seen him risk his life to achieve a result. She had seen him hurt for it.

And she had not seen then what she saw in his eyes now. It wasn't just the surprise. It had taken them forty minutes to finish with Pierce and return to the waterfront; however startled Donovan had been to see this ghost from his past amid the grime of Broad Wharf that had already passed. What remained in the dark hollows of his eyes, where he may not have been aware that it showed, was a wariness bordering on fear.

'Liam Brady,' said Donovan. They were in *Tara*'s long saloon. Donovan's first instinct, as soon as he recovered from the shock of seeing Brady, was to avoid being seen by him. By now he'd rationalized this as the wisdom of letting the man think himself unrecognized. He mightn't remember Donovan as clearly as Donovan remembered him, but if he got a good look he'd know him. 'That's his real name, the one Special Branch'll have. He must have been travelling under an alias or he'd have been picked up coming into the country.'

'Special Branch?' Shapiro's voice was sharp. If he hadn't been wedged in what was essentially a beanbag he would have strode to the cabin window and peered up the wharf. 'What's their interest?'

Donovan's eyes widened, not altogether respectfully. 'With a name like Liam Brady, what do you think?—he was welfare officer for the Ulster Protestant Action Force?'

'IRA,' said Liz. The cypher slipped between her lips like a low whistle. Murder was one thing, she was trained to deal with that. Terrorism was something else.

Donovan nodded. 'All the time I was a kid in Glencurran, Liam Brady's da was the local commandant. Everybody knew it—you needed to, there were always things you needed to know in Glencurran to keep your head from getting blown off. Liam's about twelve years older than me, he was on active service'—he twitched Liz a bleak grin—'sorry, he was a working terrorist—when I was at school. The RUC used to pick him up at regular intervals; they knew what he was about, the problem was getting witnesses into court.

'They shot him once, rather the Army did. His da got him across the border and had him patched up there. For a time after that he was fund-raising in the States, and after that I don't know where he went. I never saw him again, till today.'

'I wonder where he teamed up with Reverend Michael Davey. Europe, I suppose—aren't they just back from France? There are probably worse ways for a known terrorist to travel than as an evangelist's roadie.' Shapiro looked at Donovan. 'You knew the man—how he worked, what he was capable of. Could he have killed the girl?'

'He could, no question about it.' Donovan uncurled from the low furniture with the fluid unconscious grace of a cat and padded over to the window. 'He'll have killed people before. He'd need a reason—he's not enough of a mad bastard to go round killing girls for fun—but all the same, a reason's easy come by. She worked this neighbourhood, she'd introduce herself as soon as a gang of strange men arrived. She may have seen something she shouldn't have. Whatever Brady's here for, it's not putting a tent up and passing round a plate. He's up to something. That's a lot of equipment they have: there could be anything tucked away in it.'

'What, guns?' Liz was aware of a throbbing at her temple that meant her pulse was racing.

Donovan shrugged. 'Or drugs. One thing's for sure: Brady isn't here to spread the gospel.'

'All right,' decided Shapiro, 'we can't handle this on our own. Go back to the office and get on to Special Branch. It might be as well to tip off Customs & Excise, too, in case you're right about there being more in those lorries than appears on the manifest.

'Liz, you come with me. For the moment this is still the murder of a prostitute we're investigating. Let's see what the God-botherers have to say: what they heard, what they saw. Brady won't suspect anything if we talk to them together. After all, they were parked fifty yards from where this poor kid spent yesterday wrapped in a tarpaulin. Only my sergeant was closer. Oh, don't look like that, Donovan,' he added briskly, 'nobody's blaming you. Give me a hand out of this bloody chair before I take root.'

THERE WERE SEVEN men in the road crew and they lived in a twelve-metre caravan that had the words 'Reverend Michael Davey Gospel Crusade' painted down one side and 'Face The Future With Faith' down the other in bold red letters. Liz was amused to see that the sign-writer hadn't used enough undercoat: the legend 'Mahout Hassan & His Amazing Dancing Elephants' was still clearly visible.

They'd been told to keep themselves available and were passing the time setting out chairs in the tent. There must have been five hundred of them stacked along the canvas wall. Liz considered that wildly optimistic. Castlemere wasn't the kind of town to turn out in droves for a peri-

patetic preacher. The only time a local church filled was
for a televised *Songs of Praise*.

The crew were something of a broad church themselves:
three Englishmen, including the ganger, two Irishmen including Brady, a burly Breton with a beard and a Dutch
boy. Liz jotted down all their names and didn't look up
when Brady gave his as Joseph Bailie. In age they ranged
from eighteen to fifty. Apart from the Dutch boy who was
still learning the job, they were all powerful men, their
bodies trained by hard physical labour to a state that left
gym-freaks breathless with envy. Muscles bulged in the
arms and necks of their singlets and filled the thighs of
their jeans. They made a wildly improbable bunch of evangelists.

And of course that wasn't their job. Their job was to
transport the great marquee, erect its masts, raise its canvas
and fill it with chairs. It was their job to see that it stayed
up whatever weather an ungrateful God threw at it, then
take it all down, load it in the trucks and go through the
routine again in the next town. It was a job, like many jobs,
in which periods of intense back-breaking activity were
punctuated by spells of utter boredom.

If Charisma had waited another week to be murdered
they'd have welcomed the diversion. Once Davey got to
work they'd have little to do, barring a storm or a breakage
in the rigging, but tidy the site, drink coffee and play cards.
But right now they had enough on their hands. The first
meeting was tomorrow night, by then everything had to be
ready, and they resented being held up by a policeman investigating the death of a tom.

Shapiro talked and Liz watched. Mostly she watched
Brady. Like Donovan, she had limited faith in the power
of coincidence. Perhaps even a man like Brady wasn't responsible for every crime committed within five miles, but
his history made a presumption of innocence downright
silly. While Shapiro was talking to the crew Liz was watch-

ing Brady to see if anything that was said struck chords with him.

'It seems likely,' Shapiro was saying, 'she was put in the canal last night while it was dark. We've found the place, about fifty yards from here. Have you moved your vehicles since last night?' The ganger shook his head. 'Then fifty yards from where you were supping your cocoa someone was staggering across the wharf with the body of a sixteen-year-old girl. Did anyone hear anything—a car, footsteps, a splash?' A chorus of shaking heads. 'Did anyone go outside?'

The ganger was the oldest of the crew, a broad grizzled man like a chunk of Pennine granite chiselled off for a monumental statue that was never completed. He was a Geordie and his name was Kelso. 'I went out about midnight to look at the lorries,' he offered, his voice a bass rumble like a cave-in at a coalmine. 'We've got some valuable gear, I don't want nobody messing it about.'

'Right, good,' said Shapiro. 'Was there anyone on the wharf?'

'Nobody I could see.'

'How long were you outside?'

The man gave a mountainous shrug. 'Five minutes? I walked up one side of the lorries, back down the other. Then I went to bed.'

Shapiro nodded resignedly. Even if it was true it didn't mean that the killer wasn't there at midnight. There were too many dark places to hide. There was a light on the back wall of the timber yard, there might have been lights on some of the houseboats, that was all. It was only enough to emphasize the pools of inky shadow between. Any number of murderers could have been humping any number of bodies up and down the wharf all night and still gone unnoticed.

'What about earlier? Did you go out for a meal, to the pub maybe?'

Again Kelso shook his head. 'Bailie went down the chippie for us. It'd been a long old day: we got the night ferry out of Ostend, got into Dover about dawn, up here for breakfast. We spent most of the day unloading the gear and getting the masts up. By evening we was ready to put our feet up.'

Shapiro looked around him. 'You carry all this round with you? Can't you hire tents?'

'It's easier having our own,' said Kelso. 'We're on the road most of the year, here and on the Continent. It's one man's job to make sure there's always a tent waiting. We used to hire, when I was first with Reverend Mike. It was a nightmare. We'd get to a site with two days to get everything ready, then find that the last man who had the tent went bust and it was still in a field at the far end of the country. Or he had a use for half a mile of good rope and replaced it with the stuff he tethered his donkeys with. Or there was an accident with a gas-stove that he forgot to mention so there was a damn great hole with half a gale whistling through it. It's a mug's game. It even costs less having your own gear when you use it as much as we do.'

Shapiro nodded slowly. 'You've been doing this a while then—moving Mr Davey around.'

Kelso did some sums. 'This is the sixth year. For the first couple, like I said, we hired. Then Miss Mills, his business manager, bought this stuff off a travelling circus. Till then we'd stayed in Britain, but once we had our own gear we started going over to Europe as well. France, Belgium and Holland mostly. Last summer we did Germany as well.'

'Have you all been together those six years?'

Either Kelso couldn't see where this was leading, or he could and he didn't like it. He frowned. 'Varies. I've been with him six years, Miss Mills for five, young Rom's on his first trip. Why? How does that tell you who pushed some bimbo in the canal last night?'

For the first time Brady offered a contribution. He had a

quiet voice, the accent both like and unlike Donovan's: softer, lightly ribbed with humour. 'It doesn't. It tells him a bit about us, if we're the sort of guys to go around knifing prostitutes. The answer, Chief Inspector, is that we're not. But for the record, the guys know one another better than they know me. I've been with them seven months just. But they can surely tell you I haven't killed anyone in that time.'

It was a gentle joke to defuse the tension that had crept in round the edges of the interview. But Shapiro didn't smile: after all, it was only funny if it was true. 'Good. Well, with luck we won't need to see you again. But I imagine we'll find you here if we do?'

'For a week or so.' Kelso gave a granity smile. 'Depends how many sinners Reverend Mike finds to save.'

'Oh, Castlemere has its share of sinners,' allowed Shapiro. 'I just don't know how susceptible they'll prove to a couple of Hallelujahs and a Praise the Lord.

'Well,' he said when they were outside and walking back to the car, 'what did you make of Brady?'

'He didn't seem too bothered by our questions, did he? I suppose Donovan's right? He doesn't strike me as the terrorist type. Generally, whoever they are, whatever the cause, the one thing they have in common is a total lack of humour. They have no sense of proportion. Brady—Bailie—isn't like that.'

'I doubt Donovan made it up,' grunted Shapiro, looking at her sidelong. 'Of course he was only a kid and kids are impressionable. Maybe Brady never was the major terrorist he seemed to a bunch of thirteen-year-olds. But it would be unsafe to assume that because he can lay on the charm when it suits him he must be a decent chap underneath. I've known some thoroughly charming murderers in my time.'

Liz accepted the rebuke but not altogether gracefully. 'Well, he didn't murder Charisma. Unless Dr Crowe's wrong about when she died, none of them did. They were in Belgium at the time. That's too easily checked to be a lie.'

'True,' agreed Shapiro. 'All the same, Brady knows something.'

She stopped and looked at him, her eyes widening. There was a note almost of indignation in her voice. 'I was watching him all the time. His expression never flickered. What did you see that I missed?'

Shapiro allowed himself a small self-satisfied smile. It was one of the compensations for advancing age, that he could still show bright young detective inspectors a thing or two. 'I didn't see anything. Maybe you were too busy watching to hear what he said. We pulled her out of the canal, everyone else assumed she drowned. But Brady said the riggers weren't the sort of men to go round knifing prostitutes.'

'No, I didn't pick that up,' she admitted. 'It could have been a coincidence—the first thing that came into his head?'

'It could have been. But why would it come into his head when he knew she was found in the canal?'

'God damn!' Liz was all for going back and having it out with him, but Shapiro kept her walking towards the car.

'He'll keep. Like you say, we know he didn't kill her.'

'But—'

'I know: withholding evidence isn't the behaviour of an innocent man. But I'd like to know what he might be guilty of before I haul him in. Let's find out what Special Branch have to say, yes?' He gave a low chuckle, amused by her indignation. 'Shapiro's First Law of Criminal Investigation: never ask a question until you've a good idea what the answer's going to be.'

FIVE

OVER THE PHONE Brian Graham's voice was quiet and icily calm. 'What do you mean, you have to work tomorrow?'

Liz stood on one leg, twisting the wire like a discomfited schoolgirl, wincing at the fury latent in his self-control. She wasn't surprised he was furious. He was entitled to be furious. 'I know what I said. I said I'd keep Monday free to finish the move. I said, come what may, I'd be here. Brian, I'm sorry. I didn't expect a murder over the weekend.'

'Murder?' She detected the least imaginable lightening in his tone, as if this at least were something he could understand. 'A woman, was it?'

Liz blinked. 'Yes, as a matter of fact it was. Well, a girl.'

A sniff came down the wire. 'Find the husband. Ask if she'd recently left him to move house on his own.'

FIRST THING, MONDAY morning she found Donovan waiting in her office, looking as disgruntled as Brian sounded. 'Special Branch.' He spat the words out as if they tasted bad. 'They couldn't organize a piss-up in a brewery.'

'Don't they have anything on Brady?'

'Oh, yeah. They say he's dead. They say he died in the States, in a car crash, and the file is closed.' His voice was heavy with sarcasm. Liz guessed he'd given Special Branch as hard a time as they'd given him.

'A car crash. What—deliberate? A hit?'

'They say not. They say he was on his way to address a meeting, he'd been drinking and he tried to beat an articulated lorry through a red light.'

Mingled feelings of relief and anti-climax left Liz momentarily nonplussed. She'd been gearing herself up mentally for the worst, for the prospect that poor Charisma's death was no more than a prelude to the campaign of terror to come; and now it seemed Donovan had made a mistake. An easy mistake, it had been thirteen years... A shade light-headed, she chuckled. 'So Joseph Bailie isn't Liam Brady at all—never was any more than a carnival roustabout—'

Donovan breathed heavily. 'Boss, did I ever tell you about Glencurran? It was a one-horse town until the horse died. It's got three churches, three pubs and a betting shop, a sub post office, a general store and an agricultural supplier. It's got a two-room primary school and one bus-stop. Total population, including the outlying farms, about four hundred. I knew them all, at least to see. I'd known Petey Conway's bedbound grandmother if she got a hip replacement and turned up here as an exotic dancer. You think I can't recognize the guy every five-year-old in Glencurran knew to tiptoe around? The one guy who never got "Wash me" scrawled in the dirt on his car?'

Liz didn't ask the first question which occurred to her, which was how he had brought himself to leave such a throbbing metropolis. Instead she said patiently, 'But, Donovan, he's dead. The FBI told Special Branch and Special Branch told you: Liam Brady is no more. Bailie looks like him, that's all.'

'I'm telling you,' he said stubbornly. 'I know the man. That's him.'

Liz favoured him with a look on the incredulous side of sceptical. 'Then how do you explain it?'

'Cock-up?'

'Did you try Customs?'

'They've nothing either. They checked the crew through Dover about five o'clock Saturday morning. They weren't looking for anything in particular and they didn't find anything.' His lip curled. 'They pointed out that the duty on religious pamphlets and holy water aren't enough to tempt the average smuggler away from cocaine.' He sniffed dourly. 'Smug bastards.'

Liz smiled. By his own account Donovan went through life like the fox, every man's hand against him. Of course it wasn't true. He met with approximately the same trials and tribulations as other people; he just resented them more. At first she'd found his grim humour tiresome. Now it positively cheered her up. Her whole day seemed bright with promise when compared with the war of attrition that was Donovan's.

Her father made a formal identification of Charlene Pierce, aged sixteen, known along the wharf as Charisma. Then he passed out on the mortuary floor. When he was feeling better Shapiro had a squad car take him home; but he heard later that Pierce got out at some traffic lights and disappeared into a handy pub.

At midday—about the time her furniture and her husband were expected—Liz called Castle General and asked for Dr Crowe. She was told he couldn't come to the phone immediately— 'Up to his eyes at the moment,' said his assistant, leaving Liz to wonder if she meant it literally—but he called back in fifteen minutes with an interim report on the Pierce autopsy.

'Cause of death was the obvious—sudden massive blood loss from a throat wound that severed both carotid arteries and the trachea. She'd have lost consciousness almost immediately with death following soon after. Unless she did it before she wouldn't have screamed. Then she lay for several hours on her side on a hard surface, and only after that was she put into the water.'

'Time of death?'

She heard him sucking his teeth. 'That's a good one. It's a complicated scenario, you know? Body temperature's no guide after a few hours in cold water; the decomposition process would be affected too. I can't really expand on what I said yesterday.'

Liz knew how reluctant pathologists were to pin themselves down to times of death, even with 'give or take half an hour' as a gesture of human fallibility. But even by the usual standard, even allowing for the undoubted complications, Crowe seemed to be being unhelpful. 'If I promise not to quote you, when would you say she died?'

He chuckled good-naturedly. 'Then I'd say she was killed around midnight on Friday, and that she lay for about twenty-four hours before she was put in the canal. But those are only guidelines, and if anyone asks about this conversation I shall deny it ever took place.'

Liz liked Crowe, liked most of the pathologists she met, found them on the whole more approachable than GPs, and thought it a pity that their patients were in no state to appreciate them. 'The secret of your competence is safe with me,' she assured him solemnly.

'And I was right about her killer standing behind her, I think. It'd be an awkward movement to make a wound like that from in front. From the angle the blade was held at, he was several inches taller than her.'

'Good,' said Liz, thinking this was a bonus. 'How tall?'

Crowe sounded apologetic. 'Well, it's not going to be that much help. She was only five-foot-one. You could say he was probably five six or more, but most men are.'

'At least we can rule out midgets,' Liz said philosophically. 'All right. Apart from the neck wound, was she injured in any other way? Was she raped?'

The pathologist was slow to answer. 'She hadn't been raped violently.'

Liz's eyebrows climbed. 'There's a gentle way?'

Reproof came down the phone at her. 'That's not what I meant. Look, this was a girl who spent her working life with her legs apart. She had sex the way you use a typewriter, battering away at it whenever the need and opportunity arise. Of course she was bruised. Of course there were abrasions. And yes, she had sex on the day of her death. But it could have been earlier and not with the man who killed her. It may have had nothing to do with her death.'

'So what's he saying?' scowled Shapiro when Liz brought him up to date. 'That she was a prostitute but she wasn't killed for sex?'

Liz shrugged. 'If a girl's a prostitute, you don't have to kill her for it. You pay her for it.'

'Then why did he kill her?'

'For pleasure? We should consider the possibility, Frank. There are men who get a kick out of killing women: the ultimate domination. Prostitutes are more accessible than most women, they're more likely to meet such men. Then there's the fact that they won't be missed as quickly and the feeling that less effort may be put into finding their killers.'

'The hell for that!' Shapiro's eyes were fierce. 'Round here, *nobody's* life is that cheap.'

'We'll tell him that when we find him,' Liz promised.

For a time Shapiro said nothing more. But the air around him remained charged with his thinking so Liz stayed where she was. At length he said, 'Twenty-four hours?'

'Sorry?'

'Isn't that what Crowe said—that she'd been dead twenty-four hours when she went into the water?'

'It was a guess, but yes, something like that.'

'She lay under that tarpaulin all Saturday and nobody found her. I know the tow-path isn't Piccadilly but it's not Outer Mongolia either. Particularly at weekends there are boats passing up and down, people walking dogs, kids out for a bit of fun. And nobody found her. Nobody thought it worth examining a girl-sized hump under a tarpaulin? Somebody's dog must have smelled her and wanted to investigate. What did they do—pull it away, complain it was making them late for dinner? What kind of a town is this?'

'An ordinary town,' Liz said quietly, 'full of ordinary

people who don't expect to be confronted with dead bodies
on public paths. If your dog barks at a bit of tarpaulin you
think there's a rat in it and hurry away. Hindsight's a fine
thing, Frank. But there was nothing unusual about a roll of
old tarpaulin left out with the timberyard's rubbish. Why
would anyone investigate? You can't blame people for
walking past, any more than you can blame Donovan for
not hearing anything. It would have been nice if we'd
picked up on it sooner but nobody turned their back on her
deliberately. It was bad luck, that's all.'

Shapiro nodded dispiritedly. 'I just wonder sometimes if
we're the only ones who give a damn about law, order, the
sanctity of human life, all that stuff. If the tax-payers of
Castlemere wouldn't be just as happy with an effective public cleansing department that tidied up the mess so they
didn't have to look at it. Go into town. Have lunch in a
nice restaurant, have a drink in a wine bar, have a look
round a couple of the better shops, and listen to what's
being said. You think the place is going to be up in arms
over this? Somebody cut a young girl's throat: that's public
knowledge now. But what's Castlemere going to be talking
about? Going down three-nil to Hull Kingston Rovers. De-
lays on the motorway due to the contra-flow system. How
long it takes to get an appointment at Hair Traffic Control.
They don't care, Liz. The only reference you'll hear, if you
hear anything is What do these girls expect? and Why don't
the police do something about prostitutes?'

'You're not being fair, Frank. We worry about it because
it's our job to. They pay us to worry about it. They try not
to worry about it, not to think about it, because there's
nothing they can do. None of them, and probably none of
us either, could have saved Charisma from that end or one
very like it. Donovan tried, I imagine others have too, and
she didn't want to know. We could have locked her up.
Then the man who killed her would have killed someone
else—a young girl on her way home from a disco or out

walking the family dog, a young mother whose car broke down so she had to walk the last mile home. I'm not saying that would necessarily have been worse. But would it have been any better?'

'It would at least have reminded our local worthies that violent death isn't the prerogative of the poor,' Shapiro said savagely. At once he relented with a wry smile. 'You're right, I'm being unfair. It's just, I get so tired of policing two nations when one of them thinks there's a special lane on the ring road for BMWs and the other thinks we're part of a conspiracy against them.'

Before she left Liz said, 'What, if anything, do you want me to do about Bailie? Now it seems he isn't Donovan's friendly neighbourhood terrorist after all?'

Shapiro's lived-in face wrinkled. 'What's to do? He's in the clear as far as the crime we're investigating—they all are, they didn't enter the country until after she was dead. And if he didn't kill her, why would he be moving her body about? Surely to God that was the killer. His slip about the knife must have been a coincidence.'

'Donovan's still convinced he's Liam Brady.'

'Donovan's always convinced he's right, right up to the moment that he's proved wrong. Brady's dead. Special Branch wouldn't have closed the file without being sure.'

As she went down the corridor towards her own office she met Donovan coming up it. 'Is the chief in?'

'Yes,' she said. 'And no.'

He frowned. 'I wanted to ask him—'

'No,' she said again.

He didn't understand. 'I wondered what he thought, if it's a good idea—'

'No Donovan,' she said a third time. 'No, you may not go and see Bailie. No, you may not accuse him of being a dead terrorist. No, you may not search his belongings for Semtex. I asked Mr Shapiro and he told me, and now I'm telling you. No. We leave the man alone.'

THE VAN WAS LEAVING as Liz got home. The front door was open and there were packing cases in the hall and also at the top of the stairs. So far as she could tell from a quick glance through the windows the furniture had been decanted into more or less the right rooms.

She found Brian in the living-room, sprawled on the couch with his head tipped back and his eyes shut. She thought for a moment he was asleep. He looked exhausted, his shirt darkly patched with sweat.

But he wasn't asleep. He stirred at her entry and cranked his eyes open. 'Good day at the office, dear?'

She bent to kiss his forehead, which was about as high as foreheads go before people start talking openly about baldness. 'Not great. But probably better than yours.'

'The cooker's working. Do you want to eat now or later?'

'Stay where you are,' she said, 'I'll put something together. I'll just turn Polly into the paddock first.'

'Polly—!' From the tone of Brian Graham's voice he thought there were more important things to do.

'Be fair: today's shambles wasn't her fault, there's no reason to punish her for it.'

'Oh, see to the bloody horse,' he growled, closing his eyes again.

SIX

'SIN,' RUMBLED the Reverend Michael Davey. 'Sin and corruption.' His eyes, sharp as a diamond drill guaranteed accurate to a thousandth of an inch, scoured his congregation as if expecting to catch some of them out in pride, avarice or lust at that very moment.

'Sins of the heart. Sins of the soul. Sins of the flesh. Wherever I go, wherever I travel, always the same. People without values. Without faith. Without love: the love of God, of their fellow man, of their families, of themselves even. Because people who liked and respected themselves couldn't do half the things that happen in our society. Old men tortured for their pension money. Old women raped at knife-point. Children snatched from the streets, young girls violated by those who should be looking after them.'

Reverend Michael Davey wore a white suit, as anyone who had seen the posters would have expected, and sat in the centre of a dais raised some three feet above ground level—sat because he had no option, he was a man in a wheelchair. On his feet he would have been a hugely commanding figure, tall and broad, with a strong fleshy face crowned with a shock of springy hair somewhere between blond and white. That was the age he was, somewhere between young and old, and that was all you could know without reading his well-publicized autobiography. In fact he was fifty-two.

But the impression he gave, in spite of the wheelchair, was of a man in the prime of life and vigour. The eyes were only part of a vast natural arsenal of command. The voice was another weapon: deep, rough, with power burgeoning up through it as if it came from a fathomless res-

ervoir of passion and it was as much as he could do to keep
it from running amok and tearing the tent down.

The white suit, the commanding figure, even the electric
hair and diamond eyes, were taken straight from the chapter
on American evangelists in the Book of Stereotypes. But
the voice, resonant with its full vowels and rolling conso-
nants, came from the mining valleys of Wales. It was a
fierce, angry, Trade Union type of Welshness in which the
words rushed from him like a violent little torrent coming
off Snowdon.

'So what's gone wrong, that suddenly we have such
monsters among us?' he asked. 'There are people, you
know, who blame God. It wouldn't happen if He really
cared for us. What, rape and torture God's will? If I believed that I'd throw stones at the Archbishop of Canter-
bury and spit in the communion wine. I would not serve a
God who treated His people that way. These things are
artifacts not of God but of the Devil, and we have to confront the Devil's work, and the Devil's people, wherever
we find them.

'Know thine enemy, saith the Lord. And there's a damn
good reason for that: if we don't know him, if we don't
recognize him when we see him, he's free to work his
ravages among us. We must understand the forces of evil,
recognize them and join battle with them. In the dark streets
and the gutters. In the high-rises and the sewers. In the
places where people live, where they work, where they
drink and have their entertainment, even—God help us—
in the schools. There are no refuges from the tide of filth
and sin that washes around us. Either we fight against it or
we go under.'

That was not quite the end. There was some more of the
same, followed by a rousing hymn in which the preacher's
voice could be heard soaring majestically. A yellow plastic
bucket went round in lieu of a collection plate. Then the
congregation climbed creakily to its feet and filed out. It

didn't take long. There might have been twenty of them, mostly old ladies. Row upon row of folding seats had collected only dust.

There was a plywood ramp from the dais down to the ground sheet. With the confidence of long practice Davey rolled off the top, gathering enough speed to take him halfway up the aisle before he had to wheel. He arrived at the flap of the tent in time to bid goodnight to the rearguard.

'Thanks for coming. Come again tomorrow—same time, same place. We haven't finished here; we've hardly begun.'

When they were gone he turned to the woman standing beside him. All the fierce power went out of his eyes and his muscular shoulders slumped. His voice was soft, a low rumbled plaint. 'Oh, Jenny, what am I doing here? These people aren't interested in anything I have to say. They only came out of politeness: they'd have sat on the same seats if I'd been selling hair tonic or vegetarianism or a new political party for black lesbian pacifists.'

The woman put out a slim hand, laid it not on his shoulder but on the back of his chair. She gave him a quiet smile. 'You're here because they need you, Michael.'

'Don't tell me that, tell them!'

'When you tell them so much better?'

'I can only tell them if they'll come and listen!'

'They'll come. They always do. It's first-night blues, that's all.'

'Castlemere.' It came out as a long sigh. 'There's something—impervious—about it. Maybe they really *don't* want to know. Maybe they'd rather have the corruption than the trouble of cleaning it up. There was a girl killed here the other day, did you know?' The woman shook her head. 'She was found in the canal right by here. A young girl, a prostitute apparently. What's the world coming to? The people of this town, they see young girls working as prostitutes and do nothing to stop it; they see them murdered and dumped in their canal and still they don't care enough

to come and talk about the mess they've got themselves
into. You'd think they'd be glad of any advice anyone
could give them.'

'They were, those who came. And there'll be more tomorrow, when word's had a chance to get round. Tonight
people came on spec: they'd nothing better to do, there was
nothing on the TV, or they go to religious meetings out of
habit regardless of who's speaking. But now they know
you're something different: not just another Bible-thumper
repeating the same old stale formulae but someone who has
something important to say, something concrete to offer
them.

'They were part of something real tonight, and they
won't keep it to themselves. The posters are all right as far
as they go, but there's nothing like word of mouth to get
people interested. You know that, Michael. It's always like
this when we work a new area. We've never been here
before. Give them time to hear what kind of a man you
are, what kind of an inspiration. Then they'll come.'

'Inspiration!' he exclaimed self-mockingly.

'Michael, you are! Don't undersell yourself. Things that
other people are afraid to say, you spell out. You don't
dress it up for them, tell them it's not their fault, that they're
the victims of society. You make them face the fact that
they *are* society, that whatever power there is for change
is vested in them. You're a fine speaker, Michael, of course.
But what's infinitely more important is that what you are
and what you do actually makes a difference to people.
They'll come, because you give them something no one
else dares to: the promise of a better here and now if they
want it enough to go out and claim it. Jam today. Believe
me: for that they'll come. They always do.'

He ran a thick hand through his hair. 'I must be getting
old, Jenny. Was it always this hard?'

She laughed, affection dancing in her eyes. 'Of course it
was. Often it was harder. The first time in France they

shouted insults and tried to pull the tent down. But then they came inside.'

Davey regarded the knuckles of his right hand reflectively. 'Was it there I was arrested for affray?'

'I do believe it was,' said the woman, trying not to smile.

IT WAS MID-EVENING before Donovan went home, across Cornmarket and up the tow-path to avoid Broad Wharf. Not because he was afraid of meeting Bailie but because he'd been told to stay away from him. Donovan came from a long line of poets and wordsmiths: he could find alternative meanings in all but the most explicit of statements. Unfortunately Inspector Graham had already discovered this and spoke to him the way solicitors draw up contracts, in short sentences with minimal punctuation. He could have disobeyed her order to stay away from Bailie but he could not have claimed misunderstanding as his defence.

Dark had already fallen and the lights in the big tent threw giant shadows on to its white walls. At one point he heard the distant apologetic hum of not enough voices raised in song. Soon after that the faithful shuffled out of the tent and up the walkway to Brick Lane. Donovan grinned. He'd been right: Mavis Spurge the religious groupie was one of them. She'd throw herself at anything in a dog-collar.

Tara was a narrowboat built to carry grain and coal and general cargo on the inland waterways. Once her master and his family lived in a tiny cabin at the after end, but conversion had opened up her holds as living accommodation. So Donovan had a perfectly good bedroom and a perfectly good bed. There was no need for him to sleep on the couch in the saloon. But that as often as not was what he did, with a book propped on his knees and music playing softly on the tape-deck. If he was awake enough to get up and go to bed he usually stayed put and read a bit longer instead. So it was this night.

The tape reached its end and switched itself off unheeded. Broad Wharf was in darkness, the congregation away to their beds in the small streets of Castlemere, the preacher away to his in the Castle Hotel. Even the road crew had played enough poker and drunk enough beer and no lights showed at the windows of their caravan. It seemed that nothing stirred along the canal.

But something did stir: a shadow moving among the great still shadows that blackened the tow-path. A crescent moon was just high enough to cast a shimmer on the water, the lonely light burned behind the timber yard; but there was more than enough darkness to shield the progress of the man-shaped shade moving swiftly along the wharf. A hunting cat saw it and froze back into the alley until it passed. No one else heard or saw anything at all.

Donovan was jerked from sleep by the sudden massive conviction that he was dying. He couldn't breathe, couldn't move. Numbing weight pinned him down. His eyes flew wide, bulging with panic, but he couldn't see: either his reading light had gone out or he was blind.

Someone said, so close to his ear that he could feel the breath on his face, 'Lie still, you bastard, or I'll brain you.'

He froze at the sound. It was like a hand reaching out of his past to grab him. It was probably the accent, Donovan had never had the sort of personal dealings with Liam Brady that would have marked the voice indelibly on his mind, but the chill of recognition struck him to the heart. There was no longer any point coming home the long way: Brady must have seen him at the same time he saw Brady.

Even in the shock of the moment a part of his mind managed a grim satisfaction at this unarguable proof that he'd been right and Special Branch wrong.

The smug feeling vanished as he wondered what Brady intended to do now. He didn't suppose the man had broken into his boat in the middle of the night, switched off the light and pinned him to the couch in order to ask for news of home.

Brady may have taken his stunned immobility for compliance or he may have thought that if Donovan didn't breathe soon he'd have another body to explain. For whatever reason he shifted the hand clamped over Donovan's mouth and nose. 'That better?'

Donovan was too busy sucking in air to reply, and with Brady's knee in the middle of his chest it wasn't as easy as it might have been.

'Now listen to me, Cal Donovan.' Brady had never been a man to shout, he'd held people's attention in other ways, and he wasn't shouting now. His voice was soft, calm, even faintly humorous. He wasn't so much as breathing heavily. 'I don't want any nonsense out of you. You give me a hard time and I'll break your arm, see if that'll keep you quiet.'

'What do you want?' gasped Donovan.

'You know who I am, don't you?'

It might have been politic to deny it. 'Of course I do. Look, if you want to talk will you get off my bloody chest?'

Brady chuckled. He levered himself off Donovan; then he pulled Donovan upright and pushed him against the back of the couch. 'Now, stay you there. I mean it: give me any trouble and I'll hurt you.'

Donovan wasn't afraid of being hurt but he didn't think it would achieve anything. They should have been a fair match, Donovan the taller, Brady a little heavier. But the older man was a practised street-fighter: Donovan would take him on if he had to but he didn't want to be beaten up for no good reason. He stayed where he was. 'What are you doing here? I don't know what you want.'

Brady's face was invisible but his voice was relaxed. 'A little information, that's all. When did you spot me?'

Donovan saw no reason not to answer. 'Yesterday afternoon, when you were unloading the chairs.'

The beanbag whispered as Brady nodded. 'That's when

I saw you.' His grin was audible. 'I couldn't believe it: little Cal Donovan, scourge of the RUC graffiti squad, all grown up and helping the English police.' The voice hardened a tone. 'Then I saw you ordering them other coppers round so I knew it was true, you were one of them.'

'It's what I do.' Donovan offered no further explanation.

'Who did you tell about me?'

'Away on!' Donovan exclaimed indignantly, moving to get up. He had his breath back and thought he could move faster than Brady could reach him.

He was wrong. He rose into the path of a blow that somehow in the dark found the side of his face and sent him tumbling over the soft furniture until he fetched up in a heap against the door. Before he could defend himself Brady was on him, cranking his head back by a handful of hair. He felt the cold clean prick of steel against his throat.

Brady hissed in his ear, 'You want to try that again, Cal? I warned you, mess me about and I'll gut you. You may be God's gift to Castlemere CID but to me you're still a snotty-nosed kid with an attitude problem. Feel that? That's disembowelled better men than you. You give me some answers, boy, or I'll vivisect you.'

The problem was, Donovan believed him. He didn't like yielding to coercion, it went against the grain with him, but it would be nothing short of silly to let Brady cut his throat. He growled, 'My inspector, my chief inspector and Special Branch.'

Brady laughed out loud. He sat back, unknotting his fingers from Donovan's hair. 'Special Branch? What did they have to say?'

Donovan no longer had any qualms about answering. He'd called Brady's bluff and found he wasn't bluffing. 'They said you were dead. They said I was mistaken. Looks like it, doesn't it?'

'What about your chief? Who did he believe?'

'Special Branch.' With his face in the carpet Donovan still managed to convey disgust.

'Good. Very good.' The hand that didn't hold the knife lay amiably on Donovan's shoulder. 'Now, listen to me carefully. You were mistaken. Liam Brady is indeed dead, God rest his soul. So nobody held a knife to your throat and nobody asked you any questions. Tomorrow you can tell your inspector and your chief inspector that you were wrong, Joseph Bailie isn't the man you knew in Glencurran. They know I couldn't have killed that girl: if I'm not a terrorist either they'll lose interest in me. So will you. Won't you?'

Donovan felt the cord of his carpet pressed against his face, felt a cool spot of blood where the blade had pricked his skin, felt humiliation rise through him like a crimson tide. He gritted his teeth and said nothing.

The knife pricked behind his ear. 'I mean it, boy. I don't want to turn round and see you ever again. What I do is none of your business. You keep out of my way. If I catch you nosing round again, I'll fix you. You've seen men knee-capped, Cal, you know that's a thing worth avoiding. Unless Castlemere CID has a positive discrimination policy about detectives on sticks, don't give me a reason to come back.'

'All right, damn you,' shouted Donovan. His cheeks were hot, his eyes squeezed tight and he had to unclench his jaw to get the words out. Saying it cost him precious self-respect but there was no alternative that wouldn't cost him more. 'All right.'

SEVEN

Too TIRED and too rattled to sleep well, Liz woke early. She lay still for a while, hands behind her head, watching the sunlight strengthen through the flimsy curtain, her mind stumbling over a confusion of images drawn from her work and her marriage. She was unhappy about both, in oddly similar ways.

There was too much happening under the surface, unstated and only dimly perceived, brewing up a turmoil that she should be dealing with and could not. Poor Charisma and her cut throat. Poor Brian, whom she both loved and liked yet who once again found himself playing second fiddle to her career. This move was to benefit her career. He'd taken a set-back in his own to accommodate it: he'd headed the art department at his last school, might have to wait some time for a similar chance at Castle High. But she'd come down here with her horse and a few other treasures, and left him to do everything else alone. She didn't know what else she could have done, but perhaps that was no answer. Perhaps it was in failing to see the alternatives that she was at fault.

She wondered if breakfast in bed would cheer him up. She didn't fool herself that it would put everything right but it was at least a gesture. But he was still deeply asleep, his face pensive against the pillow with a tiny frown between the eyebrows, and he wouldn't thank her for waking him yet. She got up to see to the horse instead, sliding her feet into the boots she kept behind the kitchen door. She made up a feed and a haynet in the little store beside the stable, then—fetchingly attired in green wellies and a night-

shirt announcing 'Policemen do it with conviction'—
walked through the orchard to catch Polly.

The mare had acquired a little friend. Her nose was thrust
deep into the high hedge enclosing her field and the tip of
a small white nose peeped through from the other side.

If Liz had been here long enough to get her bearings
she'd have known the pony had no business being there,
that it wasn't another field beyond the hedge but the lane
round Belvedere Park. A forward-thinking council, an unusual thing in the history of Castlemere, had taken the Belvedere estate in settlement of taxes during the '50s and now
used the house as a town hall and the grounds for public
recreation. The lane was a bridleway.

Only when the white pony followed Polly up the hedge
and appeared at the side of the house, saddled and with its
reins dangling, did Liz realize it had gone AWOL. The
likeliest explanation was that it had dumped its rider and
set off at a spanking trot with its tail in the air to show the
world how clever it was. Some hot and grubby little girl
was probably pursuing it as fast as her jodhpur boots would
carry her.

With Polly safe in the stable Liz went into the lane with
a handful of feed. The pony was wary of her, standing on
tiptoe with its neck arched and nostrils flared. But when it
got the smell of food it threw caution to the wind and made
a dive for it; Liz snatched the rein and the pony had the
grace to acknowledge itself caught.

There was still no sign of the rider. But there were marks
in the grass verge to show the pony had come from the
park and not up the road so after a moment Liz, wishing
she were more formally dressed, led it back the way it had
come. Then she cast dignity aside, mounted—her feet hanging to the pony's knees—and let it do the work.

Rounding an overhanging rhododendron she saw a pair
of polished boots and thought the decanted rider must be
hurt, concussed perhaps. She dismounted quickly, tied the

pony to the bush and pushed aside the lower branches to
see what damage the girl had sustained.

When she saw, she stood frozen for perhaps half a minute. For another half minute she concentrated on what she
was seeing, in case someone came by and disturbed the
scene after she left. The gaping wound in the throat, ear to
ear as before. The denim jacket pulled half-way down her
back, imprisoning her arms. The putty-coloured jodhpurs
pulled down to her booted calves. She was a child, not even
as old as Charisma, and she was dead.

Then Liz flung herself back on the pony and galloped
for home, shouting for Brian as she ran to the telephone.

DR CROWE AGREED with Liz, that the similarities between
the two murders were significant. The throat wound in particular struck him as distinctive, almost as individual as a
signature.

'There are no hesitation marks. There was no doubt in
his mind, either about what he wanted to do or how to do
it. That should tell you something about him.'

Liz had pulled on some clothes, and a warmer coat than
the season dictated, without making much impact on the
deep inner chill occupying her. She'd seen many bodies in
the course of her work, some of them nastier sights than
this, but this was the first one she'd discovered. The shock
of that was like cotton-wool in her brain, keeping the syn-
apses from firing. 'Like what?'

Shapiro saw what he was getting at. 'This wasn't done
on the spur of the moment—he didn't just happen to be
here, see her and find himself overwhelmed by lust. It was
planned. Look at the jacket: that's not the sort of thing
you'd think of in the heat of a struggle. He knew exactly
what he was doing, had it all worked out. He got her off
the pony, pinned her arms, cut her throat, then went on his
way. He could have done the whole thing in half a minute.'

Liz stared. 'Not if he raped her he couldn't.'

'But did he?' He turned to the pathologist as if he thought he knew the answer already.

The large young man shook his head. 'No. There was no sexual assault beyond the disordering of the clothes.'

'He was disturbed? Again?' Liz heard her voice soaring and steadied it. 'At eight o'clock on a Tuesday morning in a country park? This is getting silly. Nobody's that unlucky.'

'Nobody's that lucky, either,' grunted Shapiro. 'What are you suggesting?—that he was disturbed in the act of rape, and killed the girl to ensure her silence, and not only did he get away without being seen but the person who disturbed him didn't notice the body? Or they noticed it and did nothing about it? And this happened not once but twice? Pull the other leg,' he suggested dourly, 'it's got bells on.'

'Then—what—?' Liz was still too shaken to follow his train of thought.

'I don't think he ever intended to rape them. He meant to kill them. His kick isn't sexual, it's cerebral: he likes killing. He didn't start with Charisma: he's too handy with that knife, too sure of himself altogether. He's done this before. But not round here or I'd know. So he travels. Maybe he's a visitor, or maybe he's moved here since his last fix. But two in five days: that's quite a habit.'

'You mean, there'll be more?'

Shapiro nodded mechanically. 'Oh, yes. The man who did this isn't finished. He's going to want some more.'

'Some more *what?*' demanded Liz shakily. 'What does he get from killing young girls?'

'Revenge,' said Dr Crowe unexpectedly. Finding the experts regarding him with interest—for motives are the stuff of detection not forensic pathology—he blushed and muttered, 'I did a course once.'

Shapiro smiled inwardly. Young Crowe might remember

what he'd been told on his course but he'd clearly forgotten who was speaking. 'Revenge?' he said encouragingly.

'Against women in general or one woman in particular. He can't handle relationships with women so he takes it out on young girls. He can't deal with rejection so he doesn't leave himself open to it: he only approaches them when he's in a position to dictate the outcome of the encounter.' He heard himself lecturing and stopped abruptly. 'Anyway, that's what they said on the course,' he mumbled.

'Indeed I did,' Shapiro agreed good-naturedly. He caught Liz's grin and returned it, glad she was recovering her sense of perspective.

What had happened was still shocking, but by degrees she was remembering how to deal with it, how to do her job. She had made the first moves on auto-pilot, out of habit, a machine running along well-worn tracks. Now her mind was catching up and she was beginning to think constructively again. She said, 'Perhaps he doesn't rape them because he can't.'

Shapiro dragged his mind away from the exotic image of a homicidal eunuch and back to essentially pragmatic Castlemere. 'Or maybe it's that, if he always intends to kill them, rape would be irrelevant. Look. Rape isn't about sex, is it, it's about power. It's men saying, "Look what I can do, that you aren't strong enough to stop me doing." But ending a human life is the ultimate exercise of power. You can't top it. Maybe he isn't interested in rape because he wants to get straight to the main course, not fiddle around with the canapés first.'

He glanced at the sad, tumbled little body now decently covered by a blanket. 'But in that case, why touch the clothes at all? Why does he want us to think he's a rapist when *he* thinks he's something better than that?'

'To confuse us?'

'Not for long. He knew what the medical examination

would show. Did he think we'd continue looking for a sex maniac in the continued absence of sex?'

'It's as if he's playing with us—challenging us to discover the real reason he kills. And he can do that,' Liz went on, developing the thought even as she was speaking, 'because there's a time limit of some kind. You're right, he doesn't live here, he may never have been here before and he doesn't plan on staying. If we don't find him soon he'll have moved on.'

Shapiro nodded slowly. 'That fits. We know he's an arrogant man—to kill twice in five days, both times in public places, the second time in broad daylight. That isn't need or compulsion, it's doing what he wants to do because he thinks no one can stop him. He thinks he can outsmart us. Not necessarily for ever, just for long enough.'

Liz was thinking back. 'If he's so confident, why the change of heart about disposing of Charisma? We assumed that he panicked and had to go back later to tidy up. But this time he hardly troubled to hide the body.'

Stuck for an answer, Shapiro only shook his head.

Beyond the screens, beyond the barrier which had been erected at the end of the lane, a car pulled up and a door slammed. Liz said, 'I've had someone ringing round the local stables, trying to get an identification on her. Maybe that's it now.'

It was a dark green saloon, discreetly prosperous, and the man hurrying towards them wore a business suit and a stunned expression. A constable stopped him at the barrier. The man tried to shake free but the policeman held him back, respectful but unyielding.

'The father?' murmured Liz, and Shapiro gave a fractional nod. 'Oh, God,' she sighed.

'Are we finished with her?' asked Shapiro. 'Photographs? Scenes of Crime? You, Dr. Crowe?' The pathologist inclined his head in assent. 'Then tidy her up a bit, would you? I can't ask him to wait till we get her to the morgue to find out whether his daughter's dead but we don't have to show her to him like this.' He moved out from behind the screens.

Despite the suit and the dark car he was only a young man. Words spilled from him anxiously as Shapiro approached. 'Alice? Is that my daughter? I was at the stables—she forgot her schoolbag—and somebody called and said there'd been an accident. A girl on a white pony. Is it Alice? Is she hurt?'

Shapiro introduced himself. 'It's Mr Elton, isn't it?—of Elton & Farrow, the accountants?'

The man ran an agitated hand through his hair. 'Yes, I'm Sam Elton. For God's sake—is it Alice? Is she going to be all right? That damn pony—!'

'How old's your daughter, Mr Elton?' Partly he needed the information, partly he was giving Crowe time to tidy up behind the screen.

'She's thirteen. She has blonde hair and blue eyes, she was wearing a denim jacket, a checked shirt and jodhs, and she was going to ride round the park then catch the bus to school. I left her at the stables—Mrs Skinner's in Cobham Lane—at seven-thirty. When I got to the office I found her bag in the car. So I drove back, and while I was with Mrs Skinner someone phoned—a policeman, someone—and said there'd been an accident. For pity's sake, Chief Inspector!' His voice cracked. 'Is it my daughter?'

Shapiro took his elbow and guided him through the barrier. 'I'm not sure, Mr Elton. From your description it could be. In a minute I'll ask you to look at her and tell us. But first, I'm very sorry to have to tell you that the girl is dead.'

The blood drained from Sam Elton's face. His mouth opened and closed twice, then his knees buckled and he went down.

EIGHT

DR CROWE had done a good job in the short time he'd had. He'd closed her eyes, folded his jacket under her head to close the gaping wound in her throat and drawn the blanket up to her chin. She still wore the Pony Club-approved hat that was designed to protect her from any misfortune she met while riding but was no defence at all against a man with a knife. Under it the long fair hair framed her face. With the wound hidden she hardly looked dead, just somehow a little more stolid than a child asleep. She couldn't have looked less like Charisma.

Sam Elton whispered. 'My baby.' Then he began to cry.

Shapiro took him home. Liz was relieved that it wouldn't be her breaking the news to the girl's mother. When Elton was safely installed in his car, Shapiro turned back and his face was grim. 'We're going to take flak on this one.'

'Because of who she was?'

He nodded. 'Because of who she was. Because of her age. Because of where and when it happened. If a thirteen-year-old girl from a decent family can't ride her pony in a public park in broad daylight without getting her throat cut, nobody's kid is safe. We have to get this man, Liz. This town's going to be in a state of panic until we do.'

'I'll start a house-to-house round the park,' she said. 'At least this time we know where and pretty well when the attack took place. People are getting ready for work about eight, someone may have seen him. The ground staff start about then too: I've got them together in the park-keeper's hut, I'll talk to them next. Somebody may have seen him this time, even if they didn't see anything suspicious.'

Shapiro indicated assent. She was making all the right

moves, a fully functioning detective inspector again. 'I'll
go back to the office when I'm finished with the family. I
want to start a search for this man's MO. I bet he's left a
trail of young girls with slit throats: we'll know more about
him when we find out where he's been. I'll get Donovan
on to that: it'll keep him away from Bailie if nothing else.'

'What about Bailie? Do we ask him about this?'

For a moment Shapiro was undecided, then he shook his
head. 'I don't see much point. His connection to the last
one was tenuous enough, to this one it's non-existent. Unless we get a description, of course, in which case we're
into a whole new ball game.' He winced. He hated using
expressions he'd picked up from Donovan.

The park-keeper's hut began life as a garden pavilion for
the family at Belvedere House. They kept their croquet
mallets and tennis racquets there. When private enjoyment
gave way to municipal endeavour it became a repository
for scythes, billhooks and pruning shears, and the place
where the gardeners took their tea and sandwiches. It was
also where they punched their time-cards as they came on
and off duty.

There were four of them: an old man well past retirement
age, gnarled and bent enough to have been undergardener
to Adam; a powerful middle-aged man, a young man and
a boy. The boy, who might have been about seventeen, was
clearly shocked. He was trying to drink from the mug of
his flask and his teeth were chattering on its lip.

Liz took their names and addresses and asked when each
had arrived at work that morning. The old man was the
foreman: he fetched the time-cards from the clock. His dep-
uty and the younger man arrived a few minutes either side
of eight; the boy, who was on a year's youth-training
course, followed them in ten minutes later; and the gaffer,
exercising the privileges of rank and age, arrived after the
police, at about eight twenty-five. The big man, Arnie
Sedgewick, had seen the white pony, complete with rider,

trotting along the bridleway as he drove his van into the council yard. He thought that might have been about five to eight.

Liz nodded. That agreed with what Mrs Skinner said, that Alice rode out of the yard at about seven-forty and should have been back by eight-twenty in order to feed her pony, change and catch the bus down the hill at eight-forty. The council yard was half-way on the three-mile ride.

'You didn't see anyone else?'

''Fraid not. Only the other lads, until the police arrived and told us to wait here.'

'What about you, Mr Carver?'

The young man shook his head. 'I never saw nobody.'

'Except the girl.'

'I never saw her neither.'

Liz frowned. 'The bicycle in the council yard, isn't that yours?' He nodded, warily. 'Surely it takes you longer to cycle through the park than it takes Mr Sedgewick in his van? If you arrived four minutes behind him, he must have passed you on the bridleway. Didn't he?'

Ray Carver eyed her sullenly. 'I don't remember where he passed me. He passes me on the road just outside or just inside the park every day: I don't remember where this morning.'

Liz said reasonably, 'It wasn't much over an hour ago.'

'A lot's happened in that hour, though, hasn't it?' he snapped back. 'I'm sorry. I don't remember where Arnie passed me. But I do know I didn't see the kid on the pony.'

'All right,' said Liz quietly. 'So maybe they were off the lane and in the bushes when you passed. That would mean you passed the spot where Alice Elton was killed within moments of the attack on her, possibly while it was taking place—while the man was still there. The pony was loose, it was on the lane when I found it; if it was still in the bushes when you passed then the attack could only just have occurred. So anything you tell me, Mr Carver, is terribly important. Was there anyone else around?'

'I didn't see anyone. No one.'

'All right. Did you hear anything—even something that seemed unremarkable at the time but which, looking back, could have been a man moving in the bushes or the child trying to scream? Anything?'

'Nothing. I'm sorry. I'd help you if I could but I can't. I'd be lying if I said I'd noticed anything.' Long dark hair tumbled over his forehead and he tossed it back out of his eyes. His gaze on her was intense. 'I can't help you catch this man by saying I saw something I didn't.'

'No, of course not,' she agreed automatically. But though there was nothing impossible about his account she was left feeling that Carver had told her less than the whole truth. She thought she'd talk to him again soon, at the police station next time.

No one else had anything to add. All of them had seen Alice Elton riding in the park, sometimes alone, sometimes with friends, but only Sedgewick admitted seeing her take her last ride. It was enough: it made it possible to say that the attack took place in the ten minutes between seven-fifty-five when Sedgewick saw her and five past eight when Liz found the pony. The best pathologist in the country couldn't have been that precise.

LIZ LEFT Detective Constable Stewart taking statements and returned home. After the activity of the last hour the place seemed unnaturally quiet, abandoned almost.

She found Brian in the living-room, drinking tea. He looked up and his face was still. 'It's just brewed. Sit down for five minutes.' He padded into the kitchen for another cup while she shrugged out of her coat.

The heat of it in her hands did as much good as the drink. She regarded him through the steam with a wry smile. 'So what do you think of Castlemere so far?'

He didn't reply, just stood watching, quiet and still. In his intelligent face she saw respect, and compassion, and a new understanding of things that had eluded him for the past eight years. He finally understood that they meant different things when, discussing their work, they talked about 'matters of life and death.' He meant whether there was enough poster-paint to get 3B through a double period and if they'd embarrass him over the nudes when he took them round the local art gallery. She meant hunting down a madman before he cut another child's throat.

Liz saw him regarding her as if they'd just been introduced and he wasn't yet sure if he liked what he saw, and something inside her shrank. He doesn't *know* me, she thought. We've been married eight years, and how I make my living has come as a shock to him! He thought it was like Agatha Christie, a neat intellectual puzzle with the bodies either off-stage or decently disposed with only a spot of blood under the watch-chain to show where the knife went in. Now it's happened on his doorstep and he knows there's nothing decorous about murder, that by the time a body's suffered enough abuse to die of it it's neither neat nor intellectual but as unrelentingly carnal as a butcher's shop-window. And if murder's not what he always thought then I must be other than the woman he thought he married in order to deal with it.

She said quietly, 'Don't look at me like that.'

His gaze didn't flicker. 'Like what?'

'Like you're watching a freak show.'

NEWS SPREAD through Castlemere at a speed governed by the electronic telephone exchange. By ten o'clock when Shapiro was driving to his office the whole town seemed to know what had happened at breakfast-time in Belvedere Park.

There was no one about. No one strolling in the spring sunshine; no young mothers chatting outside shops with prams beside them; no old people on the benches in Hampton Gardens. Most of all, no children. The Hampton Garden swings and the gaily painted roundabout hung still and forlorn. Two teenage boys and a dog hurried across the street and disappeared through a doorway.

Finally, just before he turned into Queen's Street, Shapiro saw a toddler in dungarees and tiny trainers playing in the gutter under the windows of a terrace of mill cottages. But the news must have arrived just as he did because one of the doors was suddenly flung open and a pair of bare arms, soapy from the morning's laundry that was half-done when the phone rang, shot out and snatched the infant inside.

When he got out of the car he could smell fear in the air, acrid like the smoke from the tannery chimneys when the wind was in the east. He murmured to himself, 'This town is just so far from wholesale panic,' and his finger and thumb were the width of a matchbox apart. He climbed the police station steps.

As he passed the CID room he saw Donovan hunched over a phone. 'Oh, good, you got my message. Any luck?'

Donovan shook his head, put the phone down. 'He can't have spent much time in London: the Met has nothing that fits. But they're going to put it round, see if it rings any bells.' He seemed to become aware then that Shapiro, who had only stuck his head in for an update, had not passed on his way but remained in the doorway, staring. 'What's the matter?'

Shapiro did what in the classic days of Hollywood was known as a slow burn. His voice was flat with unstated meaning. 'Cut yourself shaving?'

Donovan's hand went to his throat. He'd put a polo-neck on specially, but the collar had slumped while he was on the phone and there was a sticking plaster over his larynx. 'Er—'

By then Shapiro had also seen the black eye. He turned away. 'My office, Sergeant.'

For a moment Donovan hesitated, his hand sliding towards the phone. The words, 'Now, Sergeant,' came at him from the corridor.

HOUSE-TO-HOUSE inquiries are among the least productive way of using police man-hours. They're slow, tedious and frustrating, and the chance of any individual call discovering something valuable is only marginally better than Millwall's chance of winning the FA Cup. They're unpopular with policemen and householders alike. Nevertheless, the list of crimes which would not have been solved but for diligent door-stepping and intelligent correlation of the information collected is too long for the technique to follow the bicycle patrol and the Black Maria into history.

There were over a hundred houses around Belvedere Park whose residents might conceivably have seen (but probably had not) either or both players in the morning's drama. Those on the Castlemere side—there were twenty-eight of them—had a view of that stretch of bridleway where Alice Elton met her killer. Someone looking at the right time might have seen her ride along the park boundary, stop and turn into the bushes. Scant minutes later they might have seen a man walking briskly—probably not running, the rest of his act was too slick for him to make that basic error—down the lane to where he'd left his car. They might have been able to describe the car.

In fact no one saw anything. Of the twenty-eight houses, six had no one at home when the police called. At three, all of the residents had been in bed at eight o'clock. Nine of the households ate breakfast in the kitchen at the back of the house and didn't finish until after eight-fifteen. Of the remainder, two were eating in a morning-room at the front of the house between seven-forty-five and five past eight, and eight went out to their cars in the same period. They saw nothing either.

Or rather, nothing that advanced the investigation. Five of them remembered the child on the white pony coming down from the council yard, both at about the same time Arnie Sedgewick saw her. Nothing happened in the few seconds they had her in view. Three of them noticed Sedgewick's van. That was all.

Gradually Liz became aware that no one seemed to have seen something that should have been visible to anyone moving about at that time, something that would have been part of the park scenery for two or three times as long as Sedgewick's van. No one remembered seeing Carver ride his bicycle up the lane. A man on a bicycle wasn't so remarkable a sight as to remain indelibly in the memory of anyone who saw it, but then neither was a council van, and three people saw Sedgewick arriving for work. Why had nobody seen Carver?

She turned over the notes she made while talking with the groundsmen. Ray Carver, she read, 15 Coronation Row. She frowned: it was time she knew this town better than she did. 'Coronation Row?' she mused aloud.

DC Stewart was passing close enough to hear. 'That's one of the Victorian terraces at the back of Brick Lane.'

Liz was aware of the nearness of something important. Groping as if through mist she hazarded, 'Near Jubilee Terrace?'

Untroubled by presentiment, the constable nodded. 'Just round the corner,' he said cheerfully.

II

ONE

Liz took the stairs two at a time and ran along the corridor. She rapped on Shapiro's door but didn't wait for an answer before throwing it open. 'I've got a suspect.'

Shapiro caught the suppressed excitement in her voice and his eyes left Donovan and shot to the door. 'A real one?' But he was already talking to her departing shadow and the swift rap of her heels on the linoleum.

Momentarily torn, he wondered if it was more important to persevere with the odd tale Donovan was telling him in the hope of making some sense of it, or to see what Inspector Graham had that had brought her back to Queen's Street when experience told him the house-to-house couldn't be more than half done. But he didn't waver long. Jabbing a thick finger in Donovan's direction he said, 'Don't go anywhere, Sergeant, you and I aren't finished yet.' Then he thrust his chair out from his desk and set off after Liz at a sturdy jog.

He caught up with her outside the interview room. 'Who? Why? How? Are you serious about this?'

Her eyes sparked indignantly at him. 'Of course I'm serious! I don't haul people in here to interrogate them about multiple murders on a whim. It's one of the gardeners. His story doesn't add up. He wasn't where he says he was when Alice Elton was killed.'

'What have you got so far?'

'He'd been in the park for a while. If he'd arrived when he said someone would have seen him and no one did. But he only clocked on after the girl was dead. Also, he knew Charisma. He lives round the corner from her.'

Shapiro sucked air between pursed lips. His eyes were

cautiously optimistic. 'Do you want to talk to him alone, or—?' It was as far as he would go towards taking over the interview.

Liz smiled. 'I'd be glad of your help, sir.'

It took no stretch of the imagination to picture Ray Carver as a murderer; more than that, as a man who cut throats. Hunched sullenly over the desk in the interview room, the black hair hanging lank in his face, dark eyes smouldering on his arms crossed in front of him, he looked like a gypsy about to be hanged for stealing the proverbial sheep. He was twenty-five though he looked older. He'd worked as a groundsman at Belvedere Park for three years. He wasn't tall—about five foot eight—but well muscled under the rough work-clothes and anyway tall enough to kill the two girls in the way they had been killed.

Shapiro was unhappy that he'd been in Castlemere a minimum of three years. After two killings in quick succession he was sure in his own mind that the man they were looking for must have attacked before. But if he'd done it here Shapiro would have known. 'Where did you work before that?'

Carver muttered into his sleeve. 'Sorry?' said Shapiro.

The man straightened abruptly, his eyes flaring like coals. 'I said,' he said loudly, 'I didn't work for eighteen months. Before that I was an apprentice mechanic at Cooney's but the garage went bust.' So he'd been in Castlemere for something over five years, and not far away for longer: he spoke with a local accent.

'How long have you lived at Coronation Row?'

'I was born there.'

'Ah,' said Shapiro.

Liz looked at him sharply, not appreciating the significance. She took up the questioning. 'About this morning. Why did you lie about the time you got to work?'

Carver's gaze returned to his sleeve. 'Who says I lied?'

'I do,' she said firmly. 'If you'd been riding your bike

through the park at the time you say I'd have had half a dozen witnesses. But nobody saw you, Ray. Nobody. That means you weren't there.'

He lifted the muscular shoulders in a heavy shrug. 'So maybe I got the time a bit wrong. I don't know.'

'Maybe,' agreed Liz. 'But you couldn't have been much later because we know what time you clocked in. And if you were earlier, why didn't you clock on earlier and claim the extra money?'

She got no reply beyond another shrug.

'So then we have to wonder what might have been worth more to you than a few extra quid in your pay-packet.'

'I didn't kill her,' he shouted. 'I didn't touch her.'

'You said you didn't see her.'

'I didn't.'

'Then where were you? Everybody else in the area at that time saw her.'

Again the powerful body hunched up as if around a secret. Liz tried a change of direction. 'You knew Charlene Pierce, too, didn't you?'

'Everybody knew her,' he growled.

'In the biblical sense?' asked Shapiro. Carver didn't understand. 'Did you sleep with her?'

'No.' Then he seemed to think better of it. 'I have done. Not recently.' He looked up. 'She was a hooker, she did it for money.'

'You paid her?'

He laughed at that, a hoarse, angry laugh. 'What, you think she took one look at me and begged for it? Of course I paid her.'

'When was the last time?'

'Three, four months ago—something like that.'

'You must have known her all her life,' said Shapiro.

'Pretty much.'

'And you paid to sleep with a sixteen-year-old girl you'd known since she was a child?'

The quick temper flared again. 'She hadn't been no child for a long time. It's what she did, it's what she was: she went with men for money. If it hadn't been me it'd have been someone else. I never hurt her neither.'

'What were you doing Friday night and Saturday night?'

'Friday night I were out drinking. Saturday night I stayed in and watched the telly.'

'Where did you drink?'

'A few places. The Fen Tiger, The Ginger Pig—there were a bunch of us, we moved around.'

'Will they vouch for you?'

'Sure.'

'What happened at closing time?'

'We had a carry-out. When that was finished we went home.'

'So you were alone from, say, midnight?'

'Maybe a bit after; yes.'

'And Saturday?'

'I live alone. Mostly I watch telly alone too.'

'What you're telling us,' Liz spelled out, 'is that nobody can vouch for your whereabouts during the hours when Charlene Pierce was killed, when she was put in the canal, or when someone dragged Alice Elton off her pony and cut her throat.'

Carver rounded on her furiously. 'All them hours, and a whole lot more besides. I'm on my own, see? There used to be my mam and me, now there's just me. Apart from working hours and Friday nights, you can pin any crime in your book on me if I need witnesses to prove I didn't do it.'

'Do you use a knife in the course of your work?' asked Shapiro.

''Course I do. For pruning, grafting, cutting twine—all that stuff. Every gardener uses a knife: you'd take all day with bloody scissors.'

'You have a knife of your own? Where is it?'

'In the house. I don't take it to work with me, I use one from the tool-box. If I took my own I wouldn't have it five minutes. Load of bloody thieves up there, they are.'

Liz said quietly, 'Surely you have some friends among your workmates? A lot of people work at the Town Hall—you must have some friends.'

'Arnie Sedgewick's all right,' he conceded. Some impulse of humour tugged at the corner of his mouth. 'Arnie and me, we—' He stopped.

'What?'

'He's all right, that's all.'

It was like drawing teeth. After a little more of the same Liz and her chief conferred outside.

'Gut feeling?' asked Shapiro.

Liz hesitated, then committed herself. 'That he could have done it but he probably didn't.'

'Then why is he lying?'

She gave him an old-fashioned look. 'If we knew that we'd know everything.'

'Then why do you think he didn't do it?'

'Because he's told the truth about the things that matter. All right, he couldn't have denied knowing Charisma but he could have denied sleeping with her. We have no witnesses to that. He could have invented an alibi for one of the two nights we asked about—he must have a mate somewhere who'd lie for him. He could have said he saw Alice at the same time everyone else did; we'd have believed that. I think he's being straight with us, except for this one thing that he won't tell us about. But I don't think it's that he murdered anyone.'

'Do you want to let him go?'

'Not yet. Not till he tells me what he was doing when he should have been cycling through the park.'

Shapiro left her to it then and returned upstairs. Donovan was on the phone again. There was no one else in the CID room so Shapiro perched on a desk and waited for him to finish. 'Any progress?'

Donovan regarded his notes pensively. 'Well—maybe.'

'Really? When?'

'August of last year. Another young girl—nineteen. Another hooker: amateur, thinking of turning pro was what the investigating officer said. Throat cut back to the spine, probably by somebody standing behind her.'

Shapiro let out a thin whistle. 'That's him, isn't it? Where was this?'

'Dover.'

'*Dover?*' Then Shapiro understood his sergeant's lack of enthusiasm. 'Oh, that's great, isn't it? Now all I've got to find is someone who's been to Dover. Like, half the bloody population.'

Donovan tried to look on the bright side. 'They probably weren't all there last August.'

Shapiro glowered. 'Have you ever been in Dover in August? It *seems* as if half the population's there, setting off on its holidays or getting back with its Duty Free.'

Donovan nodded wordlessly.

After glowering a little longer Shapiro said suddenly, 'How tall was she?'

Donovan was surprised. 'I didn't ask.'

'Find out, will you? Our two have both been particularly short. If this girl was too, maybe it means our man is either short or not particularly strong himself.'

'Or just that he likes an easy life.'

'Or nothing at all,' admitted Shapiro. 'Still, find out.' Then he said, 'What's this you had to tell me about Joseph Bailie?'

Donovan leaned back in his chair, tapping with a pencil and eyeing his chief speculatively. 'What I have to tell you,' he said carefully, 'is that I made a mistake. It's been a lot of years since Liam Brady was a big man in Glencurran: last night I bumped into Bailie, accidentally, on the tow-path and I realized it wasn't the same man.

'What I'm not supposed to tell you is that he broke into my boat while I was asleep, held a knife at my throat and threatened to carve me if I didn't put him in the clear.'

Shapiro's eyes saucered. Like Liz, he'd put his faith in Special Branch records and dismissed Donovan's insistence that they were wrong as paranoia. 'What did you tell him?'

Donovan's glance was scathing. 'With his knife in my jugular, what do you *think* I told him? I told him I'd do it. I let him think he'd scared the shit out of me. It wasn't that difficult.'

Shapiro had known Donovan for five years. He had seen him afraid. Fear acted on him like alcohol, making him querulous and bloody-minded. Knuckling under might have been the sensible thing to do, at least until Brady took his knife away, but for Donovan to do it he must have thought there was more than his skin at stake. 'Then too,' he said slowly, 'if he thinks you're shielding him he can carry on with whatever it is he came here for and we can have him for more than threatening a police officer.'

Donovan gave his saturnine grin. 'It occurred to me.' One of the advantages of working for Frank Shapiro was that a man didn't have to spell out his thinking. This was also one of the disadvantages.

'What do you want to do? We could have him for assault.'

'Save it,' said Donovan, 'in case we need it later. Let him think I'm playing along. He's up to something. Give me a couple of days, see what I can sniff out. He isn't going anywhere—not while the daft bugger in the white suit thinks there's souls to save in Castlemere.'

Shapiro smiled. 'Don't you believe in the power of prayer, Sergeant?'

'If prayers were worth the breath it takes to speak them,'

Donovan said darkly, 'a lot of dead men would be alive and a lot of living men would be dead.'

Shapiro was heading back to the interview room when a call came through from the front desk saying a Mrs June May from the Town Hall wanted to see the person handling the murder investigation. He asked for her to be shown up.

'Mrs May?' he said pensively, mostly to himself. 'What on earth can the Town Hall caretaker's wife know about the murder of Alice Elton?'

Donovan looked up with an interest that was not quite wholesome. 'Have you met her?'

Shapiro knew Davy May well enough, caretaker by name but more of a butler by nature, a dapper, fussy little man of middle age who wore blazers with the municipal arms on the pocket and shoes polished enough to make a sergeant major cry. He couldn't bring Mrs May to mind. 'I don't think so.'

'You wouldn't forget. She's ten years younger than Davy. She thinks people take her for his daughter. You know what they call them up at the Town Hall?—Daisy May and June Certainly Will.'

So it was with an inkling of what she had to tell him that Shapiro greeted Mrs May at his door and showed her to a chair.

Davy May had needed a wife to take on the job of Town Hall major-domo. June Coates had needed a husband to escape the grinding routine of caring for seven younger siblings and an unappreciative father. You had to know that to make any sense of their otherwise incomprehensible union: the fastidious Mr May and his busty, blousy little wife with her fondness for high heels and low necklines.

It was nobody's idea of a match made in heaven. Where Davy cherished order, June craved spontaneity; where he worshipped routine she adored surprises; Davy believed that discretion was the mark of a gentleman while June thought it diagnostic of brain death. They had two things in common. One was a talent for cheerful hard work, the other a fondness for being at the centre of things. Davy's job enabled him to feel that all the business of the Town Hall and thus of Castlemere revolved around him. June achieved the same feeling from constant flirtations and a succession of light-hearted affairs.

As she explained, with a deeply unconvincing essay at remorse, 'I never mean no harm, sir.' She didn't even put it in the past tense. 'I just get carried away. A girl's got to have a bit of fun before she dries up and blows away.'

Shapiro smiled encouragingly. 'And Mr Carver—?'

She smiled too, cheekily, as if at a memory. Then she remembered why she was here. 'It was only a bit of a lark. We never meant anything by it. Only my Davy starts work at seven, and Ray don't start till eight. So sometimes he comes by early and we—well, we have a bit of fun together.' She tried to blush, with no discernible success.

'This morning?'

'He come in by the side door about ten past seven. We had a bit of fun. It was quarter past eight before he left. So you see, he couldn't have seen that girl. He was with me until after she was found.'

Shapiro frowned. 'But, Mrs May, he clocked in for work at three minutes past eight. Ah.' Understanding dawned. 'Mr Sedgewick?'

She beamed, like Barbara Woodhouse finally getting through to a particularly dim dog. 'Arnie and Ray are mates, see. Arnie covers for Ray when he's with me, and Ray covers for Arnie if he wants to knock off early. Fair's fair,' she said virtuously. 'You'd understand that, sir, you being a policeman.'

When it was put to him, Carver agreed that that was how it had been. He was clearly relieved to have it out in the open. 'I wouldn't have told you. Arnie's been a good mate to me, I wouldn't have shopped him for doing something they could sack him for. But yes, that's what we did. When

I'm up at the Town Hall I can't leave till Daisy ain't around. So Arnie clocks me in a couple of minutes after he's punched his own card.

'So what was I to do? Tell you I'd seen the girl when I hadn't? Probably it wouldn't have mattered, but it might have done. I couldn't have seen the poor kid. All the time she was in the park I was in June's bed.' He looked up then. There was no shadow of guilt in his gypsy eyes. 'You going to tell them at the Town Hall? You'll break Daisy's heart.'

'*I* will?' exclaimed Shapiro, taken aback. 'You don't think maybe it's a bit late to consider Davy May's feelings?'

'We always considered his feelings,' said Carver indignantly. 'That's why I arranged with Arnie, so he wouldn't see me sneaking out.'

After Carver had been sent back to his work, trying not to laugh Liz said, 'What will you do? As an officer of the law and a tax-payer, I mean.'

'Damned if I know,' confessed Shapiro. 'It's nothing to do with the investigation, that's plain enough—though we could have wasted a hell of a lot of time if June May hadn't had the wit to come down here. Let them get on with it, I suppose. Though I may drop a hint to Mr Sedgewick that fiddling the time-cards is in fact fraud.'

In the event he didn't have to. In the event, Ray Carver never again enjoyed a bit of fun with June May while her husband polished the candlesticks in the Mayor's parlour.

TWO

ALL TUESDAY the streets of the housing estates and the gardens of the leafy suburbs remained disturbingly empty, and that night the frightened people of Castlemere turned to the one man who seemed to have something to say about the obscenity stalking the town. Their vehicles—for nobody walked to Broad Wharf through the stillness of Castle Place and down the dusky waterfront—were backed up along Brick Lane, blocking the pavements on both sides and narrowing the thoroughfare to the width of one careful car. By eight o'clock Brick Lane was solid and they were parking in Jubilee Terrace.

It was hard to know what they hoped to hear from the man in the white suit. He was an evangelist, not a clairvoyant: nothing said about him and his presence here, even by himself, suggested he could toss a handful of mixed herbs at a flame and reveal the author of their distress. Yet it seemed to be something of that sort they were looking for.

For comfort, strength or guidance they could have turned to their own churches, those who espoused one—for Castlemere was a working town with few pretensions towards piety. So it was something on the metaphysical side of moral leadership that they sought, even if they could not have explained quite what, something to do with the white suit and the rolling thunder of the voice and perhaps even the wheelchair.

They seemed to feel it was more than coincidence that this stranger with his powerful personality and his crusade against evil should arrive in unpromising Castlemere at the one time anyone could remember that there was a job for him to do. They were looking for Merlin, for someone from another dimension to step into the chaos and say, 'It's all right, I have it under control.' A Welsh cripple with a burnished voice and a patched tent was just the closest they could get.

They came like children at first, shyly, shamefaced even, ready to remember urgent business elsewhere if anyone laughed. But the sight of so many others with the same idea, groping towards something they needed but could not have described, gave them confidence. They crowded together in the marquee, drawing comfort from their closeness long before the man in the white suit began to speak.

And when Michael Davey hauled himself up on to the dais by the strength of his shoulders and wheeled to face his audience, the lights behind him shining through his energetic hair like a halo, a sigh whispered over the dense rows of seating. They might not have known, as they made their uncertain way here, just what it was they were looking for; but when they saw Michael Davey, particularly when he drew that first big breath and the words began flowing from him like slow fierce lava, they knew they'd found it.

He filled the tent. When he let it go his voice soared into the eaves and wheeled around there like great birds. His voice made musical thunder like the roar in the hollow of a deep sea wave, rolling across the heads of his audience and crashing against the white canvas cliffs in a foam of pith and wisdom. His voice thrilled and quickened them.

The dais was not high enough that a seated man could be seen easily from the far reaches of the tent. From halfway back people found it easier to stand. Near the back of the tent they stood on the chairs. Because many of them had scant experience of church it did not seem incongruous to them to clap and cheer and even whistle when his vibrant words struck chords of meaning in their hearts. They thought, That's right!—that's what *I* think!—about concepts they had never before considered.

What did he say? What were the words that drew such fervour from frightened people? Reduced to letters on a cool page they would seem nothing very much, only a trite cocktail of moral certainty and righteous indignation. But how he used those flat words, those commonplace ideas! How his audience responded! How they fed each other with pain and anger and the thrill of marshalling themselves to strike back! When Davey spoke of confronting the Devil in the backstreets of Castlemere it seemed that at any moment someone would produce a sack of brands and a taper to light them with.

More like lovers than a shepherd with sheep, drawing vitality from one another, clasped together like coupling bodies on a sweaty bed they rocked to the rhythm of his rhetoric. If thine eye offend thee, pluck it out. Life for life, burning for burning. No peace for the wicked; for whatsoever a man soweth that shall he also reap. Blessed are they which hunger and thirst after righteousness. For where two or three are gathered in my name, there am I in the midst of them. Vengeance is mine, saith the Lord. Faith without works is dead.

And what was it that turned the sensible, cynical people of Castlemere into a mob intoxicated with the cordite smell of a church militant? Only fear, that makes cowards and heroes of the same dust. They looked on the wine when it was red, and changes they did not understand came over them.

Donovan had watched in disbelief as the throng swelled on Broad Wharf until the tent, all but empty the night before, could hardly hold them. He listened uneasily to the swelling voices, the disturbing unanimity of mood. He thought he should do something about it and didn't know what. All his instincts told him something sinister was happening, but the only facts were that a gospel meeting had attracted a bigger turn-out than he'd expected. He didn't know how Superintendent Taylor would react if Donovan phoned him at home to tell him that.

He thought of phoning Shapiro instead, even though crowd control was no part of a detective chief inspector's brief, but he didn't know what he could say that would justify a police presence here. For a long time he stood undecided on *Tara*'s deck, feeling the electricity in the air grow even as the light faded. Then he made a move towards the tent. There was no longer much point in avoiding Brady and he'd have a better idea what needed to be done if he could hear what was being said.

He never got there. As he moved across the dark wharf, doing nothing to attract attention to himself, a hand reached out of the shadows and hooked his elbow, swinging him into the alley where he'd found the body of Charlene Pierce. Another clapped over his mouth. He had a powerful sense of *déjà vu.*

Brady hissed in his ear, 'There's going to be trouble here. They're saying you had the man who killed those girls and you let him go. Is that right?'

Donovan shook off his hand. 'No. We talked to a guy but it wasn't him, it couldn't have been: he was in some-body else's bed at the time.'

'Well, the people in there have convinced themselves he's the one. You know what folk are like in these situa-tions: they don't wait to hear the details. You people ques-tioned him at the park after the little girl was found, then you sent a squad car for him. Did you think no one'd no-tice? That's a public park, a dozen people must have seen you arrest him. Before you had him cautioned the experts in every bus queue and every supermarket check-out in town had him tried and convicted. And now they think you've let him get away with it. There'll be no trouble as long as Reverend Mike keeps talking. But he'll be done soon and they'll leave, and not all of them are going to go straight home.'

Donovan stared at what he could see of the man in the dark. 'You think they'll go after him? Jesus Christ, he only lives off Brick Lane.'

'I don't know what they'll do,' said Brady. 'But in that tent right now there's a strong smell of hemp rope. If they start to move, and they know where to find him, you, me and a couple of wooden-tops aren't going to stop them. You know where he lives. Get him away before they go for him.'

Donovan started to say, 'I'll call Queen's Street—' but Brady interrupted. 'There's no time. I'll call the police, tell them what you're doing. But if you're not away from here before they come out of that tent you'll never get past them. And there's nothing you can do from behind.'

Donovan waited no longer. 'I'll take the motorbike.'

He took the walkway up on to Brick Lane. Traffic was theoretically barred but a motorbike could squeeze between the bollards and Donovan judged the situation urgent enough to break a bylaw or two. He accelerated between the parked cars and did a dirt-track turn, his knee centimetres from the tarmac, into Jubilee Terrace.

It was like entering a walled city. The six streets, all with classic Victorian names, formed an enclave to which the only way in was Jubilee Terrace. The dwellings were modest little back-to-backs with yards separated by narrow alleys, called in the local argot ginnels, but apart from Philip Pierce's they were respectable enough and no one who lived there thought of the place they called The Jubilee as a slum. It was quiet, there was no through traffic, the kids could play in the streets—normally they could—and nobody complained if a man kept a few pigeons. For those with no great ambition it was an easy place to live.

Donovan gunned the bike to a halt in front of Carver's house and hammered on the door, dragging his helmet off as he did so. Best of all, he thought, was if the man wasn't at home—was out celebrating with June May, for instance.

But if he was here, the sooner he'd answer this bloody door the better.

He was there. Donovan caught movement at an upstairs window followed by the sound of feet on the stair. The door opened and Carver peered at him suspiciously. He hadn't met Donovan formally and didn't recognize him. 'Who are you?'

'Detective Sergeant Donovan, Castlemere CID. Grab a coat, you're coming with me.'

Carver's gypsy eyes opened wide and he took a step back. 'You've got it wrong. I was let go. I've got an alibi.'

'I know. But there's going to be trouble here. You'll be safer away.'

Carver stared at him. 'Trouble?'

For the first time Donovan's resolution wavered. He was here on the unsupported word of a liar, thug and at least one-time terrorist. Apart from his general observation that a lot of people were at the crusade that night, and they were listening to the address with as much enthusiasm as Davey was giving it, he had no evidence that any harm was intended or likely. Now he thought about it, it seemed just as likely that Brady wanted him off the wharf for half an hour while he got on with whatever had brought him here.

If there was a problem there was no time to waste; if there wasn't, it didn't matter. He decided. 'Look, this may be a false alarm—somebody making a fool of me. But it's possible some of the God-botherers from the wharf are going to come here when they've finished their meeting. They've got hold of your name, they know we questioned you about Alice Elton's murder and don't know why we let you go. I'd like to get you out of here before that meeting winds up.'

Carver understood that. He was a man from The Jubilee, he didn't share the middle-class faith in the power of rational persuasion. If men were coming here to accuse him of killing a child, however complete his defence he wasn't going to stay and offer it when he could be on the far side of town. Subsequent vindication and abject apologies wouldn't mend broken bones.

Nodding at the bike Donovan said, 'Have you done this before?'

Carver's response was scathing. 'Can a fish swim?'

Donovan held out his helmet. 'Put that on, then nobody'll recognize you.' He mounted the bike and Carver climbed on behind him. Rather more sedately than he'd arrived, Donovan circled the block back into Jubilee Terrace.

And they were there. At the end of the road, the cork in the bottleneck. It was hard to judge how many. They looked like a wall of people across the end of the street: there might have been twenty of them or twice that number. The Jubilee was sealed off.

Half expecting them as he was, the sight shocked Donovan to the core. He'd seen mobs in Ireland but never in Castlemere. It wasn't mob country somehow. But recent events had affected everyone in town, and especially those with children of their own. They weren't natural go-to-meeting folk: they were young men who'd left their wives and children at home behind locked doors, who'd tramped the empty streets angrily and failed to find comfort in the pubs, who'd come then in a kind of cynic despair to see if the preacher had anything to offer.

And the preacher had said, in essence, that the remedy lay in their own hands. If thine eye offend thee, and all that. The Old Testament passions worked on them like strong drink, and when the meeting had finished a significant number of them felt moved to confront the works of the Devil as they'd been told they must.

To his credit, part of his brain continuing to function while the rest of it froze, Donovan did nothing to signal his alarm, either by accelerating, braking or throwing a quick turn. He continued at the same unhurried pace and turned left into the other half of Coronation Row, out of sight of the gathering in Jubilee Terrace. So far as he could see they made no move to follow him. They didn't seem sure what to do next.

At the top end of the enclave he stopped the bike. He knew the area but not like a native. 'Is there a way out?'

Defective street-lights didn't get replaced as quickly in The Jubilee as round Belvedere Park but there were enough to show the pallor of Carver's cheeks. He shook his head.

'Even on foot,' Donovan pressed him. 'Is there a back wall we can climb over, a garage roof, anything?'

'From Coronation Row.' Carver's voice was reedy, his teeth chattering as if the night was cold. 'You can cross from the backyards of Coronation Row into the backyards of Brick Lane. We might get out that way.'

Under normal circumstances perhaps: the need for a little breaking and entering would have deterred Donovan no more than any genuine resident of The Jubilee. But with a hostile gathering at that end of the walled city someone would see them, raise a hue and cry. They might conceivably reach Brick Lane but they wouldn't get any further. Brick Lane was where these people had come from, where they were probably still coming from, where their cars were parked, where those who didn't want to get involved but also didn't want to miss much would be waiting.

'We'd better get indoors. Round here somewhere, I don't want those people to see us. Do you know anybody who lives here, who'd let us in without making a row?'

Perhaps he did but Carver couldn't seem to think. He peered anxiously from one front door to another as if trying to distinguish between them. 'Never mind,' said Donovan, 'I'll flash my card at them.' He reached for the nearest bell.

But no one came. The first couple of times he rang and no one answered Donovan thought he was being unlucky. He wondered if half The Jubilee was down at the wharf as well: from curiosity, he couldn't see them going anywhere

to pray. But when time and again his summons went un-
answered, as he moved from door to door and no one so
much as opened a window to look at him, he understood.
These houses weren't empty; not all of them. At some of
them the inmates didn't know what was going on and didn't
want to. And at some they knew exactly what was going
on and, through fear or because they too believed in Carver's guilt, wouldn't raise a finger to stop it.

'You miserable bastards!' Black fury and gnawing fear
ravelled together in Donovan's mind. He didn't know what
to do. He could force an entry but he couldn't do it silently
and the sound of breaking glass would carry.

That gave him an idea. There was no time to go through
it in detail to judge if it was a good one. He waved Carver
to the bike. 'You take her. Don't ride, push. Get round the
far corner and stay out of sight till you hear a commotion.
I'm going to break into one of these houses. One of two
things should happen. Either I'll find a phone and whistle
up some help. Or the God-botherers'll come after me. If
they come up here to see what the noise is about, maybe
they'll leave the road open.

'If that happens, get out of The Jubilee as fast as you
can. Don't stop for anyone. If they try and stop you, run
them down.'

THREE

SHEER BAD LUCK defeated him. He chose a house at random and stabbed his gloved fist through the circle of reeded glass in the front door. The glass was tougher than he expected: he hit it twice without result. When it did break the noise of falling glass shattered the uneasy quiet of The Jubilee.

Protected by his leather jacket he fumbled for the catch, stumbled inside. But there was no telephone. A low-wattage bulb showed him a tiny hall, stairs and two doors. He tried the front room but there was no phone there either. He tried the kitchen. Finally he ran upstairs. He found an old man cowering on an iron bedstead in the dark.

'I need your phone.'

'I haven't got one.'

Donovan flung downstairs again and back to the street. He could hear them coming, the rumble of feet and voices mounting as they approached the corner. He had no idea what they'd do when they got here. Quite possibly nothing: they might eye one another in growing embarrassment for a few minutes and then shuffle off home. But unpredictability is inherent in any mass action, and the experiences of Toxteth and Broadwater Farm destroyed for ever the comfortable notion that, even when they were worked up, people weren't animals and common sense would intervene before anything really nasty took place.

So Donovan didn't wait to see but smashed the glass in the next door along, scrabbled for the catch and fell into the hall with an image of movement—rolling movements like a breaking sea—on the edge of his vision.

His groping hands found the phone. He dragged off a

glove with his teeth and dialled 999. While the dial returned unhurriedly to neutral he had time to think that countries which used 111 as their emergency code had the right idea. Then the line connected and someone asked him which service he required.

Then the wave of bodies that had wheeled into the street behind him surged through the open door, bowled him away from the phone and fell on him like breakers falling on rocks. Fists and boots rained on him. The arms he raised to shield his face were wrenched apart and someone hit him across the eyes.

Then the tide receded, taking its flotsam with it. When the house was empty the little tinny voice of the emergency operator was plainly audible asking with increasing agitation what was happening, whether anyone was still there, and which of the three services the caller was in most urgent need of.

Half-conscious and unresisting, Donovan was dragged into the street and dropped in the gutter. His head collided with the kerbstone: new constellations rose before his eyes. Men leaned over him. Someone shone a torch in his face.

He could make more sense of the voices than of what he could see. They were saying Carver's name and, with taut satisfaction, 'We've got him.' Someone said, 'The stinking beast.'

Someone else said, 'That isn't Carver.'

A murmur and then a silence ran through the press. A voice raised in thin anger demanded, 'Then why'd he run? Of course it's Carver.'

'I'm telling you,' said the first man, 'I know Ray Carver and that's not him.'

'Then who is he?'

They bent over him; hands fastened in his jacket hauled him to his feet. The torch blinded him. He mumbled through broken lips, 'I'm a frigging policeman.'

In the hush that fell the sound of the motorbike was clear, strong and close. Someone yelled, '*That's* Carver!'

If he'd been the man they thought, Carver would have got through the depleted gathering in Jubilee Terrace, broken bodies spinning from the wheels of the big machine, and might well have escaped. But he wasn't. He was an ordinary man; within certain limitations a decent man; a man who could have avoided trouble by either compromising his lady-friend or lying about what he'd seen but who had refused to do either. Whatever he might have promised Donovan, Ray Carver was never going to mow through a press of human bodies. He didn't have it in him. At the last possible moment, when he had either to brake or drive into them, he braked.

Road-dirt spat from under the tyres and the machine slewed wildly. People scattered before it. When the wheels went from under him Carver hit the ground hard, the bike toppling on to him, pinning him down.

For a long moment no one seemed to know what to do. The man they'd come seeking was helpless at their feet. They gathered round to look. A couple of the older men ventured forward to lift the bike off him and help him up.

A furious bellow stopped them. The young men who had led the charge up into the enclave were back, thrusting through the crowd. One of them bent over the man on the ground and pulled the helmet off. 'That him?' Voices agreed that it was.

The man straightened up, breathing heavily. He was stocky and well muscled but more accustomed to heavy labour than to running. Sometimes he was a catch-hand bricklayer, sometimes he was a bouncer at the 'Samarkand' nightclub. He didn't live in The Jubilee but he was known there. His name was Jackson, he was in his mid-thirties, and he was the father of two daughters both under ten.

He'd put a suit on for the gospel meeting but it wasn't a new suit to start with and it had aged a lot in the last ten minutes. His tie was pulled down and his collar open; sweat glinted on his face in the wink of the street-lamps. He said, 'So that's what human filth looks like.'

Carver struggled with the machine lying on his leg but couldn't shift it. His mouth moved but nothing came out. Fear shone in his eyes.

Jackson bent over him again to take the key out of the ignition. For a moment Donovan thought he'd done it to prevent Carver leaping up and riding away. Then with a shock of premonition he realized what was intended. He roared, 'No!' and heard his voice crack.

Hands held him. Someone hit him in the small of the back and he went down on his knees. The rest of what happened he watched through a forest of legs.

Jackson didn't glance at him. He unlocked the petrol filler cap. The fuel ran over Carver's leg and up to his groin. Fumes rose acrid as incense.

The sometime bouncer took out a cigarette. 'Damned if I know what we should do with it,' he said with a heavy and vicious humour. 'Anybody want a smoke while we think about it?'

So far as Donovan could see nobody took him up on the offer. But he lit his own cigarette, and held the match until it burned down to his fingertips. For the same space his eyes held Carver's eyes as they rounded with terror, terrible mewling little cries spilling out of his lips while his head shook from side to side and his hands thrust ineffectually at the machine.

When the flame burned his fingers the stocky man said mildly, 'Ow,' and let it drop.

'I WANT HIM for this, Liz.' Shapiro was speaking through clenched teeth which meant he was very angry. When he was ordinarily displeased, for instance with her, he favoured a kind of gruff sarcasm. Occasionally she had heard him angry enough, usually with Donovan, to raise his voice. But in the ten years, on and off, that she'd known him she could only remember three or four occasions when he'd been angry enough to whisper. 'Not just the bastard in the cells who did it. I want the bastard in the tent who put him up to it.'

'If we can get him.' Liz was more cautious. 'Incitement's a tricky one, Frank. You can know perfectly well what somebody meant but if the words are in any way ambiguous you're not going to make it stick.'

'That gang went straight from his tabernacle to The Jubilee. Ten minutes after he'd finished with them they were beating the crap out of my sergeant. Then they watched while one madder-than-average bastard doused a helpless man with petrol and put a match to him. You don't think that's cause and effect?'

'I'm sure Davey was responsible for what happened,' Liz said deliberately. 'I don't know yet if he's committed any offence. I've got them waiting downstairs now. I may know more when I've interviewed them.'

'Can't Donovan nail him?'

'Not specifically, no.' Liz had talked to him in the hospital while he was getting his own hurts dealt with. They weren't serious: cuts and bruises, burns to one hand where he'd tried to smother the flames, forgetting that he'd left a glove in the house with the phone. He'd seemed dazed, mostly with shock. Seeing a trapped man deliberately set on fire, hearing the shrieks hammer at his brain and trying to affect a rescue while thirty men looked on and did nothing had been the most harrowing experience of his life. The flames were reflected in his eyes as he talked. Liz knew he was seeing anything but her. 'Nobody said "Reverend Mike sent us."'

'What about Jackson? Will he say it was Davey's idea?'

'Not yet.' Liz gave a grim smile. 'He's still claiming it was an accident, that he wanted a smoke and didn't think of the consequences.'

'God help us all!' exclaimed Shapiro despairingly. 'When he'd unscrewed the petrol cap? When he had to take the key out of the ignition to do it? What does he think?—somebody looked under a cabbage leaf and there we were?' Belatedly he caught an echo of what Liz had said. 'Interviewed them? What them?'

'He has an assistant. Jennifer Mills. She makes the business arrangements, he does the talking.'

'She was there last night?'

'She's there every night, apparently. Reverend Mike's cheerleader.'

Shapiro sniffed. 'Which do you want to talk to?'

'I don't mind.' They were along so she could be candid. 'But if you take him, Frank, don't lose your temper. I know how you feel about zealots, but whether we like it or not people selling religion enjoy more latitude than people selling fish-and-chips. It doesn't make him fire-proof. It does mean that if you want to prosecute you'll have to be careful.'

Shapiro wasn't so angry that he'd lost all sense of proportion. He tugged an imaginary forelock. 'Yes, ma'am.'

She grinned at him with real affection. He wasn't one of the giants of detective mythology, one of the men to whom the conversation inevitably turned at police gatherings. But she thought he was probably as good a policeman, and at least as good a man, as those that were.

Being a Jew may have held him back. Being of no great height and inclined to stoutness would not have helped. There were no stereotypes of stardom that fitted him. At the same time she had never met anyone, police or civilian, who'd known Frank Shapiro however casually without learning to respect him. She hoped he knew that.

She said, 'Just don't tell him about the agnostic dyslexic insomniac.'

'The one who lies awake nights wondering if there is a dog?' He sighed and shook his head, making for the door.

'It's getting time to retire when everyone you work with knows all your jokes.' In the doorway he paused. 'Have somebody buzz me when Donovan comes in.'

Liz stared at him. 'Donovan won't be in today.'

Shapiro just smiled as he went out.

FOUR

JENNIFER MILLS was Liz's age or a little older, a tall, slim woman with intelligent eyes in a high-boned face under a short cap of red-blonde hair. She had a low, faintly husky voice on which an upper-middle-class accent sat lightly, a mere interesting inflection. She wore tailored casuals and good shoes. A slouch hat lay on the table before her, and beside it a packet of cigarettes and a gold lighter. She had seen no need to ask permission to smoke.

A glance confirmed what Liz had been told, that Davey was the heart and soul of the crusade but Mills was its brains. It was Davey people came to hear but Mills who put him where he was needed. In the other interview room Davey might be filling the air with gestures and rhetoric but Liz suspected Shapiro had the easier task. This intelligent, self-contained woman wasn't going to get carried away by the sound of her own voice and accidentally say what she meant instead of what was politic.

Liz introduced herself and began the interview. Almost immediately Mills interrupted: there was no hostility in her manner, but—deliberately or instinctively—she hijacked the proceedings, effectively setting both the agenda and the pace.

'I want to say at the outset that Reverend Davey and I are appalled at what happened last night. Neither of us anticipated such a thing. We want to co-operate with your inquiry and hope we can help you bring those responsible to justice. We've no wish to protect anyone capable of that kind of atrocity. The climate of fear created in this town by recent events is no defence.'

If Liz was taken aback by this manifesto she tried not to

show it. 'It must have occurred to you, Miss Mills, that since those involved came to Broad Wharf seeking the consolation of religion and left as a mob looking for blood, Mr Davey's contribution must be open to criticism.'

Jennifer Mills took from her handbag the flat plastic box of a tape cassette. 'You might find it helpful to listen to this. I tape all Reverend Davey's addresses. He doesn't use a prepared text so if he comes up with something that hits the spot it's useful to have a record. I also offer them to the local radio when we arrive somewhere new.' She smiled thinly. 'Sometimes they have a little fun at our expense but it's all publicity. This is the tape from last night. I can't prove when it was made but he refers to the murder of the child earlier in the day, and you can hear the crowd there, so it really couldn't have been made anywhere else.'

Liz put it into the machine and they listened to the musical voice, the Welsh accent emphasized by the electronics, that began low and sombre and worked its way up by degrees to first a strident intensity and then a soaring celebration of the power of the word that seemed to Liz to have less to do with religion than with the sheer grand opera of oratory.

SHAPIRO DIDN'T like opera. He mistrusted oratory—it was too easy to be swayed by the power of the speaker and fail to analyse the content of the speech—and was unconvinced of the efficacy of religion, his own or anybody else's. For every genuinely religious person he'd met he reckoned there were ten who used dogma as an easy alternative to thinking and faith as a substitute for personal responsibility. He suspected the words 'The will of God' had been responsible for more deaths than cholera.

So it was never on the cards that Frank Shapiro and Michael Davey would like one another and by no means sure that they would manage respect. But they were two middle-aged men in responsible professions with a wealth of experience behind them, and they ought to have been able to avoid insults.

Davey had been badly shaken by the events that followed his meeting, and the summons to the police station seemed to infer that they were in some measure his fault. He hadn't intended to raise a mob against anyone, least of all an innocent man. He'd listened to the tape—his memory being less reliable—and he didn't think he had instigated what happened. The Old Testament prophets he preferred didn't mince their words, tended to preach in blood and thunder, but he didn't think quoting them amounted to incitement to violence. But he was aware the police might take another view. Anxiety made him come out fighting.

'What the hell kind of a town is this?' he demanded, leaning over the table and thrusting his broad face at Shapiro's. 'You people got no self-control? Between young girls selling themselves on the streets, and people cutting throats twice a week, and people setting fire to other people because of some rumour, it's like Sodom and Gomorrah. I've been some rough places in my time but I don't remember anywhere they hold life as cheap as here.'

Shapiro gritted his teeth but couldn't stop his nostrils flaring. 'I'm glad you want to talk about the attempted murder of Raymond Carver, Mr Davey. That's why you're here.'

Diamond eyes glinted in the flushed face. 'Oh, I know why I'm here, Chief Inspector. I'm here because it's easier to sit moaning in the dark than try and get a fire going.' It was the wrong metaphor for the occasion. Flustered, he hurried on. 'When people ask what you're doing about the appalling lawlessness in Castlemere you'll be able to point at me and say, We're arresting the people who complain about it.'

'I see,' Shapiro said slowly. 'You said the police weren't doing enough to catch Alice Elton's killer, and your audience dashed off and set fire to the man we'd had in for questioning.'

'No!' Then he thought again. 'Well yes, I suppose so. But it wasn't my doing. You're blaming me for something I could neither anticipate nor prevent. On the same basis I could blame you for the murder of that little girl in the park. It's the job of the police to protect people but, boy, did you ever let her down!'

'And you think your way's better, do you?' asked Shapiro tight-lipped. 'Rabble-rousing, mob rule, and go straight to the punishment to avoid the tedium of a trial. That's the New Jerusalem you have to offer us, is it, Mr Davey?'

'I don't know,' Davey shot across the table at him, 'if I have anything to offer. But at least I am not afraid to confront the need. I'm not so scared of failing that I'd sooner pretend there's no problem. I don't sit in a snug little office two floors above the street, with my back to the window so I can pretend not to see the filth mounting up out there. I get down into it, with the smell in my nostrils and the grime under my fingernails, and I try to clean it up. I don't always succeed. Even when I do succeed, a little, there's still so much more to do than one man can ever hope to tackle. But by God, Mr Shapiro, at least I try. I do my Christian duty and try.'

Someone deliberately trying to annoy Shapiro could not have bettered that sanctimonious stridency of tone, that astringent blend of militancy and piousness. Anyone who knew him would have seen how angry he was becoming. Even a stranger such as Davey must have seen how the muscles of his face tensed and the skin round his eyes and over his jowls went white. But he still didn't raise his voice. He lowered it so that the words came out, one at a time, like the base line in a piece of martial music reserved for state funerals.

'There's a young man in Castle General because of your Christian duty. He's got third-degree burns from his waist to his knees. I'm told his life is now out of danger. I'm also told he has months or years of painful skin grafts ahead of him. Now, I don't know yet if you're legally responsible for what happened to him. But if you don't feel a moral responsibility then it seems to me that what you call your Christian duty is of less use to humanity than the bit we throw away after circumcision.'

Outrage leaves many people momentarily breathless. If it had had that effect on Davey he probably wouldn't have spat out, 'And what can a Jew know of Christian duty?'

'Jews,' said Shapiro deliberately, 'know all about Christian duty. They've carried the burden of it for two thousand years.'

Into this edifying scene came Liz Graham. She saw the anger in the two men's faces, red in Davey's, white in Shapiro's, and sighed. 'May I have a word with you outside, sir?'

'*Now,* Inspector?'

'Now, sir.'

When he'd heard the tape Shapiro had to agree that, unwise as it might have been in the circumstances, Davey's address of the previous night did not constitute an offence. 'Damnation,' he said with quiet feeling. 'I wanted the pleasure of charging the daft bastard.'

'Give him a piece of your mind instead,' suggested Liz.

'I did that,' he said gloomily. 'He gave me a piece of his in return.'

Liz offered to drive them back to their hotel but they'd come by car: a specially adapted car which Davey drove. While he was getting in—he refused her help while Mills knew better than to offer—the women stood chatting by the boot; not as friends exactly but as people with something in common.

'He's a good man,' said Mills. 'Really, a good man. But he isn't always an easy man.'

Liz smiled. 'You must have read my book.' Mills raised

an interrogative eyebrow. '"How To Apologize Gracefully
For A Bad-Tempered Boss".' She was, Liz knew, being
unfair to Shapiro but she was interested to see what she
could learn about Davey by putting Mills at her ease. They
chuckled together.

'You wrote that? I keep a copy in my handbag. Seri-
ously,' Mills went on, 'Michael does so much good. He
gives people faith in themselves. He gives them the strength
to stand up for what they believe in. When we leave somewhere, it's a better place than before we came.'

'Well, maybe,' murmured Liz, politely unconvinced.

'No, truly,' insisted the other woman. 'Enough to affect
local crime statistics.'

Knowing something about crime figures, Liz was non-
committal. 'How do you decide where to go? I mean, what
made you pick Castlemere?'

'We try to go where there seems to be a need for us. I
do a bit of driving round between stops—it's easier for me
than for Michael, so he stays behind to say goodbye and I
go on ahead. I have to arrive in every town ahead of the
tent anyway, to make sure the site we've been given is
suitable and complete the paperwork, so while I'm on my
way I look out for places we could go next time we're in
the area. I drive around, pick up the local papers, sit in on
a church service, visit a pub. You develop a feeling for
communities which are essentially strong and those which
are in danger of breaking down.'

'And Castlemere seemed to you to be breaking down?'

Mills looked at her with surprise. 'You doubt it? After
this last week? Inspector, I was first here about six months
ago. I thought then the place was in need of—well, let's
call it moral leadership. Then you had that business of the
hospital killings, and I changed the question-mark in my
diary to a tick. While we were on our way here this fresh
business with the hookers started, and now there's been a

riot. Do *you* think Castlemere knows where it's heading, Inspector Graham?'

Liz frowned. 'Charlene Pierce was a prostitute. Alice Elton wasn't.'

Mills dropped her gaze in swift apology. 'Yes, of course. I'm sorry. But you take my point. This is not a town where everything's bumping along normally. Things have gone badly wrong with the social structure of a community before events like these start showing above the surface. You may not want Michael here; that doesn't mean you don't need him.'

'How long do you plan on staying?'

'It was going to be a fortnight. After this'—she shrugged eloquently—'I don't know. As long as he seems to be doing some good.'

'How do you judge?'

Mills smiled tightly. 'That's always the hard part, isn't it?—knowing if what you're doing is for the best. No offence, Inspector, but I've learned not to take the police view as law.'

'That's a coincidence,' Liz parried amiably. 'I've stopped taking the word of the clergy as gospel.'

FIVE

BACK INSIDE Donovan was poring over the log-book by the switchboard. The left side of his face was discoloured and his right hand was wrapped in cling-film, otherwise he seemed to have got off lightly enough. But when he glanced quickly up at her and then back at the book she was aware of the tension threading through his long body like electricity.

'Mr Shapiro's looking for you.'

He nodded. 'I'll be up in a minute. I wanted to check something.'

'What?'

He stabbed the page with a savage finger. 'This. Brady told me he'd call here while I got Carver out of The Jubilee. There was a call—anonymous—but it didn't come in till ten-twenty. Now, I can't say what time I left the wharf, but it had to be fifteen minutes before that. That's a damn sight longer than it takes to get to a phone. What the hell was he doing that was more important than getting me some back-up?'

'He's a stranger here,' Liz said reasonably. 'It would take him longer than you or me.'

'Quarter of an hour?'

'Maybe.' It seemed a long time to her too. It must have felt hellish long in the midst of a mob.

He followed her upstairs. 'Are you charging Davey?'

Liz shook her head. 'He didn't do much to improve the situation but I can't show that he provoked it.'

'It wouldn't have happened if he hadn't been here.' Anger vibrated in his voice; when she looked round he looked away rather than meet her eyes.

Liz sighed. 'Go see what Mr Shapiro wants. Then I have some phone calls for you to make.'

That brought his gaze flicking back. 'I thought I'd go see Liam Brady.'

'Donovan,' she said patiently, 'he's already thumped you once. That was when you had two good hands. I don't want you leaving the office until you can deal with any trouble you meet, and I can trust you not to start any.'

'But what about *Brady?*' he demanded. 'He's supposed to be dead, and he isn't. So what's he doing here, and what are we doing about finding out?'

'We will find out,' she promised him. 'I'll tackle Special Branch this time, see if I can get a bit more sense out of them. I know it's suspicious but it may not mean he's guilty of anything. The car crash was obviously rigged. What if it wasn't so much to mislead us as to mislead the IRA?'

She'd succeeded in surprising him. 'Why the hell would he want to do that?'

'Maybe he'd had enough. Maybe he decided getting shot once was once too often and he didn't want to risk it again. What would he do? Tender his resignation in triplicate and wait for his gold watch to arrive? You know these people better than me, but wouldn't there be a lot of grief waiting for him if he said he wanted out?'

He thought about it, nodded slowly. 'Probably. His da being who he was, Liam'd know too damn much for comfort.'

Liz shrugged. 'So maybe he thought an accident was the simplest way out.'

'You mean, even his da thinks he's dead?'

'He'd have to, for it to work. When he heard it from the NYPD he'd believe it, and everyone else would believe it from him.'

'And that's why he didn't want me raking it up? He wasn't scared of us, he was scared of word getting back to the boyos. So what?—he really is working as an evangelist's roadie?'

Liz shrugged. 'Even an ex-terrorist has to live. It's work he wouldn't need too many papers for.'

He looked at her with mingled doubt and admiration. 'And the chief says I've an over-active imagination!'

She grinned. 'Yes, I know, it's all a bit hypothetical. All the same, it would fit with what we know. Including the fact that he seems to have had some help from the FBI. They wouldn't be taken in by a crash faked by the IRA to protect one of their own. They'd go through the wreckage with a microscope; if it wasn't Brady's body they wouldn't tell Special Branch it was. But if Brady was trying to leave the IRA, particularly if he was willing to trade information for some help, that's how they'd handle it. And in that case Special Branch know he's alive, and know he's no threat to us, and maybe they'll admit it if I put it to them straight.'

Liz was heading for her own office then but Shapiro heard their voices and called them both inside. 'I've had an unworthy thought. I'd quite like somebody to talk me out of it.' Liz sat down, and Donovan perched on the windowsill like an exotic houseplant kept more for its interesting habit than its attractive foliage, and they listened.

'Suppose,' he began, 'just suppose because I've no evidence for this, that it was Michael Davey who murdered Charlene Pierce and Alice Elton.' He paused but was denied the satisfaction of a sharp intake of breath. They'd played this game together too often before. He sighed and went on. 'He could have reached the scenes of both crimes—he can drive and the surface is hard enough both at the wharf and the bridleway to take a wheelchair. Neither girl would be scared of a man in a wheelchair. Alice would have got off her pony to help if he said he'd dropped something, for instance.'

'What about the angle of the wounds?' objected Liz.

'They indicated somebody standing above the victims. Are you suggesting he can get out of the chair?'

'Not necessarily,' said Shapiro, 'though it's a thought. But suppose he gets the girl to turn her back and cuts her throat. Wouldn't that give you the same wound as with the man standing behind her?' No one denied it. He continued with the hypothesis.

'He'd have no trouble moving the bodies. Probably they died on top of him; if not, all he had to do was haul them on to his knees and carry them that way. He's a strong man, remember, at least from the chest upward. Anyone in a wheelchair develops great upper body strength.

'But he probably isn't capable of rape. He can think about it, he can experience the urge, but probably he can't carry out the act. Any gratification he wants that way he'll have to get with his eyes. Hence the victim with her clothes round her ankles but no attempt at penetration.'

'But—why?' asked Liz, obviously taken aback but willing to consider it. 'Because he can't have relations with women?'

'Perhaps. But there's also a financial incentive.'

She stared at him, appalled and disbelieving. 'How can he possibly make money out of killing young girls?'

'He makes money by filling that tent. If no one comes there's no collection. Castlemere isn't natural evangelist country, a week ago the only people at his meetings would have been there to laugh at him. Even after Charisma died there wasn't any real interest, was there?'

Donovan shook his head. 'Monday night you could hear a loose screw drop.'

'But the murder of Alice Elton on Tuesday morning put the fear of God into this town, and people turned to the warrior priest. Davey made a lot of money last night, and he gained a lot of credibility which means a big turn-out for the rest of his stay here. A cynic might consider that a motive.'

'He'd have been seen,' objected Liz. 'Probably at the wharf—the place may be quiet after dark but it's not deserted, somebody was bound to see a man in a wheelchair with a body over his knees, not even once but twice.'

'It wasn't him that put her in the canal,' Donovan proposed. 'That was one of the roadies covering for him. The first time he was lucky, but he knew he couldn't hang around and he knew he couldn't go back. That's why she had to wait a day before she could be disposed of. Once the trucks arrived and he had men camped fifty metres away it was easy enough.'

'This would all depend on Davey travelling ahead of the trucks,' Shapiro reminded them. 'Do we know if he did?'

Liz looked doubtful. 'From what Mills told me, he's the last to leave when they take the tent down. I suppose he might travel faster than the lorries—that's obviously his car, it's adapted for him. But would he get here a whole day ahead of them?'

'And what about Mills?' added Shapiro, picking holes in his own argument. 'Does she travel with him? Because if she does his opportunities to go out looking for girls would be strictly limited.'

'Usually she goes on ahead. Between stops is when she looks for new towns to target. So she must have her own car, so probably Davey does drive alone. I'll find out when they arrived at the hotel, if they'd already got together or if Davey was on his own.'

'Miss Mills could tell us a lot about Davey—what motivates him, what he gets up to between shows—if he would. Will she?'

Liz shook her head. 'Don't count on it. She's very loyal. We'd have to convince her first that he'd done this, and if we can prove that we won't need her help.' They had an understanding: just because they discussed something didn't mean they believed it. This was pure hypothesis, a theoretical exercise. 'But surely he'd have been seen at the park? The neighbours saw the girl on the pony, they saw the van and they didn't see the bicycle that should have been there and wasn't. They'd have seen a man in a wheelchair.'

'A man in a wheelchair's much lower than the other men,' said Shapiro. 'The houses facing the park have all got front gardens, hedges, fences; and there's a little bit of a hedge running along the edge of the park. Maybe he was too low to be seen.'

Liz found herself nodding pensively. 'It's possible, I suppose. A man who doesn't have a family, who spends his time imposing his opinion on strangers, who can't have much of a sex-life—a man like that could build up enough frustration to want to kill the women he can't have, and go for young girls because they're easier to handle. But, Frank, it's a hell of a suggestion. If we're wrong we'll make the Nine O'Clock News.'

'That's not a good enough reason for not looking into it,' Shapiro said mildly.

'Maybe it's a good enough reason for you not to look into it, though.' She caught his eye. 'After what happened between you and him this morning, the less you have to do with this the better. Will you leave it with me?

'Donovan, find out where Davey's pitched his tent in the past. Ask if any deaths of young girls have coincided with his visits before. Mills claims the crime figures drop after one of their crusades: see if there's any truth in that. And get on to the ferries, find out if he travelled through Dover about the time of the murder there.

'And whoever you talk to, for God's sake ask them to be discreet. I do not want to read about this in the Sunday papers.'

THE CARAVAN was strictly for the use of the road crew. The preacher and his assistant had taken rooms—rooms plural, Liz checked—in the Castle Hotel, the only hostelry in town with any ambition to cater for the carriage trade.

Liz saw the manager in his office, but she was almost no time there. She had two questions for him, and his answers were such as to virtually close the investigation on Michael Davey. His rooms were booked from Sunday night. Miss Mills arrived about teatime and Davey in the middle of the evening: two days after Charisma was killed and most of a day after she was put in the canal. That didn't make it impossible for Davey to have killed her—he could have come to Castlemere secretly a few days before his public arrival—but it did make it unlikely.

Especially when the answer to her second question quite cleared him of the attack in the park. Between seven-thirty and about eight-fifteen on Tuesday morning Michael Davey was taking breakfast in the hotel dining-room. The staff were able to be accurate about the time because, barring special requests, seven-thirty was when they started serving breakfast, and they appreciated Mr Davey's promptness because it enabled them to help him to his table before the dining-room filled. They couldn't be as sure what time he finished, but he waited until adjacent tables cleared so that he could wheel himself out unaided and that was certainly well after eight. To Liz there was no material difference between eight and eight-fifteen: Alice Elton had already met with her killer. She thanked the manager and went to leave.

As she crossed the lobby a voice hailed her. For a moment, looking round, she couldn't see him. Then, lowering her gaze, she found him at waist-level, the big man in the wheelchair. 'Inspector Graham. Come to arrest me this time?'

She gave him her most gracious smile. 'Not at all. I wasn't even looking for you.' It was true, if misleading. 'I thought you'd be down at the wharf, getting ready for to-night.'

He raised a pale bushy eyebrow. 'That doesn't bother you—the fact that I'll be speaking again tonight? You're not afraid of history repeating itself?'

They had come together in the middle of the lobby. Liz found it odd talking down to a grown man as if he were a child. 'You've every right to go ahead and speak. After last night you don't need me to tell you that passions are running high, that we'd rather see you calming things down than stirring them up.'

Davey's steel-blue eyes caught hers and suddenly she didn't feel to be looking down at him any more. His voice was a sombre musical bass. 'I didn't mean to stir them up last night, Inspector. I didn't even know there was a suspect, let alone that everyone in that tent bar me knew who it was.'

'Gossip has wings in Castlemere. There's no such thing as a discreet arrest.'

'So I gather. I also didn't mean to upset Mr Shapiro. The man was only doing his job, I don't know why I let rip at him. If you would, I'd like you to convey my apologies. I'd call him myself but I'm afraid we might get started again.'

Liz smiled, against all her expectations liking him. 'We have to be able to cope with the odd frayed temper. We should be able to do it without our own unravelling but we too are only human, sometimes we say things we shouldn't.'

Davey nodded the lion head in assent. 'The other thing I wanted to say only I lost my temper first was how sorry I was about what happened to that boy. I didn't want it to happen, I don't think I could have stopped it, but that doesn't mean I can't be sorry. I'll always wonder about that: if I could have saved him. Well, both of them. There were two of them, weren't there, Carver and another man?'

'The other man was my sergeant. He lives in the area, he got wind of what was going to happen and tried to get

Carver out. Don't worry about him, he wasn't badly hurt. He's used to taking the odd knock.'

A kind of agonized scowl twisted Davey's face. 'That's a desperate admission, Inspector. I mean, we're used to it, you probably more than me, it doesn't sound so very dreadful. But it is. It's a terrible indictment of our society, that the people tasked with the business of protecting it can't do their job without exposing themselves to injury at regular intervals. Mr Shapiro mightn't believe it but I have great respect for the police. It's easy to find fault with anybody doing a difficult job. But you have to give credit for trying to do it in the first place.'

'I'm glad we have your confidence, sir.' Liz smiled and tried to leave. But one of Davey's powerful hands captured her wrist. Startled, she looked back at him, by which time he'd already released her. His head was on one side, like a supplicant schoolboy's.

'It's half-past twelve, Inspector. I was going to have a bit of lunch in the bar. Will you join me?' She hesitated and he hurried on. 'It's never much fun eating alone in a public place. Eating alone in a public place in a wheelchair is next best thing to exhibiting yourself at a freak-show.'

'Won't Miss Mills be joining you?'

He shook his head. 'She's down at the wharf, getting the tent in order. I'm not allowed to help: I'm supposed to rest until teatime. Come on—you need a break or you'll be arresting the wrong people all afternoon.'

Liz grinned. 'All right. Just a sandwich—I really don't have time for anything more.'

'Just a sandwich.'

SIX

DONOVAN SPENT the day on the phone. By late afternoon a pattern was emerging: not the one he'd hoped for, a trail of teenage girls with their throats cut at times and places where Michael Davey was thundering forth on the Old Testament virtues, but a pattern none the less. He squinted at his notes from different angles as if seeking a hidden message. Then he went to consult Inspector Graham. She wasn't in her office so he tried Chief Inspector Shapiro.

Shapiro looked up, glowering, at his unheralded appearance. 'Does it ever occur to you, Sergeant, that you could march in here one day and find me making mad passionate love to Miss Tunstall on top of the desk?'

The thought had not occurred to Donovan. Partly because Superintendent Taylor's secretary, like Shapiro himself, had reached an age that militated against cavorting on office furniture, and partly because he knew his chief's private vice and it was not middle-aged ladies in lisle stockings but forty winks when business was slow.

'Sorry, sir.' He gestured with his hands, one full of papers, the other wrapped in cling-film. 'Nothing to knock with.' His face brightened. 'I could kick.'

Shapiro sighed. 'Just clear your throat and give Miss Tunstall time to recover her confusion. What do you want?'

'I've been phoning round the places this travelling circus pitched its tent before coming here, and I've turned up something a bit odd.'

Shapiro waited but Donovan didn't go on. 'Yes?' he said at last, irritably.

'This improvement Jennifer Mills claimed in crime figures following their visits is open to debate. You might get something if you massaged the figures enough, but the kindest interpretation is that Miss Mills has a touching faith in her employer. Mostly the statistics fluctuate about how you'd expect, with one exception. Several divisions noticed an increase in drug offences after Davey left town. Not while he was there, after he left. They didn't think much of it, only mentioned it as a curiosity. But about the third time I heard it I started taking notice. Small towns they are, mostly, that never had much of a drug problem before. I asked across the Channel too, but so far as I can find out there's been nothing similar following the European tours.'

Shapiro stared at him, appalled. 'Dear God, Donovan, what are you saying?—that Cardiff's answer to Billy Graham is a drug-runner?'

The prospect cost Donovan no grief. 'Why not? It's a good cover. Who's going to strip-search a peripatetic preacher in a wheelchair?'

The gears were grinding almost perceptibly behind Shapiro's eyes. 'How often does he cross the Channel?'

'Twice a year in each direction. They do winter and summer in England, spring and autumn on the Continent.'

'That's just two trips a year when they could bring stuff into England. It isn't much. If Davey's set up a drug-running operation you'd think he'd want to milk it for more than that.'

'How it pays depends on how much he carries, not how often he makes the trip. Look, most drugs entering Britain now come from Europe. Some of it comes sewn into tourist souvenirs but the profitable way is to shift it by the ton. Customs know that: they search ships, open cargoes, strip the odd juggernaut to the wheel-bearings. But unless they have precise information they still miss a hell of a lot.

'So suppose you're a well-known evangelist with your own tent, three big vehicles, two cars and a good reason to cross from Europe to England twice a year. You're not going to invent excuses to make extra trips. You're going to stick to your schedule, pack your trucks with as much stuff as you can hide from a routine inspection and sell it in small lots as you travel. After a few months you go back for more.'

'I suppose you could hide quite a cache in a lorry before it became too obvious,' Shapiro ruminated.

Donovan consulted his notes. 'A ton of cannabis is worth about £2.5 million. A ton of cocaine would make £150 million. With what you could hide in a lorry you wouldn't need extra trips.'

Shapiro went on looking at him for a long time. 'Am I going to get a rocket over the size of our phone bill?'

Donovan chuckled darkly. 'You want me to do a thorough job, don't you?'

'What does Inspector Graham think of this?'

Donovan looked away. 'I don't know where she is.'

'POLIO, SAID MICHAEL Davey. He gave a rueful grin that knocked ten years off his face. 'Pity, really. It would've been worth more to me, professionally speaking, if I'd been mugged.'

Liz smiled too. 'How old were you?'

'Nine. I've had time to get used to it. There are compensations. I'm never stuck for a seat.'

'Have you'—Liz encompassed his life-style with a gesture—'been doing this long? What do you call it, a campaign?'

The grin deepened with just a hint of mischief. 'I call it a mission. You'd use another expression. Don't deny it: you might be more tactful than Mr Shapiro but I doubt you've any more time for it than he has. I've yet to meet a police officer who thinks I'm worth the space I take up. It's funny, really, because so far as I can see we're on the same side. I could understand it if I was encouraging people to nail one another to barn doors. But all I'm doing is trying to make them better people. What's so anti-social about that?'

'Nothing,' Liz agreed. 'The problem is that when people feel strongly about something—moral revival, gay rights, animal welfare, whatever—they see everything in black and white. If I'd been there last night I might have agreed with everything you said. But I'd also have foreseen what you didn't: that if you bring together a lot of angry, frightened people who don't know which way to turn and give them a blood-and-thunder speech about rooting out the evil in their midst, they aren't all going to break up quietly and go home when you've finished.'

Davey nodded a wry acceptance. 'I should have anticipated it. Truth is, it never occurred to me. I'm a preacher, see. One of the ironies of the job is that it's not evil people but good ones who come to listen. I'm always preaching to the converted. And you don't expect decent law-abiding, God-fearing, go-to-meeting folk to turn into a lynch mob.'

'Perhaps preachers don't. Policemen do.'

His voice was husky. 'I wish you had been there last night.'

Liz thought she was changing the subject. 'Have you and Miss Mills been together long?'

A shield dropped in front of his eyes, distancing. A cool crept into his voice. 'What do you mean, together?'

She blinked. 'I understood she was your business manager. Perhaps I've got it wrong.'

Davey seemed relieved. 'No, that's right enough. It's just, people jump to conclusions. A man and a woman travelling together...' His voice warmed. 'Jenny's my strong right arm. More than that, she's all the bits I'm not best favoured with. She's my legs, my wits, my patience. She organizes me. Give me a crowd and I can move them: give me a map and a diary and I'm lost. Before Jenny came along I used to run round in circles, the same half-dozen towns all the time. You can't call that Outreach, can you?'

'She must be a great help.'

'It's Jenny makes it all possible. I have' —he made a self-deprecating gesture with one hand— 'a certain reputation for doing faith transfusions. When we go back to places after a year or so people thank me for what I've done for them. Nobody ever thanks Jenny, but without her I'd be helpless. She came from a good family, had real prospects. She gave up everything to come with me. I'll always be grateful.'

Liz smiled. 'I'm sure she knows how much you think of her.'

'Oh, Jenny knows. There's nobody in the world I respect more than Jenny. We have a very nice, satisfying working relationship.'

But Liz had talked to Jennifer Mills and knew something which apparently Michael Davey did not: that his business manager would have liked more than respect and a satisfactory working relationship.

DONOVAN WAS TIRED, his hand was sore and he'd given up waiting. He was heading for the door when Liz came in. 'Oh, Donovan. I was hoping I'd catch you.'

'The chief's been looking for you,' he replied obliquely.

She nodded without comment. 'Did you get anywhere with the phone calls?'

'Maybe.' He told her what he'd told Shapiro. At some point during the telling, almost unnoticed, she steered him away from the door and back upstairs.

When he'd finished she sniffed dubiously. 'It sounds like you're trying to pin half the crime in Europe on this man.'

Donovan stiffened. 'I'm not trying to pin anything on him. I'm reporting what I've been told: that in several of the places he's visited there's been an upsurge in drug-related crime.'

'There's been an upsurge in drug-related crime most places in the last few years,' Liz said reasonably. 'Anyway, you can't both be right: Mr Shapiro suspecting him of murder, you suspecting him of drug-running.'

'Why not?' A hint of belligerence was creeping into his manner.

'Because it makes no sense. If he's got narcotics worth millions hidden in his lorries he's going to be on his best behaviour, not out hunting young girls to kill. Besides, I know for a fact that he didn't kill Alice Elton: he was in the dining-room of the Castle Hotel at the time. So he didn't kill Charisma either. I'm not even going to wonder if there are two homicidal maniacs using the same MO.'

'All right, so he's not the killer. What about the drug figures? You reckon that's a coincidence?'

'Could be,' she said lightly. 'Tell you what: get on to Drugs Squad, let them know what you've found, see if it makes any sense to them. Tell them about Brady too, that rumours of his death have been exaggerated and if he is up to something this could be it. They're the experts, they'll have a good idea if your statistics mean anything.'

Apropos of nothing, except that he didn't make small talk and there was meaning in everything he said even if no one else understood it, Donovan asked sourly, 'Have a nice lunch?'

Liz felt herself flushing. 'What's that supposed to mean?'

'You've been talking to Davey. What did he tell you?—that he's just your ordinary everyday prophet, his hobbies are saving the world and macrame, he wouldn't dream of whipping up interest by killing young girls, and it never occurred to him to raise a mob and send them after a scapegoat.'

She was about to deny it but changed her mind. 'Yes,' she said calmly, 'that's about what he said. Not the same degree of rhetoric but that figures: people who have something to say say it, people who haven't just make a lot of noise. You're good on ideas, Donovan, I'll give you that.

What you're not good at is recognizing the difference between the improbable and the downright bloody ludicrous.'

On a better day Donovan would have agreed with her. He knew his strengths and weaknesses as a police officer: they were the same as his strengths and weaknesses as a man. He was energetic, resourceful and single-minded in the interests of his friends and his job. He hated to think he could be wrong about either. He wasn't often wrong about friends: he didn't make them easily, by the time he was ready to consider them friends he knew them well. Enemies he made more readily so he was more likely to misjudge them.

But he thought that Inspector Graham was letting personal feelings colour her judgement. He believed that what he'd discovered warranted proper consideration, not brushing under the carpet because it didn't accord with what she thought she'd learned about the man over a ploughman's lunch.

He came to his feet abruptly, uncoiling like an angry snake. The blood glowed darkly in his face and his eyes were hot. 'Coincidence? You think it's coincidence that everywhere this guy goes he leaves a wake of crime behind him? Drugs, murder? You probably think what happened to Ray Carver was a coincidence too. Just one of those things that happen now and then: people go to a gospel meeting, sing a few hymns, then they run riot and set someone on fire.'

Liz breathed heavily at him. 'I didn't say that. If it's any comfort to you, Donovan, what happened to Carver is going to give Michael Davey nightmares for a long time. But it wasn't deliberate and it wasn't malicious. If there'd been a case against him, don't you think the chief would have charged him? He wanted to. But there wasn't so he couldn't. Whether you like it or not, legal responsibility for the attack on Carver begins and ends with the man downstairs.'

Donovan was too angry to leave it at that. Words poured from him in a bitter torrent, the accent as always thickening in direct proportion to his fury. 'So Mr Davey's having trouble sleeping, is he? So he bloody well should. So am I; and I doubt Ray Carver's getting much either. He's no skin left between his knees and his navel, and I watched him barbecued. But I see now Mr Davey's the one wc should be sorry for. People thought unkind things about him, didn't they?'

'Donovan,' she began, her voice rising as her own temper frayed.

'Do you know what burning human flesh smells like?' he shouted in her face.

Her cheeks hot with outrage she stared at him, her breast surging with contradictory urges: compassion because it had been a deeply disturbing experience, anger—at him for refusing to accept her judgement, at herself for not managing his outburst better—even an odd little impulse of protectiveness towards Davey. She teetered on the brink of saying too much, of meeting Donovan's aggression with aggression of her own.

But she conquered it. Without taking her eyes off him she got up from her chair, picked up her bag and walked to the door in masterly silence. Donovan was left alone in her office, awkward and confused, aware he'd gone too far again, wondering if she'd be back or if she was finished, considering the strong possibility that he was.

SEVEN

ONLY WHEN he was sure Liz wasn't coming back did Donovan leave the office. But he didn't go straight home. He was looking for two things: Liam Brady and a fight.

At the tent the crew were preparing for the evening meeting. The tall woman was supervising from the modest eminence of the dais, a clipboard in her hand, a cigarette held lightly between her lips. She wanted the seats arranged with mathematical precision and an Order of Service—fresh from the local copy-shop, it was only Wednesday but what had seemed an adequate supply had already run out—on each. She gave her orders confidently and didn't have to repeat herself too often. Donovan stood in the flap of the tent taking a malicious pleasure in the sight of the mad dog of the Provisional IRA lining up chairs and laying out prayer-sheets at the behest of a woman with an eagle eye and a clipboard.

Jennifer Mills saw him too. She let him watch for a minute while she arranged things to her satisfaction. Then she said, 'I'm afraid you're too early for the meeting.'

Being on duty prevented him from replying as he would have liked. 'I'm looking for someone.'

'We're rather busy just now. Could you come back later?' The well-bred voice remained friendly but it really wasn't a question.

Of course he could have come back later. His boat was a hundred metres away: he could have gone home, made himself a meal, come back when Brady had finished work. But Donovan was in no mood to co-operate. 'No.' He put his hand inside his jacket, reaching for his warrant card.

The Geordie, who was nearest, reacted as if Donovan

had produced a hand-grenade. He glanced up casually to see who was arguing with his boss, then in a split second his whole manner changed and he launched himself at the man in the entrance. One big fist locked on Donovan's wrist and the other on his throat. The impetus of the attack carried both of them out of the tent and they crashed into the generator throbbing industriously outside. The machine caught Donovan in the small of the back, knocking the wind out of him, but the collision did nothing to loosen Kelso's grip. He kept coming, bearing down on the younger man, bending him backwards over the machinery with all his weight and strength. His eyes glaring into Donovan's were filled with cold resolve. For a fleeting moment Donovan thought the man meant to break his back.

Then it was all over. Brady came sprinting out of the tent behind them, and gripped Kelso's arm. 'For God's sake don't throttle him, he's another frigging peeler!'

From a range of centimetres Donovan watched the man's eyes come back to life. The heavy brows stapled down in a puzzled frown. He released his grip on Donovan's throat and let him straighten up. 'Then why's the bugger pulling a piece?'

'I wasn't.' Even to himself Donovan's voice sounded rusty, creaking through his bruised larynx. He produced the card.

Kelso looked. He pursed his lips in thought. He reached out and solicitously straightened Donovan's jacket. 'Whoops.'

Brady steered Donovan away as a mother might a fractious child. 'There we are now, Sergeant, no harm done. I suppose it was me you were looking for?'

'Yes. No.' Donovan was so taken aback by what had happened that for a moment he couldn't remember. 'That lunatic tried to strangle me!'

'No, he didn't,' Brady said patiently, as if he might persuade Donovan that he'd imagined it. 'It was self-defence. He thought you had a gun.'

Donovan's voice soared incredulously. 'Why would he think that?'

Brady stared at him. 'This may come as a surprise to you, Sergeant, but Castlemere is a dangerous town. People get hurt here. People get killed. OK, so the gaffer over-reacted. He's feeling a bit twitchy. We all are. The whole bloody town is, or hadn't you noticed? The guy made a mistake, that's all. Now, what was it you wanted?'

All Donovan's instincts told him that it was not an honest mistake, the result of normal caution exaggerated by recent events. But he couldn't prove it. He hadn't been hurt, Kelso hadn't produced a weapon, and it was possible to put Brady's interpretation on the facts. He saw no point in pursuing the incident, though he was not ready to forget it.

Anyway, his earlier grievance took precedence. He rounded on Brady, throwing the calming hand off his arm. 'All right. I want to know why it took you fifteen minutes to get to a phone last night. Fifteen minutes, when you could have walked to Queen's Street in five.'

'I'm a stranger here,' Brady said reasonably. 'Is Queen's Street where you have your nick? I don't know where that is.'

'And you couldn't find a phone? There's one in Mere Basin three minutes away. There's one at the end of Brick Lane. You could have tried the boats: at least two of them have phones. You could have knocked on a few doors in Brick Lane—'

'I could have got myself caught up in that mob,' Brady reminded him. 'You were hardly away when they came out of the tent. I couldn't get through them. I went up the tow-path to the basin but the phone there had been ripped out. I tried the flats over the basin: there were plenty of lights on but nobody was answering their bell. This is a scared town, you know that? Finally a man answered and I told him to call the police. Fifteen minutes? I dare say it was. It was still the best I could do.'

Donovan was inclined to believe him. He felt the anger running out of him, weariness taking its place. 'Yeah, OK. It's just, if the cavalry had arrived even two minutes earlier it wouldn't have happened. That's all the time it was from that mad bastard set Carver on fire till the wooden-tops put him out. It was the petrol. I got to him but I couldn't make any impression on it.'

Unconsciously his hands were repeating the futile pawing gestures that had achieved nothing beyond adding burns to his own list of hurts. All he had to fight the fire with was his jacket which wasn't voluminous enough to wrap round and smother the flames. He desperately needed help, begged for it, but no one in the ring of men responded. They just stood watching the screaming man burn. Then sirens wailed round the corner into The Jubilee, the crowd scattered and a constable ran over with a fire blanket.

Brady looked from Donovan's hand to his face. 'I'm sorry. If I could have got you those two minutes I would have.'

LIZ WENT straight home. Brian had a stew simmering. She put her arms round him. 'Just what I need.'

He dropped a kiss lightly on top of her head. 'I thought you might get home at lunchtime.'

'Sorry, I couldn't.' She collapsed into a chair. The dining table was still stacked with tea-chests, they'd be eating off trays for a while yet. 'I had someone to see.'

She had nothing to hide from Brian. She had taken advantage of a chance meeting to seek information that might have had a bearing on an urgent inquiry. It was irrelevant that no useful information had emerged and that she'd enjoyed lunch more than she'd expected. They had said and done nothing she was reluctant to tell him. On the other hand, it almost seemed to be investing the meeting with too much significance, to come home and tell her husband about it. Something less than professional. If she had nothing to hide, equally she had nothing to confess.

In the end she made a wholly justifiable decision for the most trivial of reasons: so that she could throw it in Donovan's face. 'That evangelist with the tent by the canal. Michael Davey.'

Brian blinked. 'Evangelist? Whatever has he been up to?'

'Probably nothing. There've been some odd coincidences but that's likely all it is. But Donovan's gunning for him after what happened in The Jubilee and I felt I had to look into it. But I know now he wasn't there when the girl on the pony was killed, which is as good as saying he had nothing to do with any of the murders.'

'*Any* of the murders?' Brian echoed weakly.

'Sorry, I keep forgetting you don't know the ins and outs of this. The same killer seems to have struck at least three times: the two girls in Castlemere and one in Dover. But one of them couldn't have been Davey which really means that none of them were. Coincidence.'

'So what's the problem?'

'There isn't one.' Then as an afterthought: 'The problem's Donovan. He's convinced Davey's doing something illegal, if not murder then perhaps drugs. There's no evidence. He sees that more as a challenge than the natural end to a line of inquiry.'

'He's your sergeant,' Brian said reasonably, putting the tray in front of her, 'tell him to drop it.'

'And if he doesn't?'

Brian shrugged. 'I suppose, in the last resort, you get Frank Shapiro to slap him down.'

Liz scowled. 'That's what I'm trying to avoid. You said it: Donovan's my sergeant. If I need help to handle him, what credibility do I have left?'

'Listen,' Brian said, 'he isn't a child. Kids in fourth form have no choice but go to school, whether they see the point or not. Them I expect a little trouble from. Teachers can leave tomorrow if they don't like what they're doing. The education system is not, nor should it be, geared to the needs and aspirations of teachers. I'd have said the same was true of the police. Don't be afraid to read him the Riot Act. You know Frank'll back you.'

'I know that. That's why I'd rather not put either of them in that position. Donovan has his faults, God knows, but he's worth—' She gave a little snort of laughter. 'It sounds silly, but he's worth nurturing. I want him on my side. I don't want to turn him into another time-server waiting for his pension and going by the book because that way nobody can blame you no matter what the outcome. He's a better copper than that. With all his failings, he does at least *care* about what he's doing. That's not so common I can afford to waste it.'

'Can you afford to have him playing by his own rules?'

She shook her head. She'd pulled out the pins that held her hair in its brisk no-nonsense pleat as she'd come through the door and it tossed on her shoulders in a corn-coloured riot. 'I had a run-in with him this afternoon. By tomorrow, either he's ready to toe the line or he starts looking for someone else to work for.'

EIGHT

'THERE'S SOMETHING going on there,' insisted Donovan when they met on Thursday morning. 'I honest to God don't know what, but something. They do not behave like normal people.'

'Of course they don't,' said Liz, exasperated. 'They aren't normal people. They're a bunch of gypsies led by a man who thinks he has a mission from God. What standard do you judge them by?'

'Any standard you know will still leave them behaving like people with something to hide. I went over there last night—'

'Did you?' murmured Shapiro, with just enough emphasis to make Donovan stumble.

'Er—and that Geordie came down on me like a ton of bricks. And Brady said' —this time an elevated eyebrow was the extent of Shapiro's interruption—'that he thought I was pulling a gun. Now you tell me: what kind of people is it that assume an inside pocket contains a gun? And what kind of company are they for a genuine missionary?'

'I imagine,' Liz said caustically, 'they were employed more for the strength of their arms than for any great religious conviction. Davey believes in God, Mills believes in him, and I imagine the rest of them believe that the labourer is worthy of his hire. That's a rough life they lead, living in a caravan parked mostly on waste ground. Look where we put them: begging your pardon, Donovan, but Broad Wharf is not the most salubrious part of town. They're probably used to the occasional trouble-maker, find it wise to jump him first and search his pockets afterwards. They didn't know you were a copper.'

'Brady did. If he did, why didn't Kelso?'

'Maybe they've better things to do of an evening than talk about you,' growled Liz.

Both of them, in the quiet of their own homes the previous evening, reviewing their last undignified exchange, had resolved to strive harder for a calm professional relationship untroubled by the clash of their different, sometimes conflicting styles. They had decided that such an accommodation should pose no problem to two intelligent, adult people who, differences notwithstanding, shared a mutual respect for one another's abilities. Moreover, there were selfish reasons for them to make it work. Donovan thought his job might depend on it. Liz thought her credibility might.

Only minutes into the meeting in Shapiro's office, Liz's resolution went out the window, and Donovan's went winging swiftly after it.

'Are you telling me,' he demanded, 'that nothing about this setup seems wrong to you? You can't smell it? You don't have a deep gut feeling that, evidence or no evidence, there's something going on here that we need to know about?'

'No, I can't say that,' allowed Liz. 'But I also can't say what you just said—"evidence or no evidence". People are entitled to be odd; it's only if we have reason to suspect them of crimes that we have a right to interfere. That means facts not feelings, and the fact is that Michael Davey didn't kill Alice Elton. As for your drug statistics—well, we all know what statistics are like. Jennifer Mills thought the same ones showed that crime had dropped in the wake of the crusade. Have you been on to Drugs Squad?'

He glowered. 'They thanked me for the suggestion, said they'd give it some thought.' There was a small chorus of nods and sniffs. All three of them knew what that meant.

Shapiro said, 'This man Kelso: do you want to do *him*

for assault?' He was getting tired of asking Donovan this same question.

Again Donovan declined. 'If we haul him in, whatever it is they're up to they'll put it on ice. Let him run. I'd sooner get him for pushing drugs than for pushing me.'

Liz breathed heavily. 'Drugs again. What drugs? This isn't hypothesis, it's sheer guesswork. Do you want to search their vehicles for drugs? Would that satisfy you?'

He shook his head. 'If they're well enough hid for Customs to miss them we wouldn't find them either. Not without turning them inside out, and we can't justify that. Not yet. What I'd like is to keep an eye on them. See where they go when they're not setting out chairs and hymn-sheets. See who they meet. If we can catch them with a known dealer, then we have reason to suspect. Then we take them apart.'

Shapiro nodded slowly. 'Sounds reasonable. Inspector?'

Liz agreed. 'After last night, though, it might be better to put someone else on it. They all know Donovan's face now.'

Donovan got in fast, before Shapiro could concur. 'Sir, I live there. I can watch them without them knowing. I can move about without them getting suspicious. If you put someone else on them he'll only have the edge until they spot him and then they'll know we're interested. With me they can only wonder, and they won't even wonder unless I have to follow them somewhere they've no reason to be.'

Shapiro weighed it a moment longer then decided. 'All right, Sergeant, you take it. Two conditions. If you follow them off the wharf, let me know. And if you so much as suspect there's a deal going down, you call for back-up. If you're right about them and they spot you, you'll need more than your warrant card to fend them off.'

Liz didn't argue. 'What do you want me to do?'

Shapiro gave her a weary smile. 'I want you to catch the

man who murdered Charlene Pierce and Alice Elton. I can't offer a single suggestion that might help you do it.'

She smiled too. 'Perhaps I'll pay another visit to The Jubilee. They'll be a bit shaken after what happened to Ray Carver, perhaps they're ready to talk now. When we asked round after Charisma was killed it was like asking the walls if they'd seen anything. Perhaps if we try again someone'll remember seeing her with a customer that night.'

Shapiro wasn't hopeful. 'He met Alice, killed her and was away from the scene inside a very few minutes. Why would he hang around with Charisma long enough to be spotted?'

'Probably he didn't, in which case it's a wild goose chase. But it was dark, it's the sort of area where people mind their own business, perhaps he felt safe enough to talk to her for a little while. He probably made some sort of arrangement with her to get her into the alley. Or perhaps someone saw him before he met her. Yes, it's a long shot. I don't know what else to do.'

Shapiro shook his head lugubriously. 'You'll never make chief inspector this way.'

'Running out of ideas?'

'Admitting it.'

She grinned. 'If Special Branch call back while I'm out, will you talk to them? I've told them their information is incorrect, that Brady's alive and he's here, and asked for guidance as to whether we should consider him a threat. If they knew, if they're helping him to disappear, the answer should be no.'

'If they tell us the truth.'

'And if he isn't making fools of them. Oh no, whatever they say, I'd like to keep an eye on him. But if they genuinely believe he's dead, perhaps we should haul him in and ask him why he's not.'

'And tell him that Donovan told us about Brady jumping him on his boat? I don't know, Liz. I'm not sure Donovan isn't right—that the best thing we can do for the moment is wait and watch. If he is up to something, almost the best thing we have at the moment is that he thinks he's safe.'

It made sense. She nodded. 'Fair enough.' She went out, closing the door behind her.

Donovan hurried after her. 'Ma'am?'

'Yes?'

He stood awkwardly in the corridor as if he had more limbs than he knew what to do with. His eyes were low. 'About last night. I'm sorry. I was out of line.'

She watched him for a minute, then said coolly, 'Yes, you were.' She seemed about to walk on when a thought hit her. 'How long did you wait for me?'

He looked up quickly to see if she'd forgiven him sufficiently to joke about it. But her face was straight and he couldn't tell. 'About an hour and a half,' he mumbled.

Liz said nothing more but departed, chuckling.

SHE WAS RIGHT about one thing: the mood in The Jubilee. When she was here before, after Charisma died, nobody wanted to talk to her. Time and again as she worked round the Pierces' neighbours her knock at a door elicited only a fractional movement at an upstairs window. Seeing the uniform the householder then kept his or her head down until by repeated hammering Liz made it clear that she wasn't leaving. When she finally got someone to answer it was never worth the effort. They listened stony-faced, their eyes giving nothing away, and when asked what they had seen or heard the answer was always nothing.

They weren't afraid, not then. They didn't even seem to be protecting anyone. It was just that they had made a lifetime habit of not co-operating with the police and didn't see the murder of a working girl, even a local one, as reason enough to change. Working girls getting their throats cut was like rent-collectors getting mugged and sub-postmasters getting held up on pension day: a fact of life.

Nothing in the faces of those she spoke to suggested that they found it intolerable.

That was on Sunday. It was now Thursday. In the meantime a young girl had been murdered in a public park, a young man had been run down and burned by a mob under their very windows, and the whole town was in a state of hysteria. The normal trickle of everyday comings and goings had dried up. People moved around in groups or not at all. Castlemere's children might have followed Hamelin's into a hole in the ground. Many of them were being kept off school, others were being delivered and collected in gangs surrounded by watchful adults.

When the children were safe inside some of the adults turned vigilante, pacing the streets in tight-lipped knots, peering intently at the faces of anyone they met, even other vigilantes. As if they might see the mark of Cain on the face of the murderer. As if they would know what to do if they did. Others sought the solace of religion. They didn't blame Michael Davey for the episode that put Ray Carver in the burns unit of Castlemere General.

Or perhaps they did, and in some way they could not have explained took it as proof that this man at least cared enough about their plight to try and do something. The police said Carver was innocent; if so it was all very unfortunate. On the other hand, perhaps Reverend Davey knew better than the police. One thing was sure: people could die waiting for an arrest.

But one consequence of all the dirty water that had rushed under the bridges since Sunday was that the second time Liz went door-stepping in The Jubilee people were ready to talk to her. They still checked from their upstairs windows, but now seeing police outside they hurried to open the door.

It speeded the process, made it less frustrating, but in fact nothing helpful ensued. Assorted witnesses had seen one another and, a little before one o'clock on Saturday morning, Charisma herself. None of them had seen a strange man.

Liz stayed with the house-to-house until there seemed to be no more mileage left in it, then she sent the team back to Queen's Street. She didn't follow at once. She needed a new line of thought on this, and she'd already had everything Shapiro had to offer. She was no distance from *Tara;* a walk along the tow-path was a good way to clear her head; and if Donovan, watching for suspicious activities, happened to see her and ask her aboard, or join her in her stroll, she was not too proud to pick his fertile mind.

In the event she did not see Donovan, though he probably saw her. Indeed, he wasn't keeping much of a watch if he did not. For as soon as she emerged on to Broad Wharf a deep musical voice hailed her and Michael Davey came towards her, propelling himself with purposeful thrusts of his powerful arms.

The white suit was for business. Off duty he dressed like any other middle-aged man with a lawn to mow or a car to wash, in jeans and a rugby shirt in the Welsh colours. On his feet he wore trainers. Because they hardly touched the ground they stayed cleaner than most people's trainers. However, the wheels of his chair were filthy and a bearing needed oiling.

'Mrs Graham. Were you looking for me?'

She shook her head. 'Not this time.'

Unconsciously or by design his face fell. 'Oh. Dammo.'

Liz smiled. 'Nothing personal. I just felt like a walk. We don't have any parks in the middle of town, just the canals.'

'Funny things, canals. We think of them as the next best thing to nature, a piece of countryside sneaking into town. But actually they're industrial engineering on a grand scale. Every cubic foot of water in them represents a foot of earth taken out by a man with a spade and a barrow.'

'You should talk to my sergeant, he's a canal buff.' She stopped just short of telling him, or reminding him if he already knew, that Donovan lived on the wharf. Careful, girl, she thought: you liking the man doesn't mean Donovan's wrong.

Davey laughed. Two young men fishing turned their heads at the echoing sound. Michael Davey had spent too many years projecting his voice and personality into the furthest reaches of a tent to hold discreet conversations now. 'I've spent more hours by canals than the average bargee. Don't know why but as soon as a local authority sees an application to erect a marquee they ask themselves where the nearest canal is. They must think the water'll come in handy for baptisms.'

Liz chuckled. 'You don't go in for total immersion then.'

'Only if I misjudge the edge of the tow-path.' He made a sudden lunge for the rim: Liz was startled enough to grab his chair. He spun to face her, his eyes merry. 'It's a dangerous place, the tow-path. Nobody should walk here alone.'

'Not just now, anyway,' Liz agreed grimly.

It was all the invitation he needed. He swung the chair into line with her, measuring his pace to her stride. 'You don't mind?' he asked belatedly. 'I mean, if you came here to think—'

She glanced at him, intrigued. 'How did you know that?'

He shrugged like a mountain shrugging. 'You're a police officer in the middle of a murder investigation: I doubt you're here for relaxation.'

She nodded. 'It's hard to think in the office when there's this much going on. You need to clear your head from time to time. There's a level at which useful things are going on but you can't access it for all the rubbish that gets piled on top. You have to clear the decks sometimes, see what's there.'

Davey was silent for a moment. Liz glanced at him and glimpsed a battle going on behind his eyes. Then he looked up and said, frankly though with obvious reluctance, 'Shall I go away? Can you think better alone?'

She laughed and shook her head. 'No. Talking helps too. That's part of the problem: we're constantly talking to each other, recycling the same ideas. It helps to talk to normal people—people who aren't intimately involved.'

'Normal?' he echoed on a rising note. 'Bless you for that. Most people reckon I'm about as normal as a three-pound note.'

Liz smiled again but didn't contradict him.

They walked—or she walked and he accompanied her—east towards Cornmarket. They left the houseboats behind, and on their left the warehouses along Brick Lane became more and more derelict until they ended in the wasteland that stretched all the way to the shunting yard.

'Could have been worse,' Liz said casually, looking round. 'The council could have put you here instead of Broad Wharf.'

He said morosely, 'We got a redundant abattoir once.'

'What got you started in this line of work?'

He looked at her in surprise. 'You heard the tape.'

She was taken aback, momentarily wrong-footed. 'Yes, of course. But—'

He stopped his chair, forcing her to turn towards him. His voice hardened, became resonant. 'But what? You thought I made it up? You think it's a performance I put on?—like pretending to do magic, you can't see how it's done but nobody really thinks you've sawn a lady in half. I'm sorry to disappoint you, Mrs Graham, but I don't have any tricks. I can't do anything clever. The only gimmick I have is the white suit and that was Jenny's idea: looks good on the posters, see. Apart from that, what you see is what you get. I tell people how to better their lives. You could say that's presumptuous. And I don't always achieve what I set out to. But by God, *I* believe what I'm saying. It isn't an act. If I wanted to act for a living, even in this chair I could make better money a damn sight easier.'

Without thinking Liz touched his shoulder contritely. 'I didn't mean that. I know this is important to you. I just wondered if you'd always been a preacher.'

He seemed aware that he'd over-reacted. He closed his eyes for a moment. 'Sorry. Yes, I was a lay preacher back in Wales. I was an assistant librarian in the week, and every Sunday I set off for some obscure little meeting-house in one unpronounceable valley after another. I did it for twenty years. Then I took a long hard look at it all and asked myself if I wanted to do it for another twenty years. And I didn't. So I found a theological college that would take on a forty-year-old cripple.

'I never saw the crusade as my life's work. I thought it was something I could usefully do for a few years after graduating and before I had the experience to run my own congregation. If I'm honest, I suppose I thought it would show those people who'd wondered if I was fit enough to do the job. Only I got hooked. I made an awful hash of it to start with, but I still knew it was something I wanted to do well. I was helping people in a way that I hadn't even in the meeting-house days, reaching people who had no other minister, no other church. It was me or nothing. I sweated blood for them.'

He smiled fondly. 'Then Jenny came along and got me properly organized. You wouldn't believe the difference she made. In two years I was preaching all over Europe, we had our own tent, we had the trucks and the road-crew—it's like being a pop-star, all I have to do is turn up and do my stuff. Everything else Jenny and the boys take care of. They make it all possible. Dammo. Now I really am sounding like an actor.'

Liz chuckled. 'I imagine there's a bit of the actor in every preacher. Just as there's a cynic in every police officer. It goes with the territory.'

Davey's broad face was sombre again, compassionate even. 'That's self-defence, isn't it? I may be talking about vile and violent matters but I'm talking to decent people. You have to deal with terrible people. Somehow you have to protect yourself against their vitriol wearing you away. Anyone might be a cynic in the same circumstances.'

They'd reached the end of Cornmarket where Doggett's Canal joined the main system. Davey looked into the yawning pit of the empty lock, the exposed timbers black with age and rank with weed, a noisome stew of mud and rubbish and a little water in the very bottom. 'Where do we go from here?'

'Back, I'm afraid. They're supposed to be putting a bridge here so that you can walk out to the Levels. It's a toss-up whether anyone now living will see it. The local Restoration Society want to get the lock working first, to open up the route north. They beaver away down there every summer, apparently, but all they've achieved so far is to saw off the handrail.' Rusty spikes on top of the lock gate showed where it had been.

Davey stared. 'You mean people used to walk across there?'

'So I'm told. It took a steady hand and a head for heights but you could do it. Now you have to walk half a mile up the spur to the next bridge.' She grinned. 'Unless you're my sergeant, of course, in which case you stroll across with your hands in your pockets and glare at anyone who won't follow. I told you about him, didn't I?'

'Oh yes,' Davey said glumly. 'You told me about him.'

They turned back. Liz picked up the conversation where they'd left of. 'There are terrible people but probably not as many as you think. Most crime isn't violent, it's against property. But it's the Moors Murderers and Yorkshire Rippers, and this man we've got in Castlemere right now, who fill the newspapers; naturally, they're shocking crimes and it's the papers' job to report them. And we remember them long after we've forgotten last week's burglary. But statistically they're very rare. You're more likely to be kicked to death by a donkey than murdered by a psychopath.'

Davey was frowning. 'I know that's the official line. But I can only speak as I see, and what I see—wherever I go almost—are insane crimes whose only possible motive is to inflict pain and anguish. It isn't my imagination, Mrs Graham. You've had two young girls murdered in the past week and your town is up in arms. But every time we put the tent up the local papers are full of something just as bad. In Le Havre it was a girl too, butchered on the street. In Portsmouth it was a Gosport man who'd smashed his baby's head against the wall of a public car-park, and in Bristol an old woman burned to death in her flat when kids put firelighters through her letterbox. How can you say these are rare events?'

Liz shrugged helplessly. 'Because I know what the figures are. Perhaps, travelling round as you do, you see places at their worst. And I don't suppose it's the quiet backwaters where you can have a reign of terror with a feathered whoopee-whistle that you visit.'

For that he flashed her a quick grin. 'Well, that's true. We go where we think we can do some good. But still,' he insisted unhappily, 'I look around me and I don't see your green and pleasant land. I see dangerous people and scared people. I see communities on the edge of chaos.'

Liz shrugged that off. 'You've been unlucky. Come back in three months. Once we've got this man the hottest story in the *Castlemere Courier* will be silage run-off killing fish in the canals. It's like I say: you're seeing us at our worst.'

'Will you catch him?'

'Oh yes,' Liz said with conviction. 'We have to.'

NINE

FRANK SHAPIRO'S maternal grandfather lived his whole life in the Warsaw ghetto. He wore a long black gaberdine coat and a round hat trimmed with fur. From early manhood to the day he died he had a full beard, and when he was thinking he used to stroke it as if it were a cat asleep on his chest.

Shapiro's father was born in England. Not knowing what lay ahead for European Jewry, as a young man he was scornful of ghetto ways and confident that the way for a modern Jew to prosper and earn respect was not segregation but integration. He became a solicitor's clerk, dressed like other solicitor's clerks, and though he kept a kosher home, at midday he ate with the other clerks. He considered his religion a personal matter, not secret but private, and was philosophical when work kept him from getting home for the start of the sabbath on Friday afternoon. He wouldn't have been seen dead in a black gaberdine and fur-trimmed hat. But he still wore a beard, a neatly pointed one which he fingered pensively when faced with a complex piece of law.

The rather solid child who was destined to become Detective Chief Inspector Shapiro of Castlemere CID grew up during the war and post-war years so had no illusions about being as English as the next man. It was not religion that set him apart, for if he'd had any less he'd have had none at all. He didn't keep kosher, he didn't hurry home on Fridays, and when he remembered the major festivals it was with the faintly embarrassed air of a man pretending to be Father Christmas for his children.

What set Frank Shapiro apart was four thousand years

of history locked in his genes, and about that he could do
nothing at all. Unless he changed his name he was never
going to pass for Anglo-Saxon, and anyway he didn't want
to. With all its contradictions, what he was suited him. He
suspected he'd have been an outsider even if there'd been
no overt reason for it: the last boy in his class to be picked
for teams, the last man on his relief to be told they were
going for a drink after work. He wasn't an aggressive loner
like Donovan but he had no talent for joining in. He didn't
join clubs, was content to watch the world through a window.

Frank Shapiro didn't grow a beard at all. That didn't stop
him stroking it when he was deep in thought. He was thinking now, frowning at the telephone he'd put down minutes
ago and fingering his chin. Finally he picked the phone up
again and dialled.

DONOVAN HAD spent an unprofitable afternoon watching
for signs of drug-dealing at the mission. But none of the
crew had left the wharf, and of the few people who ventured there, with dogs or to check moored boats, none
seemed to have business at the encampment. The only person he saw approach or be approached by anyone from the
mission was his own inspector, and even at his most jaun-
diced he'd never suspected her of dealing in proscribed
substances.

That didn't mean he was glad to see her. His first thought
was that she was coming to *Tara*, which was like putting
up a sign reminding the people he was watching of his
presence. But then Davey intercepted her and they strolled
off up the tow-path, and he didn't see where they went after
that.

Now Shapiro wanted to see him. He could hardly refuse.
He was officially working, though sitting in his own living-
room with his feet up, a pot of coffee beside him and the
stereo playing so quietly it might have been humming to

itself, wasn't everyone's idea of work. And nothing that had happened so far suggested he would miss much by leaving the wharf for half an hour, particularly since the mission was entering the busiest period of its day. If Brady or Davey or any of the others had someone to meet, the best time would be morning, with no one around, or later when the wharf would be awash with urgent seekers after truth and a man seeking something else could pass unnoticed.

'Fen Tiger, ten minutes?' he suggested.

'My office,' countered Shapiro, 'in fifteen?'

But they settled for the pub because it overlooked Mere Basin. Tall black buildings that had once been warehouses and were now apartments and offices arched over each of the four canals that met there and stopped the eye travelling as far as Broad Wharf, but the same tow-path passed under the window. Anyone leaving the camp for a meeting, or anyone going there for one, would probably come this way. The alternatives, Cornmarket and Brick Lane, were each a longer walk to the town centre.

Donovan was there when Shapiro arrived, hunched in a corner by the window. Without taking his eyes off the tow-path he took a fierce draught from the glass in front of him. Partly it was the grim way he did it, with more dedication than enjoyment, and partly that the accent conveyed a certain stereotype, but Donovan had a modest local reputation as a drinker. Only close friends and barmen knew that what he was drinking mostly wasn't alcohol, and most of the time he spent in pubs he was listening.

When he saw his chief Donovan pointed at his glass and raised an eyebrow, but Shapiro shook his head. Evening it might be but his day was far from over. He squeezed in behind the table, envying Donovan his young man's narrow hips.

'I had a call from Drugs Squad,' he said by way of greeting. 'I don't know what to make of it.'

Donovan's gaze flickered between Shapiro and the window. 'About—?' The tilt of his head semaphored the mission.

Shapiro was non-committal. 'It wasn't the chap you phoned, it was his governor looking for your governor. Nice chap, we had a pleasant little talk. But what he was saying was, "Butt out".' For Shapiro this was outrageous slang.

Donovan's eyebrows climbed. 'Just that? No explanation?'

'Not even when I asked for one. All he'd say was that we had no need to be concerned.'

'What did you say?'

'I said I needed to know what the situation was. I said that if he was running an operation on our manor I'd make sure we stayed out of his way.'

'And?'

'He refused to answer.'

Less and less of Donovan's attention was on the towpath. He stared at Shapiro with coals in his eyes, like a dog scenting game. 'Then he is. I *knew* it; I knew there was something going on. But they should have told us before this. Do they not trust us? Do they think we're going to go round there blabbing—?'

He finished so abruptly, so obviously in the middle of a sentence, that Shapiro peered into his face. 'Sergeant?'

Casual acquaintances always saw the same side of Donovan: a Celtic dourness both relieved and underlined by a strain of humour so black they never knew whether it was safe to laugh. People who knew him better had glimpsed other things: a fierce loyalty, a volcanic temper, a childishly stubborn tenacity, even the rare smile that transformed his narrow face with unexpected gentleness.

But even Shapiro, who had known him longer than most, had never seen him nonplussed. His eyes dropped and flicked away, flitting between nearby objects as if seeking a safe place to land. Above them his brows drew together and his lips formed a question-mark. He looked at Shapiro and the question was in his eyes as well. But he didn't voice it, and when he saw curiosity sharpening his chief's gaze he looked quickly away. Incredibly, he blushed.

'For crying out loud, Donovan, what is it?' A sudden stab of the intuition that had got Shapiro where he was told him. The muscles of his face went slack and his voice breathy. 'You're not serious. You think someone at Queen's Street is passing information? And Drugs Squad *know* this, and that's why they're leaving us out in the cold?'

His tone grew hard with anger. 'What the hell gives you the right to think that about your colleagues?' But the intuition continued evolving: the anger passed too, giving way to a kind of stunned understanding. 'My God, you've seen something. From that bloody boat. What did you see?'

At moments of stress and confusion people fall back on the habits of a lifetime. They don't think, they do what has served them in the past. Donovan clammed up. 'Nothing.'

Shapiro's eyes went fierce and he leaned over the table. 'Don't play games with me, sonny. We're talking about the integrity of this department and the possibility that it may have been compromised, or at least that someone thinks it's been compromised. You know something about this. I want to know what. Your duty, the only duty that matters, is to me. Everything else comes second. If we're being prevented from doing our job by someone at Queen's Street I want to know who, and how, and why, and how deep the rot goes.'

'Rot!' Donovan echoed scornfully. 'It's nothing like that. It can't be. A coincidence, that's all.'

'What is?'

'It's just Drugs Squad behaving the way Drugs Squad does. They think they're smarter than the rest of us and don't like having to play with us. They keep secrets for the hell of it.'

'Sergeant, what did you see?'

Donovan gave up prevaricating. He was going to have to answer sooner or later; indeed, if he'd thought quicker he'd have answered sooner. For all his avuncular manner, his amiable expression, his spreading waistline and his penchant for tweed suits, so that he might have been mistaken for a professor of English Literature in one of the less demanding universities, Shapiro had a gin-trap mind. Once he had his quarry he didn't let go, and he wasn't likely to start with one of his own sergeants.

Besides which the man was right. If Drugs Squad had the idea that information was leaking out of Queen's Street, they needed putting right. Donovan didn't believe there was a leak. He thought it an untimely coincidence. But he also thought that Liz was sailing into trouble and someone should fire a shot across her bows. He'd tried himself, clumsily, and only succeeded in antagonizing her. Shapiro would do it better.

'Inspector Graham's been seeing Michael Davey.'

Shapiro's expression didn't flicker. 'Since we interviewed him at the station?'

'Twice that I know of. She had lunch with him yesterday; this afternoon they met at Broad Wharf and wandered off towards Cornmarket. I don't know where they went then.'

Shapiro nodded slowly, giving the information time to sink in. 'Anything else? Any violinists getting out of stretch limousines?'

Donovan grinned. However things were done in Miami, in Castlemere the drug pushers had day jobs in shoe-shops or as plumbers, and met their suppliers in the firm's van with a girlfriend acting as look-out. It wasn't true to say there was no drug problem in Castlemere; more that the drug problem had yet to become a problem. Of course, that could change. Jimmy Scoutari for one was waiting for a crack at the big time.

'Nothing. I'd like to get back for when the meeting starts, though. If anybody's going to slip away on the quiet, that's when.'

'All right, Sergeant, you get back.' Shapiro climbed to his feet. 'Leave the other thing with me. There's probably nothing to worry about but I'll make sure.'

They left The Fen Tiger a minute apart, Donovan slouching back along the tow-path, Shapiro heading for his car and, after a moment's consideration, the house on the edge of Belvedere Park.

WHEN HE SAW a car that wasn't Liz's in the drive Shapiro decided against ringing the bell. They might be better talking in the office tomorrow. But as he turned in the road another car came up the hill and flashed its headlights. Liz stuck her head out of the window. 'Looking for me, Frank?'

He was about to deny it, mumble something about the scene of the crime and go away. But he recognized the impulse as cowardice and refused to give in to it. 'Can we talk? Privately?'

She eyed him oddly but made no objection. 'Come down to the stables: the mare's very discreet. Actually,' she added gently, making the point, 'so is Brian.'

'I know that. As a matter of fact it's Brian I'm thinking of.'

In the tack room, surrounded by leather, jute and sacks of feed, he explained. Liz heard him out in silence but with mounting anger. Her lips compressed to a firm line and her eyes blazed. By the time he'd finished Shapiro fancied steam was coming out of her ears.

But she didn't shout at him. Partly out of respect for his rank, partly because they were friends, but also because the thing was too important. She knew if she left any doubt in anyone's mind that there might be some substance in this allegation her career was over. She wouldn't make detective chief inspector. She would have to fight to stay where she was, and even then she might fail. So she wanted to be sure that every word she said was clear, and clearly understood. She couldn't afford to lose her temper.

But she saw no reason to disguise the outrage she felt. Her voice was icy. 'What cause have I ever given you to think you couldn't trust me?'

'None,' he agreed readily. 'Liz, I don't think that now. I think you may have been unwise. I want to know what the situation is between you and Davey so I can put Drugs Squad straight.'

'It's none of their business!'

'It *is* their business,' Shapiro corrected her, 'if it's making them take bad decisions. If they're not confiding in us because they're afraid something they say could get back to Davey, they're doing without local back-up that could be useful and they're running the risk of our investigation inadvertently interfering with theirs. Even if they're groundless, their suspicions could wreck two important operations.

'I have to tell them they're wrong. I could do that now. I could do it with a clear conscience, because I know you'd do nothing to compromise a police action. But I may not be believed by people who don't know you unless I can give them facts. How often have you seen this man? How long have you spent with him? Why?'

She didn't answer immediately. 'This is down to Donovan, isn't it?'

Shapiro sighed. 'He saw you at the wharf. I had to drag it out of him like pulling teeth. I hope I don't have to get it out of you the same way.'

Liz had been angry with superiors before. She controlled it then and she controlled it now. Her eyes speculated on his face. 'Very well, sir,' she said deliberately. 'The facts are these. I've spoken to Michael Davey on three occasions.

The first was at Queen's Street, in your presence, after the riot in The Jubilee. The second was in the Castle Hotel yesterday: I went to find out what time he left the hotel the morning Alice Elton was killed. After I'd established his alibi I saw him in the foyer and, still wondering about Brady's involvement, asked about his work. Because it was lunch-time we talked over a ploughman's in the bar. I left the hotel about one-thirty.

'I saw him again this afternoon.' Her eyes smoked. 'Of course you know that. I was on my way to see Donovan when Davey came over. I didn't want to draw attention to the surveillance so I said I was going for a walk and he invited himself along. We talked about his mission, about the state of society and the prevalence of crime. He did most of the talking.' Deadpan, she added, 'He made no attempt to obtain information from me.'

'How long did this take and where did you go next?'

Her resentment was unmistakable. 'Half an hour, forty minutes? We came back along Brick Lane, then I returned here and I suppose Davey went back to his tent.' Her lip curled. 'I was back on duty by four o'clock. I think you'll find it takes longer than that to have an affair with a man in a wheelchair.'

Shapiro was embarrassed, but more than that he was concerned. 'Liz, nobody's suggesting that. But you know how even a casual friendship can be misconstrued if it's with the wrong person at the wrong time.'

'There is nothing wrong with Michael Davey!' she snapped, exasperated. 'We suspected him of inciting the attack on Carver but the evidence is that he didn't. We wondered if he could have killed the girls, but the evidence is pretty conclusive on that point too. Now Donovan's got some crazy idea about drugs, and because Drugs Squad are co-operating even less than usual you've convinced yourself that they're watching Davey and because I've talked to the man three times they think I'm a security risk.

'It's nonsense, Frank. Even if it was true, the timing's all wrong. If Drugs Squad was watching the mission they were doing it long before I met Davey; they'd have told you then if they were going to. Either they're not interested in him, or they never had any intention of involving us. Like so many things, this is a figment of Donovan's imagination.'

She was right about the timing. Shapiro squirmed. 'It's not Donovan's fault. Maybe it's something we cooked up between us, but he wouldn't have said anything if I hadn't insisted. And yes, Drugs Squad do tend to act as if the rest of us were a different, not wholly compatible species. But Liz, that still doesn't make it sensible for you to be seen with this man. Donovan has been known to be right, on rare occasions. If he's right this time Davey's distributing illegal substances. That's one good reason to avoid his company.' He nodded towards the house. 'Brian's another. You're a married woman.'

She gasped with indignation. 'You think I need reminding of that? How dare you, Frank? You're my chief inspector, not my confessor or my marriage guidance counsellor; and in fact if you were all three it would still be none of your business. How often do I have to say it? There is nothing going on between me and Michael Davey. Nothing to compromise my work, nothing to threaten my marriage, nothing to stir my conscience. I can't say it plainer than that. I'm amazed at having to defend myself against so frivolous an accusation.'

Shapiro raised a hand, half in apology, half to ward off her fury as if it were a blow. 'Liz, I was worried about you. If you tell me it was a misunderstanding then of course I believe you. But you don't need me to remind you how disastrous an indiscretion can be for a police officer. It's like Caesar's wife, isn't it?—if we're not above suspicion somebody with an axe to grind will find some way of capitalizing on it.'

'That's just it, isn't it?' Liz said quietly. 'Caesar's wife. When did you last have this conversation with a male detective? If I was a married man, and I'd met a woman we'd ruled out of our inquiries, and we'd had a sandwich in a hotel bar and walked for half an hour by the canal while she told me about other people who'd come under suspicion, it wouldn't have occurred to you I was doing anything but my job. You certainly wouldn't have discussed it with a junior officer.'

He'd have liked to say she was talking rot. But there was some truth in it. He spread his hand in another of those hereditary gestures. 'What can I tell you? You're right but it doesn't alter anything. It's the burden you carry. You have to be twice as good as any male officer before people will admit you're up to the job; you have to be three times as good as any male applicant before you'll get your promotions; and you have to be four times as sure as any man that there's no overlap between your professional and private lives or people will say that was always the risk with using women in CID, that they'd become emotionally involved.

'I'm not saying it's fair, I'm saying it's a fact. It was how things were when you joined the police, how they were when you joined CID, and if it's going to change it'll be by your efforts and those of women like you. And to get into positions where you can make changes you have to play by the existing rules. I know it's hard. I told you ten years ago you were going to find it hard.' He smiled suddenly, remembering. 'You told me that if all you had to be was twice the man of any toe-rag currently sitting behind an inspector's desk it'd be a doddle. Minutes later you stuck your head back round my door and said, "Present company excepted".'

They were able to laugh at that and it eased the uncharacteristic tension between them. Shapiro said, 'What should I do about Drugs Squad? I can call them and put them straight. But if you're right it could do more harm than good.'

'Do nothing,' she said. 'Drugs Squad don't know me from a hole in the wall. I don't think they know Davey: they're just covering themselves in case there's something going on they should have been aware of. I imagine that by now they've checked, decided there's nothing in it and thrown away the piece of paper with your number on it. There never was anything to support the idea. Some crime figures whose very nature is to fluctuate seemed to be fluctuating in a significant way. All right, it was worth querying. But I can't think why we're spending so much time on an imaginary drugs connection when we've got the ripped bodies of two teenage girls in the morgue.'

As if reaching a decision Shapiro gave an emphatic nod. 'You're right—let's get our priorities straight here. If Donovan doesn't come up with anything tonight I'll reconsider the surveillance. Davey's people are out of the frame as far as the murders go; if Drugs Squad aren't interested either I can't justify the time.' He paused then and his eyes slid away as if he were wondering whether to add something. 'Er—'

Liz gave a tight-lipped smile. 'No, Frank, I have no plans to meet Michael Davey again. But for the record, I won't hurry up side-streets and hide behind dustbins if I see him coming.'

She walked him back to his car. As he was getting in she leaned over and said quietly, 'By the way, Frank, you've just spent half an hour alone in a secluded outbuilding with a married woman.' His startled glance as he drove off was all the reward she needed.

III

ONE

AFTER NIGHTFALL the glow of the marquee was almost the only sign of life on the waterfront. The people in the houseboats kept their curtains drawn and their hatches locked in these uncertain times. Any dogs that needed walking were being marched up and down within sight of their owners' front doors, and anyone with business that couldn't wait either drove or got a taxi, however short the distance.

But people still came to the mission. Perhaps not in the huge numbers of that second night, with the horror of a murdered child fresh in their eyes, but still enough of them to count the crusade a success. At least in its own terms. A cynic might have asked what it would actually achieve, treating Jennifer Mills' crime statistics with the same misgivings as the local CID.

But if it achieved nothing else, for the two hours that they were there people who would have been troubled and afraid sitting in their own living-rooms took comfort and courage from the nearness of so many others sharing their anxieties. They didn't know where it was all going to end but they knew they didn't have to face it alone. Thousands of people in Castlemere felt as they did. The man in white wheeling himself round the low dais was almost unnecessary. They felt better just for coming here and sitting all together, raising shaky unpractised voices in hymns of salvation. But when Michael Davey began to speak, in that slow deep voice that built up its power like a rolling stone turning into an avalanche, expressing their half-formed feelings in words that were both strong and simple, assuring them that what they believed instinctively was right and good and could be harnessed for action, night after night it came as a revelation.

So it wasn't mere nostalgia to think that the world they lived in had been going steadily downhill since they were children! It was so, and clever articulate men like Reverend Michael Davey thought so too, and even knew what to do about it. Not that he claimed, or they expected, to resolve the world's problems in a fortnight of meetings in a marquee. But he gave them confidence in their judgement, a determination to be heard, powerful arguments that might not have occurred to them and a sense of the importance of what they were doing. He filled them with the heady joy of communal zeal.

The power of the man filled their breasts and brains and left them thinking they could tackle anything—vice, violence, malice, malevolence and greed—while the power of his words rang in their ears. He fed them his strength and they grew great with it. It acted on them like wine: with his words and the sheer scale of his personality rolling over them they caught a glimpse of glory.

Outside on the wharf, where the only light was the glow of the tent and the only sound the swell of voices lifted in praise, a dark figure moved silently between the shadows.

LIZ AND BRIAN moved the last chest into the last space in the hall, fitted the last drawer, plonked the last potted plant on top and declared the move complete. It didn't matter that the sideboard would have to be resited if they hoped ever to seat more than three at their six-seater dining table, that the television was sitting on the carpet in a nest of its own wires or that the spare room was so full of furniture that wouldn't go anywhere else that even the smallest, most uncritical guest could only have been inserted with a shoe-horn. For now it would do. They could live like this until they had the time and energy to do better.

They opened a bottle of wine to celebrate, couldn't find

the glasses, collapsed on the settee with the bottle and a pair of pottery mugs.

After a while Brian said, 'What was Shapiro being so furtive about?'

It was a moment for relying on gut instinct. She could tell him what had passed between them, or give him the abridged version. If she told him it might cost him some fleeting concern; no more, she didn't think he'd believe it. But she could spare him even that by keeping her silence. She didn't think gossip on the subject would reach much further than the Queen's Street canteen.

She smiled, lying into his shoulder as they sprawled on the couch. 'That was Frank being tactful. He's a very good police officer: it's personal relationships that give him problems.'

Brian's chin was on top of her head: she could feel him chuckle. 'If it's personal perhaps I shouldn't ask.'

'Actually,' she said, squirming round so she could see his face, 'you should. It's personal to me, not to Frank. He's afraid I'm being swept off my feet by an evangelist in a white suit and a wheelchair.'

She told him what had happened: all that had happened and all that anyone thought might have happened. She was watching his eyes all the time. He knew it wasn't as light a matter as she made out; but he seemed to know too that there was nothing she wasn't telling him. He said soberly, 'It must be difficult working under a magnifying glass like that.'

She shrugged. 'It is a bit. But we're used to it, all of us. We always have one eye on how our actions might look to an outsider. It just hadn't occurred to me that as a woman I was especially vulnerable. Perhaps it should have done.' Her head tilting, she looked at him from the tail of one eye. 'In the same way that male teachers have to guard against the fertile imaginations of teenage girls, I suppose.'

Brian's expression was scathing. 'Oh, sure. They queue

up after Home Economics to make passes at me. Listen, all the way through the Permissive Society everyone was talking about free love and the death of morality, and I was wondering when I was going to get my share.'

'And?'

'Still waiting,' he said lugubriously.

Liz thought the subject dropped, but after a pensive silence he came back to it. 'What's he like, this preacher?'

She took a moment to arrange her thoughts. 'Larger than life, but somehow it's all real. Your first impression is that it's an act. But as you talk to him, listen to him rather, you realize that's how he is: that isn't a line he's spinning you, it's what he believes.

'He's a very big man physically, and that spills over into everything he does. He shoves himself around with these big powerful hands, and when he can't express himself in words alone he stops wheeling for a moment to make some grand gesture. But it isn't rhetoric: he's absolutely sincere. The words rush out of him as if his brain's boiling them up too fast to catch them, but even in full flow he's totally coherent. You have the feeling of a huge agile intellect caged inside that vast crippled body.'

'Do you like him?'

Again she took a moment to think. 'I don't know. I find him—fascinating, I suppose. The sheer chained power of him. It's like standing on a volcano and feeling the rumble. He's an intensely passionate man. You start off thinking it's rather immature to feel that strongly about things, but next thing you know he's grabbed you by the mind and shaken your ideas to the roots. When you listen to him you begin to understand how Hitler could turn a sophisticated modern nation into a barbarian tribe essentially by oratory alone.'

'Charisma,' suggested Brian.

For a moment Liz thought of the little tom with her

slashed throat and didn't understand. 'Oh—yes. Yes, certainly. A dangerous thing, Charisma.'

A little later still Brian said quietly, 'Frank was right about one thing, wasn't he? You are just a little in love with this man.'

Liz twisted like an eel in his arms and stared up at his face, and couldn't for the life of her be sure if he was joking.

IT WAS A NIGHT for confidences. After the gospel meeting broke up Davey and Jennifer Mills left the crew to finish and set off for their hotel. Because Davey's car, unlike a motorcycle, couldn't slot between the bollards on the walkway they headed up the tow-path to Cornmarket and back by Brick Lane. Given the roughness of the ground, it took them longer to drive from the wharf to the Castle Hotel than it would have taken a fit man to walk.

It wasn't wasted time. It gave them space to talk.

'It was a good night,' Mills began, blandly enough, lighting a cigarette.

Davey smiled bleakly into the blackness ahead. 'There's nothing like the fear of God to get hands into pockets.'

Mills didn't glance at the cash-box on the back seat. 'Yes, it was a good collection. I'll count it later. But that isn't what I meant. I meant, you were good tonight.'

He refused to be mollified. Some internal irritation was gnawing away at him. 'According to you I'm always good.'

She turned her head, smiling at the side of his face lit by the instruments. 'Are you picking a quarrel, Michael?'

He shook his head wearily. 'Don't mind me. I'm—a bit out of sorts, that's all.'

For a moment she said nothing more. Then, her voice flat, stripped of the humour that lubricated the occasional friction between them, she said, 'Do you want—?'

'No,' he said quickly. 'That's not it.'

'I don't mind.' The least edge on her words suggested however that this was not wholly truthful. 'If it'll help.'

Davey shook his head again. 'No.'

She peered at him, trying to read his expression in the dimness of the car. 'What is it, Michael? What's troubling you? Is it that man who got hurt?'

'No, not really. I mean yes, I am bothered by it, I still think I should have seen it coming, done something to prevent it. I mean, I got those people there: I must bear some responsibility for what they did.'

Mills turned her slim body towards him, demanding his attention although the rough road required his eyes. 'No, Michael. With all due respect to you, they came because of what's been happening in this town. If they hadn't come here they'd have gone somewhere else: a bar, a street-corner, somewhere. Instead of singing hymns they'd have got drunk. They'd still have got angry, the boy would still have been hurt. You're not responsible. Blame whoever killed those girls; blame the police if you like, for stumbling round blindly when they should have the killer behind bars; but don't reproach yourself. You do nothing but good wherever you go.'

He put out one bear's paw to touch hers. 'Dear Jenny. What would I do without you picking me up when I fall, kissing the sore bits better?'

'I can't imagine,' she said briskly. 'Now tell me: what's really bothering you?'

He gave up trying to keep it from her, tried to make light of it instead. But the shake in his laugh betrayed him. 'I think I'm in love.'

Jennifer Mills froze from the inside out. Ice-water bathed her spine; premonition stole her breath away. 'Michael. Who? How?'

'I—I can't,' he stumbled, a gleam of tragedy in his eye. 'It's not possible.'

She governed all his days. Whatever he needed, as a

preacher and as a man, she obtained for him. She didn't
believe he could have been seeing a woman without her
knowledge, so it was not so much intuition as deduction
that led her to the improbable truth. She still hadn't breath
enough to do more than whisper, but the pitch of her whisper soared. 'The *policewoman?*'

As if he'd slapped her she turned her face from him, her
body quivering with fury. She anticipated difficulties all the
time. It was her job, to anticipate and forestall them. But
she had not anticipated this, and she was shaken to the core.

When she got her brain back in gear it was the practical
implications she turned to first. 'How far has it gone?'

He darted her a glance at that, desperate and hunted. 'It
hasn't. How could it? She's conducting a murder investigation and I'm in a wheelchair: we can't exactly slip away
and book into a motel as Mr and Mrs Smith.'

'But you'd like to?'

'Oh, Jenny,' he said, and the unhappiness in his voice
stabbed her to the heart. 'It's like—having half of something all your life. And you get used to having half, and
tell yourself half is enough, and maybe the other half
doesn't even exist. And then by sheer chance one day you
find that other half. Only it belongs to someone else and
you've no right to it. But you *feel* like you have a right,
you know?—as if having the half of it all this time entitles
you to the rest.' He glanced at her uneasily, unable to
fathom her expression in the near darkness. 'Am I making
any sense?'

She understood him well enough. She'd have liked to
tell him to stop feeling sorry for himself, that it was nothing
but spring fever and the best he could do was get on with
his work, but she couldn't. She knew it went deeper than
that, that hopeless as the wanting was it was anchored in
his soul by roots so strong that ripping it out would leave
a great bloody crater. She sat as rigid and white as a woman
carved in marble, and inside she was raging with a passion

that would have startled those who knew her at the monstrous unfairness of it. She knew what it was to want something you couldn't have.

But she didn't answer him until she had the turmoil under control and could open her mouth without giving vent to it. 'You hardly know her.'

'I *know* that. Jenny, I know how absurd this is.'

'Have you said anything to her? Does she know how you feel?'

'Of course I haven't,' he said scornfully. 'What would I say? "Here's my alibi, Inspector, here are my fingerprints, and by the way will you leave your husband and run away with me?"' Then his tone softened. 'All the same, I think maybe she does know. People do, you know, when other people are attracted to them.'

Her eyes gaped at him but he seemed oblivious of their meaning. She said tightly, 'You don't say.'

He stopped the car with a lurch, careless for once of how skilfully he manipulated the controls. There was entreaty in the gruffness of his voice. 'Jenny, help me here. I don't know what to do. I know what I ought to do but...' He tailed off, unable to think of a reason to do what he wanted instead of what he should.

By degrees Mills regained her composure. If she was shocked it was not her place to show it. She was his fixer: of course he told her that he'd embarked on a relationship that could jeopardize everything they'd achieved. She took a deep breath.

'Michael, what do you want me to say? It's all right, go for it? The world owes you a bit of happiness? That may be true but it really isn't relevant. She's a married woman. Other men can go lusting after married women but you can't.'

He slapped his useless legs furiously. 'Why not? Because of these?'

'Of course not,' she snapped, 'that's only a physical

problem, I never saw one of those defeat you yet. You can't get involved with Mrs Graham because of the man you are and the job you do. How can you tell other people how to behave if you're embroiled in adultery? Oh, I know it's been done before. But not by you. Whatever you are, Michael, you're not a hypocrite. If you can't speak from a platform of absolute honesty you won't speak at all. You couldn't lie to save your life.'

'So maybe it's time to think of doing something else,' he countered. 'Maybe I've already done all the good I'm going to. Maybe now it's time I looked for something else to do, let someone better equipped carry the torch.'

Mills shook her head. 'You don't mean that. This isn't just a job to you, it isn't even just a way of life. It *is* your life, your reason for living. Your reason for getting into that chair and hauling yourself round the country when it would be so much easier to settle down quietly somewhere and live on welfare. It wasn't much of a hand your God dealt you but I'll say this for you, Michael, you never looked like throwing it in before.'

'I'm not talking about throwing it in,' he retorted angrily, 'I'm talking about retiring. I'm fifty-two years old. I'm due a bit of happiness. If not now, when?'

She sighed. 'God help me, Michael, if I thought it would make you happy I'd give you my blessing. But you've never taken anything you didn't earn: how are you going to live with taking another man's wife? You'd be wretched. And it'd be the end of this love affair between you and God. He might forgive you but you never would. He's your best friend and you'd never be able to look Him in the face again.

'Michael, your whole life's been one of sacrifice. It's what you are, where your authority comes from. I can't see you getting anything but despair out of sacrificing your mission for your own desires.'

'What if it's what she wants too?'

'Her soul's in her own keeping,' Mills said coldly.

'And mine is in yours?' His voice was bitter.

'You wouldn't be talking to me if you were comfortable with this. You'd talk to her and tell me what you'd decided. You know there's no future in it. Yes, you could give up everything for her and tell yourself that turned it from a spot of adultery into a great romance. But you'd regret it for the rest of your life. Believe me, Michael, I know. *You* know. We both know what's important to you, and whatever this fire in your blood is telling you right now, it isn't the satisfaction of the flesh.'

She wasn't saying what he wanted to hear. Hurt and under siege he responded with a cheap jibe. 'That's easy for you to say.'

She was his friend. They'd been together five years. She'd given up everything for him: her friends, her prospects, any life outside the mission. Faithful and uncomplaining, she'd put his needs ahead of hers in every particular; she'd done things for him that only close friends would do. She deserved better than that. Icily she turned away. 'Act your age, Michael. Stay away from her.'

He was bitterly ashamed of himself. That didn't make his burden easier to bear. A stubborn anguish ran through his voice. 'I don't know, Jenny. I don't know if I can.'

TWO

THE GOSPEL meetings began shortly after eight and lasted a couple of hours, the last enthusiasts straggling away about ten-thirty. Sunset was around half-past eight.

Donovan reckoned there were two prime times for something to happen: about nine when the meeting would be in full swing and the wharf dark so that a careful man could move around unseen, and about ten-fifteen when the faithful would throng out of the tent and a man could pass unnoticed among them. On the whole he favoured the earlier time: the more people who were around, the harder it would be to find privacy. But when he slipped off *Tara* under cover of dusk and took up his watch from the alley where he found Charisma it was with the bleak knowledge that he might be standing here for ninety minutes before anything happened, or three hours before he could assume nothing was going to happen.

What he was hoping for—though with the mission here for a fortnight there was no reason for it to be tonight—was that someone from the camp would slip away for a meeting with a leading light of the local drugs trade. Eight months ago it would have been Jack Carney or someone acting for him. But where he was now there were men in peaked caps to discourage nocturnal excursions, and if any of Castlemere's lesser gangsters had taken over where Carney left off word had not reached CID.

That made it harder to crack down on but, if anything, more important. If the mission was smuggling drugs the quantity on offer could be enough to confirm Scoutari, or whichever of the pretenders made the deal, as top dog. Stopping him now would prevent a lot of misery. Donovan hadn't much sympathy for people who took drugs but on a purely practical basis supposed that, as with tetanus, prevention was better than cure.

If he was right about this, and he knew there was room for doubt, what they stood to gain was worth more than his time alone. He hadn't asked for help because of the risk that he was wrong. If there were no drugs it would be hard enough to apologize to Shapiro for wasting his own time without having to account for someone else's. Also, if Drugs Squad were involved the danger of giving the game away increased with every extra body employed.

The first indication that it mightn't be a wasted vigil came soon after he'd settled himself in the dark passage. The door of the caravan opened and the bearded Breton emerged. The glow of the tent showed him stretching, wandering about aimlessly, then taking a seat on a mooring bollard with a clear view of *Tara*. Donovan had left a light burning in his bedroom to suggest occupation.

After a minute the caravan door opened again. Donovan heard footsteps and two figures passed between him and the water. One, from the shape of it, was Kelso. The other could have been Brady. The Breton stayed where he was, watching the wharf and the boats.

In daylight Donovan could not have followed without being seen. But the darkness was undiscriminating: it covered their secret activities and it covered his. He let the two men get forty metres ahead—any closer and they might have heard him, any further and he could have lost them— then slunk out of the alley and along the wall. He watched the look-out, silhouetted against the glimmer of the water, but there was no sign that he'd been seen. Of course, the man was looking the wrong way. Hugging the buildings on his left, and when they ceased to be buildings the shadow of the broken walls, Donovan followed the two men to Cornmarket.

There was a bad moment when he heard the sound of

running feet on the tow-path behind him. He shrank into a bricked-up doorway and the man trotted past without knowing he was there. A moment later the murmur of voices told that the running man had caught up with the others, clearly believing that their departure had gone unnoticed and he could now do more good closer to the men he was there to protect. In that he was right. It certainly made Donovan's job harder.

They followed the tow-path—the two men first, the Breton ten metres behind, Donovan forty metres behind him—to the lock, then turned for the shunting yard. Where the diminishing cover of the derelict buildings petered out and the wasteland of Cornmarket began Donovan dropped further back. The only other thing he could do to avoid being seen was abandon his pursuit and he wasn't prepared to do that.

The shunting yard came down to the tow-path, victims of the same march of progress. Inside were only the carcasses of dead rolling-stock. It was a good place for a quiet meeting: one man on the path could stop anyone creeping up unnoticed. When the other men entered the yard the Breton stayed behind.

Donovan was half expecting that, had already decided what to do: cross the spur at Doggett's Lock, run like hell up the far side and cross back at the stone bridge half a mile further on, coming down on the shunting yard from the unwatched side. At least, he assumed it would be unwatched. There was only open country beyond, and nobody in his right mind would cross the lock in the dark.

Since the handrail went almost nobody crossed in daylight. Once he caught some boys daring one another and put the fear of God into them. He didn't consider this hypocrisy: he knew he could cross safely, was fairly sure they could not. He hadn't done it in the dark before. At least it was dry: the black timbers went as slick as oil in the rain.

It occurred to him—belatedly, Shapiro would have

said—that a squad car in Brick Lane could intercept anyone leaving. He had a mobile phone; now something was definitely happening he would have asked for back-up if he could have made the call without giving himself away. But it was a still night, even soft voices would carry. He thought he'd be out of earshot once he reached the bridge.

He crossed the lock like a wire-walker, head up, arms lightly spread, feeling with his toes for the stumps of the handrail waiting to trip him. When he was safe on the other side he allowed himself a little half-smile and wondered why he'd thought it would be difficult.

There was some low scrub along the bank. He hugged it, bent double, until he'd passed the look-out, then he began to run. There wasn't a proper path on this side but there was a track and the ground was level. He loped swift and easily as a wolf until he reached the hump-backed bridge where the tow-path switched banks.

Squatting behind the parapet he had the mobile in his hand when he heard the car. There were no lights and he couldn't tell if it was arriving or getting ready to leave, but the men from the mission were on foot so this was the buyer. They'd hardly complete the deal at this meeting. A smart supplier wouldn't deliver till he was ready to leave town: the last thing he wanted was a greedy dealer putting the stuff round while he was still in the area. They were here to show samples of the merchandise and to agree a price.

Donovan was afraid that he was too late: that he'd taken too long crossing the lock and the buyer was leaving. However quickly Shapiro acted he couldn't stop the car leaving Cornmarket, and once it joined the traffic it would disappear. The only chance of an identification was if Donovan got close enough to see. If the driver would switch on his lights he could get the number, maybe the backwash of the instruments would show him a face. He shoved the mobile back in his pocket and made for the sound.

He hadn't missed as much as he'd feared. Reaching the rendezvous first the car had waited in darkness and silence for the men from the mission to arrive. At the sound of footsteps the driver started his engine, announcing his presence and preparing for a swift departure if at any point that seemed a good idea. But he still didn't turn his lights on.

A door opened and a man got out on the passenger side. The brief flare of the interior light showed a muscular figure of medium height with straight long hair slicked back in a pony-tail. Then the door closed and the light went out. It was the merest glimpse, he was still fifty metres away and the man's back was towards him, but Donovan recognized him.

It was no surprise. Jimmy Scoutari had been one of the prime contenders to replace Carney since word got round that the Castlemere Godfather wouldn't be home for Christmas. He was a younger man—though too old for a pony-tail—and lacked Carney's style. Scoutari saw no point in posing as a legitimate businessman with offices and a Filofax and standing orders to some of the town's more prominent charities. He was interested only in those things that made him money or made him feared. Carney was a gentleman thug: Scoutari was a player.

He wasn't as clever as Carney so he wasn't as dangerous, and probably he wouldn't last as long, but as a nasty piece of work he bore comparison with the all-time greats. Donovan's last reservation about this vanished. The men from the mission might conceivably have fancied a walk, the car might have lost its way in Brick Lane, but Jimmy Scoutari was here to buy drugs.

Then Donovan made a fundamental miscalculation of the kind that had dogged his career. No one doubted his courage, his commitment or his integrity, but Liz was not the first senior officer to mistrust his judgement. The sensible thing to do at this point was creep back to the bridge and use his mobile to tell Shapiro what was happening. There

was nothing more he could do. He couldn't arrest a minimum of five men, some of them undoubtedly armed and
all of them dangerous, single-handed.

Besides which, he didn't have to. Nothing vital was going to happen now. They weren't going to swap vast quantities of drugs for vast sums of money and vanish from the
face of the earth. Donovan's wire-walking had achieved all
he should have wished for: he'd witnessed a secret meeting
between men from Davey's mission and a known criminal.
With that information Shapiro could go to work on both
parties and would find evidence enough for convictions.
There wasn't even any hurry. There would be a final meeting between Kelso and Scoutari before the mission left
town when they could be taken with the goods in their
possession.

But Donovan wanted more. Always he wanted more. Instead of retreating he crawled forward, hoping to overhear
what was being said. The inevitable consequence of that,
that he couldn't then use the mobile without himself being
overheard, didn't occur to him until it was too late.

Though the cinder surface of the yard grew a thriving
flora of weeds there wasn't cover enough for a grown man.
But a row of wagons was rotting away at the end of the
line five metres from the car: if he could reach them un-
detected he could crawl between the great rusting wheels
until he was almost as close to the action as the players.
He'd get a better view of their boots than of their faces but
he should hear their conversation while the inky shadow
under the bogies would keep him safe.

The meeting hadn't yet got down to business. The two
sides were still jockeying for advantage. Picking his way
across the open ground, Donovan was acutely aware that
if Scoutari decided it was time to view the merchandise and
the car lights came on he was a dead man. When the bulk
of the last wagon came between him and them he melted
against it in weak-kneed relief.

He could hear clearly. Kelso addressed Scoutari with stolid politeness as 'Mr Scoutari'; Scoutari addressed Kelso as 'You'. They talked numbers. Donovan was startled by the range of drugs on offer, as if the mission were a travelling emporium: heroin, cocaine, cannabis, Ecstasy, LSD. Scoutari was interested in them all. They haggled over quantities and price.

They reached a provisional agreement, then Scoutari wanted to test samples. Kelso produced a fat envelope from his pocket, Scoutari produced a torch. They used the bonnet of the car as a table. For some minutes Scoutari wielded tiny implements that glinted in the torchlight and sniffed or tasted the results. Each time he grunted a grudging satisfaction.

Donovan kept wishing someone would shine the torch around, catch a few faces. He knew who he was watching, with the possible exception of the man he only thought was Brady, but he'd have liked to be able to say he'd seen faces. But the beam remained resolutely on hands: Kelso's dealing out the samples, Scoutari's picking through them. He set the torch on the bonnet and worked within its beam. Once, adjusting the angle, he let it slip and the vibration of the ticking engine rolled it on to the ground. Someone picked it up and put it back.

Finally they reached the bit Donovan was keenest to hear: details of how money and merchandise would be exchanged. Kelso wanted a delay, Scoutari wanted his hands on the goods. They compromised: a week hence, with the proviso that Scoutari wouldn't put it on the streets until the mission left town.

The meeting broke up. Scoutari put his torch in his pocket and got back in his car. Without farewells, still without turning his lights on, the driver moved off immediately and the sound of the engine faded towards Brick Lane.

That left the massive figure of Kelso standing apparently lost in thought and the half-bricks and ankle-high weeds.

Donovan couldn't think what he was waiting for, why he didn't leave too. After a moment he realized uneasily that he'd lost track of the man with him. Maybe he was taking a leak. It was too late to search the place now; even so...

He wasn't kept wondering for long. He was lying belly-down under the wagon and something tapped the sole of his foot. It could have been any lump of metal of approximately the right size and weight but the message raced along his nerves that it was a gun. He exhaled raggedly and his insides clenched.

Brady's voice said amiably. 'Come on out, the show's over.'

Options skittered through Donovan's mind. It didn't take long: there were almost none. He could come out quietly and see what they intended. He could come out fighting and hope to get away in the confusion. He could come out backwards and face Brady or forwards and face Kelso.

He chose, by a narrow margin, the devil he knew, squirming round under the wagon to come out by Brady's legs. He'd been right about one thing: it was a gun. He saw it now, unmistakable even in the dark, before Brady turned him quite gently and pushed him against the wagon. In a sardonic imitation of an American drawl he said, 'Assoom da position.'

Donovan spread his arms slowly at shoulder level, spread his hands against the rotten timber. The muscles of his back knotted in fear. No one could see but his eyes were shut tight.

Even trying to be discreet Kelso's bull voice boomed, a kind of roaring whisper. 'Have you got the bastard?'

'I have.' Brady's hand rested nonchalantly on Donovan's shoulder, it's purpose not to restrain him but to detect the changes in muscular tension that would give him an instant's warning if Donovan decided to fight.

The heavy man's footsteps crunched on the broken surface as he hurried round the wagon. Before he appeared

Brady said softly in Donovan's ear. 'You may not believe this, boy, but I'm going to try and save your life.' Then he hit him, once, hard, with the gun across the back of his head.

THREE

'CAL? ARE YOU THERE?'

Brady had been sitting beside the long still form on the floor of the wagon for something over an hour before he heard a change in the rhythm of Donovan's breathing that suggested he was on his way back from the abyss. But there was no reply and his torch revealed no movement in the bloodless face. His eyes were imperfectly shut, like carelessly drawn blinds, so that a white line showed under each. Brady let the light rest on Donovan's face and after a moment, slowly, his eyes closed.

Brady sighed. 'Ach well, sleep while you may. It's going to be a long day.'

He'd been worried he'd hit Donovan too hard. It's not easy to judge: too light a tap only makes your adversary angry, too keen a swipe and you have a corpse on your hands. Nor had he had much time to work it out. He'd been afraid that Kelso would come raging round the wagon like a wild bull and kill the detective before he could weigh the consequences. He thought he'd be safer out cold. Not many people have the stomach to murder an unconscious man.

When Kelso got there to find him already on the ground he goggled. 'What happened?'

'He tried to run,' Brady said. 'I stopped him.'

'Is he dead?'

'Shouldn't be.'

Kelso bent to look closer. 'Hellfire,' he exclaimed, startled, 'it's that copper!' Like Brady he'd seen that there was someone under the wagon when the torch fell, but there'd been neither time nor light enough to see who. 'God Almighty, what do we do now?'

'One thing we won't do,' Brady suggested, 'is panic. There may be no need. If he was on official business he wouldn't have been alone—the place'd be crawling by now. He must have seen us leave the caravan and followed on spec.'

'How much do you suppose he saw? What did he hear?'

'Most of it, I guess. I'll ask him when he wakes up.'

'How did he get past Danny?'

'How should I know? He lives here, he knows his way round. We were unlucky, that's all.'

'*Unlucky?*' Kelso's voice soared for a moment before he remembered he should be whispering. 'Bailie, he's a copper. We're not going to buy him off and we're not going to scare him off. If he leaves here we all go down.'

'So what do you want to do—kill him?' Brady's manner was casual, untroubled.

'I think we have to.' Then he looked at the still face, moon-white against the dark clothing, and balked. 'I don't know. Maybe Scoutari'd take care of it.'

Brady was scathing. 'The Malteaser.' The fact that earlier Scoutaris came from Malta did not in fact make him a Malteaser but Kelso knew who he meant. 'Oh, he'd do it all right. He'd enjoy doing it. But you'd pay through the nose, and if he doesn't make it watertight we'd all end up talking to policemen. You kill a cop and they pull out all the stops, you know? They've already shown an interest in us; he lives within spitting distance of where we're camped; they're not stupid, they've got to suspect us.'

'I'm damned if I'll drop everything and run!'

'If we run they'll know they're right. We wouldn't reach Dover. I don't want to do life either, OK?'

'Then what?' Kelso was prodding the inert body with his foot. Brady thought that if Donovan stirred he'd probably kick him unconscious again.

'I'll see to it,' he said. 'Carefully, and at the right time, and it'll look like an accident. To get past Danny he must have crossed that lock. Tricky job, that. A man could fall, knock himself out, drown in two feet of water.'

Kelso nodded energetically, obviously relieved. He reached for Donovan's feet. 'I'll give you a hand.'

'Not *now*,' exclaimed Brady. 'Look, so far we're looking at—what?—ten years, out in seven. He dies and you can double that. I'll do it when I'm sure we can get away with it.'

'We could be here a fortnight. They'll start looking for him tomorrow.'

'They won't know he's missing,' said Brady. He gave an impish smile. 'I'll call in sick for him. We're from the same part of the world, nobody'll even wonder if it's him. I'll say that hand of his—mine—is playing me up and I've gone down the hospital. Before anybody thinks to check he'll have turned up in the bottom of the lock.'

'With us still here?'

'Why not? We've no reason to run. Accidental death: the guy took one chance too many. His mates must know he does things like that, they won't suspect a thing. They'll probably wonder how he got away with it till now.

'All the same,' he went on thoughtfully, 'it might be as well to finish our business before the body turns up. There's bound to be some activity down here before they rule out foul play. Call Scoutari and bring the deal forward to tomorrow night. As soon as it's done Donovan has his accident. Then the cops can poke around as much as they like: we can sit on our hands till we leave town.'

'What if they search the gear?'

'Why should they? And even if they do they won't find what Customs missed. Be cool, there's no problem.'

'What do we do with him till then?'

Brady glanced at the wagon. 'I'll keep him here. Nothing'll happen tomorrow, and if the cops come to the camp after he's found they won't ask about tonight. Sure, weren't they talking to him after this?'

Kelso regarded him with a new respect. 'How did you get so good at this?'

Brady laughed out loud. 'The same way the hare gets good at running: dodging the hounds in the bloody heather. I played this game in Ireland when even the traffic cops carried guns. By those rules, either you get good or you end up in Milltown Cemetery.'

'Talking of guns.' Kelso held out his hand and Brady passed him their weapon. 'Don't want him getting his hands on it.'

'No chance,' said Brady.

Kelso helped him put Donovan in the wagon, then he collected the Breton and left. Brady settled himself on the floor to wait. Donovan was still unconscious but that didn't stop Brady holding a quiet one-sided conversation.

'You haven't changed a bit, have you, Cal? You couldn't leave well enough alone, could you? You couldn't just wait a few days and see what was going to happen.'

He didn't expect a reply and there was none. To all practical purposes alone, Liam Brady sat in the dark in a damp wagon smelling of rot and old grain, with his knees drawn up to his chest and his arms clasped round them, and thought as if his life depended on it.

By midnight he knew what to do. He had to make some calls. Donovan's mobile meant he didn't have to risk being seen. It's an ill wind, he thought grimly.

Around midnight, too, Donovan began to surface. He'd been drifting for some time, his senses washing in and out like a slack tide. When the ache in his head was insistent enough to reach him through the fog his hands moved, loose and uncoordinated towards the source of his discomfort. His breathing came quicker, turning to a groan.

Brady bent over him. 'Cal? Can you hear me?'

Donovan's head rolled at the sound, starting a surge of pain that made him whine. 'Wha—? Who—?' His voice was a frail ghost. He'd been out too long to pick up where they'd left off when Brady hit him.

'Listen, Cal, you and me's got to talk. I know you're not feeling great but try to concentrate, this is important. It's a bad situation but maybe not as bad as you're thinking. I had to hit you, for both our sakes. Now I have to keep you here. Make it easy, hey? I don't want to hurt you any more. I can get you out of this if you'll trust me.'

There was no response. Brady peered at Donovan's face and couldn't tell if he was listening or if his senses had slid away again. 'I'm trying to save your neck here, Donovan,' he said, exasperated, 'the least you could do is stay awake.'

He waited a moment then tried again. 'Cal, listen to me. You don't know what's going on here. Will you just do as I ask?—go along with me while I get it sorted? Twenty hours is all I need. Nobody's going to hurt you. Kelso's happy to leave you to me. Twenty hours, then I'll tell you what it was all about and you'll be out of here.

'What do you say? You won't be too comfortable—I'll have to tie you up if anyone comes; if Kelso or the Malteaser thought I'd let you go we'd both be dead men. But when it's over you'll understand. You'll see why it was worth it. What do you say? Will you help me?'

Donovan's battered brain was digesting it, mulling it over, thinking at once too well and not well enough. When he had the answer he slurred, 'I know who you are.'

Brady thought he was wandering again. 'Of course you do. We grew up in the same town.' He grinned at a sudden memory. 'You wrote "Paisley For Pope" on my car.'

'Not that. I know what you're doing here.'

And Brady saw in his eyes that he did, and his heart sank. In trying to win Donovan's confidence he'd said too much. Now the risk was doubled—more than doubled. Before, the only man who knew had every reason to keep the secret. Now he shared it with someone whose feelings towards him were ambivalent and whose head wouldn't be his own for a couple of days.

Brady chewed the inside of his cheek. Perhaps neither Kelso nor Scoutari would come back here. Perhaps, even if they did, Donovan would hold his tongue. But he wouldn't bet his life on it. If they thought of it one or the other would want to know how close the police were—if Donovan really had stumbled on them by chance or if there was a net closing in. If they were determined to know, he'd tell them. Anyone would.

That gave Brady a dilemma. He could make sure Donovan wouldn't answer questions, however persuasively put. But if he hit him again he could hurt him badly. He could tell anyone who asked that he'd already conducted an interrogation and there was nothing to worry about; but men whose liberty was at stake might not take his word for that.

He could hope to wrap things up before Donovan became an issue. But the earliest the deal could now be done was this evening, and that left more than enough time for something to go wrong. Then Brady could wave goodbye to seven months' hard, difficult, dangerous work. That was the best that could happen.

In fact his choices were fewer and simpler than that. He could call the thing off now, to protect Donovan and himself, or carry on with all the risks that entailed. Twenty hours. A blink of the eye on the cosmic scale. A whole lifetime to certain exotic butterflies.

He eyed the author of his problem coldly a moment longer. Then he said with conviction, 'No, you don't. If you did someone'd get it out of you with a cigar-lighter. So you know nothing. Understand? Nothing about me beyond the fact that I used to be in the IRA. Forget the rest, hold on to that. That's our passport out of this. If they believe I'm prepared to kill you we'll be all right.'

'We'd be all right if we left now.'

Brady bared his teeth in a grin of no humour whatsoever.

'You've blown my cover, boy. Thanks to you I have to wind this up three months ahead of plan. I'm not going in empty-handed.'

'These people are going to want me dead,' said Donovan. 'You want to risk my life for the sake of your track record?'

This time the grin was genuine if fierce. 'Why not? I'm risking mine.'

Brady still had the mobile phone. Donovan held out his hand. 'Let me call my chief. If this is above board he'll go along with it, and I will too.'

'Away on! Your chief will hear from my chief when this is over, not before. I'm only discussing it with you because you haven't the wit to keep your suspicions to yourself.'

Donovan thought he could get the mobile and settle it that way. He lunged for it. But in his current state he had neither the speed nor strength of the older man and Brady snatched it easily out of his reach.

'Leave it alone, will you!' Brady glared at him, tempted to spare himself trouble by hitting Donovan again and be damned to the consequences. But his conscience pricked and instead he dropped the mobile on the floor behind him and stamped on it. 'There. Now will you give me peace?'

Donovan groaned. 'That's the second one of those things I've lost this year. You should see the frigging paperwork.'

Brady didn't know whether to laugh or cry. 'Co-operate with me and I'll buy you a new one. All right?'

Donovan thought about it. He licked his lips. 'If this operation matters that much, maybe you reckon it's worth keeping going. How do I know you won't do what they ask and kill me?'

'You'll know,' Brady smiled. 'When I point a gun at you and pull the trigger, you'll know then. If I miss, I'm on your side.'

FOUR

FRIDAY MORNING found CID like the saloon of the *Mary Celeste*. There was plenty of evidence that people had been there, should still have been near by: coffee cups half finished, sheets of paper stuffed into typewriters, pens lying in open phone-books, jackets over the backs of chairs. There were just no people.

Shapiro, pausing *en route* to his office, considered the scene morosely. If somebody reported a stolen handbag he'd have to deal with it personally. Great, he thought: we've got two murders on the go so the only detective with time to pick up a phone is the chief inspector. Good morning, madam—no, I'm sorry, my constables are all busy— will I do?

In fact it wasn't quite that bad. DC Stewart came back from the collator's officer while he was still standing there. 'Were you looking for me, sir?'

'I wasn't looking for anybody in particular. But I thought there'd be someone here. Where are they all?'

It wasn't that big a squad so Stewart knew. 'Scobie's with the CPS, Morgan's beating up the photo-copier, Sergeant Donovan called in sick. Inspector Graham's talking to the lads downstairs.'

'What about?'

Stewart shrugged. 'All she said to me was, if she wasn't getting the right answers maybe she should ask some different questions.'

That was Liz being cryptic: there was no point trying to work it out. Sooner or later she'd explain. Shapiro set off for his office again; again he stopped before he got there.

'I saw Donovan yesterday evening. He seemed all right then.'

'It's his hand, sir. He thinks it might be infected. He's taken it down the hospital to see what they say.'

'How improbably sensible of him.' Shapiro retired behind his door.

He'd hardly sat down when he heard Liz's swift steps on the stair. So her mood preceded her and it was no surprise when her face came round his door alight with possibilities. As if she were a hunter who, after long and tedious work in the coverts, had seen the russet flash of a fox's brush.

'Frank, I think we've been rather stupid about this. We all assumed we had a basic idea of who we were looking for: a man who wasn't necessarily very tall, who possibly had sexual difficulties, who hated women and took it out on young girls. Dear love us, we even wondered if a man in a wheelchair would fit the bill! But there's a simpler explanation for why they weren't raped. What if the killer isn't a man but a woman?'

Shapiro blinked. 'You're not serious.'

'Yes, I am,' she insisted. 'Think about it, it makes sense.'

He thought. 'Women use poison. Sometimes they use guns, or run people down in their cars. How many women commit murder with a knife?'

'Not many,' admitted Liz, 'though it has happened. But the reason isn't psychological, it's physical. Women don't go in for close-quarters murder not because they're squeamish but because mostly their victims are stronger than them. To kill a man, the average woman has to do it at one remove—a gun, a car—or there's every chance he'll turn the tables on her. Most women attacking a man with a knife would end up in casualty themselves.

'But that's not a problem where the victims are all young girls. Any grown woman would have been stronger than Alice Elton, and most would have been stronger than Charlene Pierce—she didn't exactly look after herself, did she? Also, a woman would have had that vital element of surprise. We're all just a little wary about men we don't know, but who gives a second glance to a woman standing in a doorway or strolling in the park? Unless she's obviously drunk or has a safety-pin through her nose, nobody thinks that a woman in a secluded place could be up to no good. People who'd cross the road to avoid meeting a man in the same circumstances scarcely notice that she's there.'

Shapiro was still wrestling with the idea. Liz Graham was an experienced detective: he knew better than to dismiss out of hand anything she thought promising, even if it went against all his expectations. 'All right, allowing that it's possible, how do we find out?'

'I want to do the house-to-house again, at The Jubilee and round the park. I know,' she hurried on, anticipating objection, 'it'll take manpower we could be using elsewhere. But I really think this is the way forward, Frank. I've talked to the lads who came doorstepping with me, and we were all asking the same question: Did anybody see a strange man? I want to go back and ask if anyone saw a strange woman.'

There was too much to do to waste time repeating an exercise that had already proved futile. If another girl died while limited resources were tied up pursuing so tenuous—some might say frivolous—a lead, the next mob would be after his blood.

But she was a good detective. She didn't indulge in frivolous investigations. If he believed in her, perhaps he should trust her instincts too.

Finally he nodded. 'Do it.'

IT TOOK LESS time than Shapiro had feared. Armed with knowledge it had taken hours to accumulate last time—who was still up and about the night Charisma died, who was awake in the houses round the park when Alice Elton met her killer—Liz went straight to those people who were at least potential witnesses and didn't trouble those who slept from eleven to eight-thirty.

Even so she might have learned nothing useful. When he heard her return ninety minutes later he quietly put down the papers he was working on and waited for her. Until he knew what, if anything, she'd discovered there seemed little point continuing. He listened carefully, and believed he heard in the metre of her approaching tread not merely hope this time but triumph.

She entered his office with a knock so peremptory it was no more than her knuckles brushing the door as she wrenched at the knob. Radiance like an aura flooded the office. 'That's it, Frank—that's the breakthrough. It was a woman. I even know what she looks like.'

Shapiro breathed out, half a sigh and half a prayer. 'Sit down and tell me what you've got.'

She took a moment to compose herself. 'I've got witnesses. People saw her, Frank. But they thought nothing of it because we all assumed the killer was a man.'

'What did they see?'

Liz knew what he was asking. 'Not the actual attacks. But there are several sightings of her at relevant times and places. She was seen in Brick Lane on the night Charisma was killed: the first time at about one o'clock near Jubilee Terrace, when she seemed to be waiting for someone, then half an hour later at the other end of Brick Lane walking quickly towards the town centre.

'Suppose she met with Charisma soon after the first sighting. They talked, then they took the walkway to Broad Wharf. Perhaps the woman said she had some business for her, or offered to pay for a magazine interview—something like that. When they reached the alley she got behind Charisma and cut her throat. Then she bundled her out of sight under the tarpaulin, and then she left. She'd have no trouble reaching the end of Brick Lane in time for the second sighting.'

Shapiro was nodding slowly. At this stage it was about all the comment he was prepared to make. 'What about the park?'

Liz's face glowed with satisfaction. 'One witness puts a woman fitting the same general description on the bridleway at about the time Alice Elton was coming through the council yard, a few minutes before she was killed.'

Shapiro watched her through narrowed eyes, seeking the flaw in her reasoning. But there wasn't one. 'There's nothing about either of these killings that a woman couldn't have managed if she was determined enough. It didn't require strength or even speed so much as the element of surprise. There was no sexual assault: she disordered Alice's clothes to make us think there'd been an attempt at intercourse but it was interrupted. She knew we couldn't be sure if Charisma was raped; ditto the girl at Dover. Alice was stripped to confirm the connection between them and reinforce the natural assumption that the killer was a man.

'We kept asking the wrong damned questions,' said Liz. A note of self-reproach crept into her voice. '*I* did: I can hear myself now. "Did you see a man hanging round?"— "Have you seen any strange men?" And of course the answer was no. When we asked if they'd seen any strangers we started getting some answers.'

'Good work, girl.' There was nothing patronizing about his approval, it was genuine admiration and some relief. 'What put you on to it?'

'You did.' His eyebrows expressed doubt so, with a certain sly pleasure, she explained. 'Last night, when you were telling me how the road to obscurity for a woman detective is paved with attractive male suspects. You said that in order to succeed I had to be better at the job than a man. In the early hours of this morning I found myself wondering if a woman couldn't have done this job too.

'When Morgan and I went back and did the house-to-house properly several people said they'd seen a woman but hadn't mentioned it because we'd only asked about men.' She gave an angry little shake of the head. 'That was careless. I hope to God Alice Elton didn't die of semantics.'

Shapiro's expression was rueful. 'If you mean did she die because police officers are human beings and as such incapable of seeing through brick walls, men's souls or particularly dense fogs, then the answer may well be that she did. But we're not to blame for things we could only have prevented by being more than we are. We do our best: inevitably that means making mistakes sometimes. You've less to reproach yourself for than the rest of us. At least you realized where we'd gone wrong.' He reached for his pen. 'This description you have. How general is it?'

Liz scowled. 'Too damn general. It fits about a quarter of the female population, including me.' She remembered what she'd been told but checked her notes anyway. 'She was wearing a light raincoat and a printed headscarf on both occasions. A skirt in Brick Lane, dark trousers at the park. Not sure about the height: either tall with an average build or average height with a slim build. No hair colour because of the scarf. None of the witnesses think they'd know her again—too dark the first time, too far away the second. Two of them mentioned a noticeably quick walk but that's not surprising in view of what she was doing. Oh, and no handbag. Nobody saw a bag.'

'It could have been in the hand, or over the shoulder, furthest from them.'

'It could. But most women habitually carry their bag on one side—it feels downright odd on the other—and this woman was seen from both sides, walking left to right at the park, right to left in Brick Lane. I'd sooner think she didn't want the bother of it when she was planning some energetic exercise. Also, she wouldn't want to risk dropping something personal.'

'So the fact that she didn't have a bag with her doesn't mean she doesn't use one.'

'No. But it may mean she carries more in her pockets than most women do. The knife, tissues to clean any blood off herself, perhaps a mirror to check with. She can look at her coat, see that she hasn't been splattered, but if she's walking round with blood on her face somebody's going to notice. At the first light she comes to, or if it's daylight as soon as she's in the clear, she's going to whip out a mirror. Nobody'd give her a second glance: we women are always checking our make-up, aren't we?' She smiled tightly.

'The light-coloured raincoat doesn't seem a great idea.'

'It is if it's plastic. She can clean it up in a moment, spotlessly. Blood on a woven fabric, however dark, would be hard to remove that completely.'

There was a long silence as they put it all together. Then Shapiro spelled it out. 'So we're looking for a woman of at least medium height and slimmish build, who owns a light-coloured waterproof—possibly with some unusual items in the pockets—and a printed headscarf; who's been in Castlemere for at least a week, and who was in Dover last August. Why does she kill young girls?'

'Why does anyone murder people they don't know?' countered Liz. 'It's either madness or evil. I expect when we find her she'll trot out a list of reasons that seem to make sense to her; and when her defence counsel calls in a psychiatrist he'll trot out a quite different list that seems to make sense to him. But we're dealing with an abnormal mind: perhaps we shouldn't expect to understand.'

There was another long silence but Liz knew the discussion wasn't finished. She could almost hear the cogs grinding in Shapiro's head. At length he looked up, straight at her, and said, 'I know someone that description could fit. So do you.'

As soon as he said it, she did. Her eyes widened, then

narrowed. She was running through what they knew and what they believed, looking for parallels. 'She fits what we have of a physical description. She has business that takes her through Dover—I'll check the exact date but we know they go back to Europe for the autumn. She was in Castlemere when Alice Elton was killed. More than that: Davey was eating breakfast alone that morning. Why?—two people staying in a hotel together normally take breakfast together even if they split up afterwards. And you could argue that someone devoting her life to a religious crusade has an abnormal mind.'

It was Shapiro's turn to play devil's advocate. 'Charlene Pierce was killed, hidden, put in the canal and pulled out again all before Jennifer Mills arrived in town on Sunday night.'

Liz shook her head. 'We don't actually know when she arrived, only when she checked into the hotel. We do know she and Davey travelled separately—he booked in a couple of hours after she did.'

'She goes ahead to finalize the arrangements, make sure everything's ready for when the tent arrives,' mused Shapiro. 'So how come she got here a day and a half after the road crew? If it's her job to liaise with the council, book hotel rooms, get the posters printed and put up—all the stuff that takes time—she should have been here days before she was.'

Liz nodded energetically. 'And if she had everything arranged in advance and didn't have to be here first, why didn't she travel with Davey? Because she didn't or they'd have booked in together. Two hours between her arriving and him arriving is both too long and nowhere near long enough.'

'Now, don't let's get excited,' Shapiro admonished. 'There could be a perfectly sensible explanation. Perhaps everything was fixed up so she spent a few days looking for other places the mission could visit. Perhaps if we ask her she'll produce hotel receipts for a night in Nottingham or a night in Cambridge and she'll say that's what she was doing—planning the next season's itinerary.'

'And perhaps if we ask at the Town Hall,' said Liz, 'we'll find that she was here at the end of last week to pay for the site and arrange the insurance and everything.' She picked up his phone and dialled from memory.

'Fancy that,' she said, deadpan, as she put it down again. 'Miss Mills saw the Works Manager at the Town Hall on Friday morning. They visited the site, finalized the details, then she told him she was heading for the Midlands but she'd be back for opening night.'

'And of course, that may be what she did.'

'Of course. Or she may have hung around until Friday night, met with Charisma, then set off for the Midlands to give herself an alibi. Not that she expected to need it but just in case. If she could find a motel that would take her in at three in the morning she could even have a receipt for Friday night. Unless we had good reason to check the details, we'd accept that as putting her elsewhere at the material time.'

The more sure he was that they were on the right lines, the softer Shapiro's voice fell. 'So she could have done both the murders here. And she could have done it before: there are a few days every couple of weeks when she's on her own in a strange town, before the rest of the circus arrive. No one made the connection before because it was a matter of record that Davey's crusade didn't arrive until after a murder had taken place. Instead of drawing attention to her, effectively the timing gave her an alibi.'

'What Davey said, about how the papers were full of atrocities wherever he went: I thought he was exaggerating, but he meant it quite literally. He was seeing more of these things than we were because he was following the murderer round the country. Dear God, he even told me the papers in Le Havre were full of a murder when he got there. A young girl butchered on the street, he said. I never thought—'

'Of course you didn't,' Shapiro said calmly. 'We none of us paid that much attention to what he said. All right, we'll get them in here again—both of them, he can tell us more about her than anyone else. I'll have her room at the hotel searched: it's the same weapon that's been used and reused, she must have it somewhere. Living out of a suitcase she won't have that many places to hide it. And when she says where she spent last Friday night we'll check with them what time she arrived. Any later than two in the morning—unless it was Aberdeen—and I think we have a case.'

'Where's Donovan? He'll want to be in on this.'

Shapiro scowled. 'I don't make arrests for the purpose of entertaining my sergeants. Anyway, he's at the hospital with that hand of his.'

'I bet he'd be back pretty sharpish if someone got word to him,' murmured Liz.

They separated, Shapiro taking WPC Wilson to the hotel, Liz proceeding with DC Morgan to the wharf. They were confident of finding both the people they wanted in one place or the other.

BUT THEY WERE out of luck. Both Davey and Mills had been at the Castle Hotel an hour before but neither was there now and both cars were gone: Davey's big automatic and Mills' vermilion supermini. Shapiro thought about following Liz to Broad Wharf, decided he could use the time more profitably searching Mills' room. He explained to the hotel manager and they went upstairs.

Knowing what he was looking for it was absurdly easy. The raincoat was hanging in the wardrobe with her other clothes. It wasn't plastic, it was rubberized cotton of the kind used to make riding mackintoshes. It was putty-coloured, styled as a trench-coat with big patch pockets.

Handling it carefully—he could see no traces of blood

but the microscope at Forensics had younger and sharper eyes than his—Shapiro felt in the pockets. In one there was a thick wad of tissues and a packet of moist cleansers. In the other was a folding mirror and a printed scarf.

But they couldn't find the knife. It wasn't in the coat or any of her clothes. It wasn't in either of her suitcases. It wasn't in the chest of drawers or slipped between the mattress and the divan. It wasn't reared up primly in her toothmug. So far as they could see it wasn't anywhere in the room.

Shapiro felt a twinge of unease under his ribs, like heartburn. If it wasn't here she must have it with her. Perhaps she kept it in her car: a woman travelling alone into the grimmer parts of strange towns might claim with some justification, moral if not legal, that she needed some means of self-defence. And they did have the coat. If she was planning another murder, surely she'd have taken that too? It was much more likely that she was down at the marquee setting up the evening performance.

But the cars weren't at Broad Wharf either. Liz asked the men who were getting the tent ready but they hadn't seen Davey all day and Mills had only put in a brief appearance around noon. She would normally have been here before now to oversee their work.

The big Geordie grinned at Liz. 'It's desperate complicated, see, putting chairs in straight lines and putting a bit of paper on each one. We'd likely get it wrong if she didn't keep an eye on us.'

Liz smiled back. 'Tell you what. Do the best you can in the circumstances.'

'You think she'll be impressed if we get them all facing the right way?' Kelso was rather enjoying this, exchanging banter with a detective inspector who didn't know he had her sergeant under guard in a railway wagon three-quarters of a mile away.

'Actually,' Liz said honestly, 'I don't think she'll give a toss.'

Before she left she asked, indirectly, about the knife. 'Does Miss Mills keep anything of her own down here: a bag, papers, anything?'

Kelso traded a shrug with the nearest of his colleagues before shaking his head. 'Nothing. All her stuff's at the hotel.'

Being this close she thought she'd take five minutes to bring Donovan up to date. She'd tried to call him but his mobile seemed to be on the blink; she'd left a message at the hospital but he mightn't have got it. Looking up the wharf she saw a glow behind *Tara's* curtains that suggested he was at home.

But she could get no reply to either a knock at the door—she felt sure Donovan called it something more nautical than that—or a sharp rap at the window. He must have left the light on by mistake. So he'd been at the hospital all day. Perhaps they'd kept him in. It was odd that he hadn't let Shapiro know. Or perhaps he'd called the office by now and found them both otherwise engaged.

As she clambered ashore, a manoeuvre Donovan performed with disdainful ease and she had yet to complete with dignity intact, the heel of her shoe went as if drawn by magnets to a crack in the gangplank, lodged just long enough to trip her and then, as she clutched at the rail, came off her foot as if it had never heard of laces. It described a graceful parabola *en route* for the spot where *Tara's* stern curved away from the wall and the water waited. Liz heard the smug plop with the resignation of someone who had never doubted where that shoe would end up.

She hobbled back to her car and called Shapiro. 'I just dropped my shoe in the canal,' she reported flatly. 'I'm going home for another pair.'

There was the briefest of pauses. Then he said, reassuringly, 'Of course you are.'

FIVE

THERE WAS A CAR outside her house: not Brian's, he'd gone to his new school for a look round before starting work on Monday. She thought she didn't know anyone with a big light-coloured car like that. Then she realized with a genuine shock whose it was. She didn't even check the controls for confirmation.

She stood foolishly for a moment wondering what to do. Hurrying away half-shod would be pathetic, calling for help an overreaction; going inside would seem odd, hobbling in search of him would be painful. So she was still standing there wondering when the distinctive crunch of narrow wheels on gravel preceded him round the corner of the house.

He'd heard her car. He said by way of explanation, 'I was talking to your horse.'

'Have you been here long?'

He thought. 'Quite a long time, yes.'

'How did you get my address?'

He flashed his winning smile. 'I asked round till somebody told me.'

'You've no business here.'

The massive shoulders shrugged as ingenuously as a boy's. 'I wanted to see you.'

'You know where my office is.'

'It wasn't police business I wanted to see you about.'

'Well, it's police business I want to see you about.' She sighed then. He was no threat to her. It was contrary to conventional wisdom, but before she did anything else she had to find another pair of shoes. She opened the door.

'Come in while I change my shoes.' Then she looked at the step. 'Oh—can you?'

He smiled at her consternation. 'No. But it doesn't matter. Get your shoes, then come back. I really do need to talk to you.'

When she was comfortable she walked him round to the paved area at the back of the house, looking down the garden to the orchard. The mare's long face watched them curiously over the stable door.

'Before we start,' said Liz, 'do you know where Jennifer Mills is?'

Davey could not have looked more astonished if she'd asked where his mother was buried. 'Jenny? Down at the tent, I expect. She usually is by this time.'

Liz shook her head. 'I've just come from there. They haven't seen her.'

'Why are you looking for Jenny, for heaven's sake?'

'I'll come to that. What are you doing at my house?'

His gaze dropped. 'I had to see you,' he said compulsively, as if it were a mantra. 'I had to talk to you.'

'About what?'

His eyes came up then, steel flecked with flame, raking her. 'About us, of course!' There was a kind of breathy desperation in his voice, terribly different from the massive self-possession that rang from him when he addressed the faithful.

He'd succeeded in startling her. She didn't know what to call him: they'd started using first names but now it seemed an unwise intimacy. She avoided the issue, said baldly, 'There is no *us* to talk about.'

'You know what I mean,' he said urgently. 'You must feel it too. I didn't want this, I didn't come looking for it. It's tearing my life apart, for God's sake. My work's the only important thing I've ever done, and because of you I don't know if I can go on doing it.'

'Me? What have I done?' That sounded phoney even to her. She winced.

Davey managed a little twitch of a smile. 'You haven't done anything. I haven't done anything. But something's happened between us. Don't pretend you haven't noticed.'

'Michael, stop this,' she said firmly. At least it was her own voice this time. Then she spoiled it by lying. 'I don't know what you're talking about.'

'You do,' he insisted roughly. 'I know you do. You feel what I feel. You don't know why, or where it's come from, or what it's for. I know you don't want it. It could ruin everything for you: your home, your marriage, your job. Your self-respect. But you feel it. If we were two people without responsibilities to anyone in the world but ourselves, we wouldn't be discussing this on the patio.

'What do you think?—that I'm less of a man, that I don't have a man's feelings, because my legs don't work?' His voice soared with sudden outrage. 'Or is that the problem here? You can't see yourself making love to a cripple? They're all right for companionable little strolls by the canal or a bite of lunch, then you can go home in a warm glow of satisfaction and tell your husband about your good deed for the day. But to make love with? I mean, that really would be gross, wouldn't it?'

She didn't mean to but, moved by his pain, she put her hand on his. The nerves jumped under her palm like electricity. 'Michael, for heaven's sake. You're talking as if you have some rights over me. We're casual acquaintances, that's all. I like you, Michael, I've enjoyed talking to you. But it's absurd to pretend there's anything between us. I love my husband.'

She thought a moment longer, wondering whether to add what had come to the tip of her tongue, deciding at last that she should. 'I don't know if this is what you want to hear but just for the record, if it was my husband in that chair I don't believe it would make any difference to how

I feel about him. Find a woman who loves you, Michael, and she won't think of it as making love to a cripple.'

Remembering then that there was a woman who loved him like that, and that as soon as they could find her the police would put her behind bars, Liz fell silent.

'But I don't want a woman,' he cried. He was almost shouting, Liz was sure her new neighbours must be all agog. 'Not just that. I'm not so desperate I'll take any woman who'll look at me. I want you. You: Liz Graham. I want you enough to give up everything else for you—and don't think that's an easy thing, my work matters to me. But having you matters more.

'So tell me to get the hell out of here and stop annoying a married woman. Slap my face if you want, tell me I've no right to feel this way. Tell me I'm some kind of hypocrite, preaching morality to other people when I've no more self-control than a schoolboy in the throes of his first crush. But don't tell me I've imagined this thing between us, don't tell me that you haven't felt it too, and don't tell me all I need is a good lay. I've been laid by professionals, girl, and it's like a Chinese meal; you're full for half an hour, then you're hungry again.'

She didn't know what to say to him. He was right, there was something between them. An attraction; something. It wasn't of her making and she had no use for it but he hadn't imagined it. It wasn't going anywhere but at least as a moment in time it existed.

'I'm sorry,' she said at last. 'I'm sorry if I've hurt you. I'm sorry if I've let you think there was some sort of future for us. There never was, and it never occurred to me you felt this way. You're an interesting man, Michael, and you're good company. But if you're asking me to give up things that matter to me, then the answer's no. I like the life I have.'

That left no room for misunderstandings. Her directness sank through Davey's expression until it struck bottom, jarring his eyes. For a moment shock and disappointment made the big face, robbed of the spirit that animated it, pale and fleshy. He looked as she had never seen him look before: like someone weakened by an illness from which he would never completely recover. The magnetic power of the man, the massive personality, were shrunk into this cumbrous body, constrained by its inadequacies. For a moment she saw the wreck of a human being he would have been without the strength of his mind, his heart and his faith to sustain him.

Then like a blind falling he shut himself off from her gaze. The muscles of his face resumed their usual contours, his eyes hardened, his wide mouth compressed to a line. His voice was low but perfectly controlled. 'Then there's no more to be said. I'm sorry to have troubled you, Mrs Graham.' He turned the chair and headed back to his car, his progress over the gravel ponderous but unstoppable like a supertanker with a ten-mile deceleration, the unoiled wheel still squeaking.

Liz leapt to her feet and hurried after him but he wouldn't break his rhythmic progression, forcing her to jog backwards before him. 'Michael, wait. I have to ask you about Jennifer Mills. I have to find her, quickly.'

'What?' They'd reached the front of the house. He opened the door of his car, began the laborious work of getting behind the wheel.

'Jenny Mills. I have to talk to her. Where is she?'

'I don't know. The hotel?'

'She's not there either. My chief's there.'

Davey paused then, staring at her. 'Why are you looking for Jenny?'

So she told him. 'She may be able to help with our inquiries into the deaths of Charlene Pierce and Alice Elton. Among others.'

He didn't believe her. He barked a laugh. 'Don't be absurd.'

She didn't argue with him. 'Tuesday morning you had breakfast in the hotel dining-room alone. Why?'

'Jenny had hers in her room. She was tired, she had a bit of a lie-in. What's wrong with that? She'd been on the road for days, then she spent all Monday getting the tent ready for opening night.'

'Did you travel together?'

'No, I came over on the ferry. Jenny was off round the country—I don't remember just where: Midlands, was it?—planning next season's schedule. Inspector, you're not serious about this?'

'Of course I'm serious,' she said quietly. 'A woman was seen at the park where Alice Elton was murdered while Jennifer Mills was supposedly having breakfast alone in her room. It could be a coincidence. But it's important that I talk to her right away.'

When he realized she was in earnest his confusion turned abruptly to anger. 'You're mad. Jenny? She's my right arm.'

Liz breathed heavily. 'Michael, this isn't about you. Or only in a way. It's about Jenny and the fact that she may have killed several young girls.'

'Why ever would she?' He was genuinely amazed at the suggestion.

'We'll ask her that when we find her.'

Finally he seemed to be thinking about it. 'Young girls. Hookers?'

'Not the last one but probably the others.' She waited.

'Jenny—knows something about hookers.'

'What do you mean?'

He flashed her an angry, embarrassed look. His cheeks were flushed. 'Jenny knows where girls like that hang out. Even in places we've never been before.'

Liz's sensibilities had taken a beating in the last half hour and she wasn't as quick on the uptake as she might have been. The puzzlement in her eyes infuriated him.

'For me, damn it! I told you, Jenny looks after me. She gets me what I need. That too.'

Then she understood. Not only what he was saying but what it meant. They'd been stuck for a motive, even the sort of motive that would seem reason enough in the abnormal mind of a serial killer. But that would do.

Her voice was a stunned whisper. 'You mean, you sent Jennifer Mills out to procure prostitutes for you?'

'I could hardly go myself, could I?' he snapped back. It didn't seem to occur to him that doing without would have been an alternative.

'No,' Liz agreed faintly. 'Michael, the woman's in love with you. And you sent her looking for young girls for your bed?'

That took him completely by surprise. For a moment he gaped at her like an idiot. But by the time he found his voice he was ready to disbelieve, finding it easier to scoff than to deal with the possibility. 'In love? Jenny? Be your age.'

Liz found herself growing angry on the missing woman's behalf. What she'd done—if indeed she'd done it—was almost incomprehensible. But Liz was beginning to understand where the despair driving her had come from. 'You think she's an old maid? She's twelve years younger than you. And she's known you a lot longer than you've known me. Why is it all right for you to be in the grip of a great passion you can't control, that you're willing to risk everything for, but absurd that she might be?

'Couldn't you *tell*? I knew from talking to her for half an hour. You must have seen the way her eyes light up when she's near you.' She gave a little angry laugh. 'Or do you think women glow like that all the time, because it's how they react to you? You're a bloody dangerous man, Michael Davey. You drop matches into dry undergrowth and deny all responsibility for the fire.'

He hauled himself into the car and slammed the door.

'You're mad,' he repeated furiously. 'I think you've imagined all this. Jenny wouldn't hurt anyone. If she loves me it's like a sister. All she ever wanted was what was best for me. When I told her about you—'

Liz's eyes widened. 'You told her about me? About—?'

'She warned me. I should have listened. She's a good woman, she knows what I need, what's important to me. I thought I could turn my back on everything I've done, go after what I wanted for once. She knew I couldn't. She knew loving you would be the ruination of me. I should have listened to her.'

He started the car with a fierce twist of his wrist and drove off at speed, the wheels spitting gravel, leaving Liz standing literally open-mouthed beside her front door.

But before she had time to work through the implications of what he'd said the phone rang. She hurried inside.

It was Shapiro and he came straight to the point. 'Are you alone?'

She gritted her teeth. 'I am now. Michael Davey was here when I arrived but he's just left.'

She thought he was going to drag her over the coals for seeing a man at her house when they'd already been the subject of talk. But instead he said, 'Listen to me, Liz. Stay inside. Lock the doors and windows. I'll be with you in five minutes.'

Surprise piling on surprise left Liz hardly knowing what to say. 'Frank? What's this about?'

'We've spotted Jennifer Mills' car. It's parked round the corner about fifty yards from your house.'

SIX

ALL THE TIME Davey had been baring his soul on the patio the front door had been standing ajar. It didn't mean Mills had got inside but it meant she could have done.

It would be consistent with what they knew, or believed, of her. She was an intelligent, obsessive woman with apparently no life beyond the crusade. She was hopelessly in love with a man who failed not only to reciprocate but even to recognize this, to the staggeringly insensitive degree of sending her to procure his prostitutes. Of course she hated young girls: not only the street-girls who served him but all the young girls with their plump bodies and their china-doll faces and their idiot giggles that sparked a glow in him when all her devotion earned only ashes. She killed out of rage, frustration, jealousy and revenge.

And something more?—because even a woman labouring under the triple lash of an obsessive personality, unrequited devotion and callous emotional abuse could still not have seen Alice Elton as a rival. Poor little Alice, trotting her pony through the park, why did she die? Only because she was available? Because the pain and rage had built up to such a pitch within Jennifer Mills that she had to let it out, and Alice was the first girl she met?

But the meeting was too unlikely, too contrived: Mills had sought her out, and sought her in a place and at a time she could not expect to find prostitutes. It was as if Alice had something different to contribute. As close as Liz could approach it, the unique thing about Alice's murder, that set it apart from those of Charisma and the other toms, was its utter wantonness. As if it were specifically designed to shock. As if Alice were no more than a tactic in her killer's campaign, not even so much against Davey as against the world in general.

Now he'd told her that he loved Liz Graham, meant to give up the crusade for her so that Mills would never see him again. His choice was particularly cruel. Liz wasn't a sluttish teenager he could lay and pay: she was an intelligent professional middle-class woman on the brink of middle-age—the same sort of woman as Jennifer Mills. It had been possible till now for Mills to tell herself that Davey wasn't interested in commitment, used the girls to scratch an itch because his work didn't allow him time for a real relationship. She couldn't believe that any more. For Liz Graham, and not for her, he would make time. The rejection was personal.

And, which made it worse, Liz was married: he couldn't even love her honourably. She threatened everything Mills cared about. Now she'd followed Davey to Liz's home: her purpose could only be guessed, but it was likely that she intended to deal with her rival in the manner she had practised.

Five minutes until reinforcements arrived. Liz would have been wise to wait outside, but she was damned if she'd be driven from her own house by a tragic neurotic woman. She'd as soon be found locked in the bathroom with the curtains drawn as meekly waiting on the front step for Shapiro to arrive. Pulling on her sheepskin gloves and Brian's leather jacket for protection, she began working her way through the rooms.

It was an eerie sensation. This was her home, and every time she opened a door she half expected a banshee to come at her with a stiletto. The bubble of safety was pricked.

Finding no one on the ground floor, checking cupboards and under tables and anywhere else a woman might hide, Liz moved quietly upstairs. All but the main bedroom were piled high with tea-chests, rolled-up carpet and furniture still seeking a home. A small troop of Boy Scouts could have been camped amid the chaos and she wouldn't have known unless they started to sing 'Rolling Along On The Crest Of A Wave'. She worked carefully through each room but found no sign of an intruder.

When the cars arrived she went down to open the door. DC Morgan's habitually rather hang-dog expression fell off his face in surprise, and Liz remembered that in the warmth of a spring evening she was dressed for the north face of the Eiger. She peeled off the coat and gloves, but not quickly enough to escape Shapiro's notice.

'You've searched the house then.' His voice was flat, conveying nothing, but Liz knew he'd tear strips off her when they were alone. 'No sign of her?'

'I checked every room.'

'Outbuildings?'

At that she turned paler, gave a quick shake of the head. Morgan took off at a run with Liz following at an anxious jog and Shapiro at a brisk walk. By the time he arrived at the stable Liz had checked the horse and Morgan the tack-room and they'd found nothing.

'Sir.' The voice was DC Scobie's but for a moment they couldn't see him. He was beyond the hedge separating the Grahams' garden from the bridleway. 'Do we know if she smokes?'

Liz thought back to the interview at Queen's Street. 'Like a chimney.'

'Two fresh cigarette ends, ma'am, with lipstick on them.'

'Bag 'em,' Shapiro said briskly. To Liz: 'Where did you talk to Davey?' She indicated the patio. Shapiro's eyes took measurements. 'Close enough to hear. What would she have heard?'

Liz told him. He looked pensively down the orchard, the trees twisted with age, capable of bearing only the hardest, sourest fruit. 'So he offered to take you away from all this, you declined and he left in a huff.' Liz nodded. 'Maybe she has no more quarrel with you. Maybe her quarrel now is with Davey. Where did he go?'

'He didn't say. We were past making small talk by then. You know, I really think he expected me to pack a bag and leave with him.'

Shapiro said soberly, 'If you had I don't know what Mills would have done.'

'What will she do now?'

He thought. 'She won't run, even if she knows we're on to her. All her emotional investment is in Davey: I can't see her doing anything that'd mean leaving him. But she knows by now that she's running out of time, she heard you tell him as much.

'And then, knowing that he was prepared to throw away all her years of devotion, everything she'd done for him, in order to be with you, must have brought the thing to a head. He doesn't love her, he'll never love her. He thinks the idea of her loving him is ludicrous. She knows now exactly what she's worth to him. Any decent secretary could take her place. She's sacrificed lives to him, not least her own, and he was going to dump her for a married woman. There's no going back for them, and no way forward either. I think she'll reckon this is the end.'

'Suicide?' breathed Liz.

Shapiro's tone was sombre. 'Yes, that's probably the bottom line. The question is, will she want to kill Davey first?'

Twice during the long day Brady left the wagon for half an hour. Both times he insisted on tying Donovan with a length of electric flex. Donovan complained but in the end he submitted, mainly because he had no choice. Brady was afraid that if someone checked and found the prisoner free and unguarded, that carelessness would cost them both their lives. Also, he was aware that Donovan might be gone when he got back. Donovan let himself be tied because he knew if he didn't they'd fight and he'd lose.

So he complained but sat still while Brady roped his wrists behind him then pushed him on to his side and tied his ankles. 'How's that?'

Donovan couldn't sit up. 'Bloody.'

'Good.'

When he returned, with hours to kill and nothing better to do they talked. Kneading the ache out of his arms Donovan said, 'How did you get involved with Drugs Squad?'

Brady shrugged. 'I couldn't go back to Ireland. This was the same sort of work.'

Understanding hit Donovan like a train and his jaw dropped. 'You were a supergrass? For the Army?'

'Special Branch.' Which explained their too easy acceptance of the myth of his death. They knew who he was and what he was doing, were in the habit of covering for him.

'Jesus. How long?'

'Seven years.'

Liam Brady was his father's son, he entered manhood believing that armed struggle was the way to reunite Ireland. That was before Claudy. 'You won't remember Claudy,' he said, 'you were only a wee lad. But I was twenty, which is an impressionable age. Three cars blew up in the main street and nine people died. There was no warning. The boyos were going to phone from Dungiven, only they had trouble getting through. All Ireland was stunned. It was such a tiny, harmless little place, and afterwards there was damn all of it left. Even the Provos were ashamed of what was done at Claudy.'

'So you turned informer?' Donovan could not rid his voice of the incredulity which would have been the universal reaction in Glencurran, even among those who hated the IRA. It was a small town with small town prejudices, and they lived on in the back alleys of his mind as the accent lived on in his speech.

'The opportunity came and I took it.' Brady grinned. 'That's when I started working up a reputation. As long as everyone knows you're a mad bastard who eats English babies you never have to prove it. I may have been the least effective soldier the IRA ever had but by God I looked the part.'

'But the Army shot you,' objected Donovan. 'Didn't they?'

'I was shot,' agreed Brady. 'But not by the Army. That was the da's lads. They finally worked out why so many things went wrong that I'd had a part of. They came for me one night with a gun and a black bag. I had the devil's own luck, but they were taking me for interrogation when the car was stopped at a road-block. All hell broke loose: the Brits were firing at the boyos, the boyos were firing at the Brits; the car broke through the blockade but one tyre was ripped up and it ran into a ditch.

'Everybody was trying to get the hell out at once: when I found myself on the road I ran like blazes, never mind that my hands were tied behind my back and there was a bag over my head. One of them finally remembered what they'd come for and dropped me as I ran. But the Brits were right there, there was no time to finish the job. They scattered and most of them got clear. I just had wit enough to tell the soldiers who I was, then I passed out. I woke up three days later in the military wing of Musgrave Park. And that was the end of my contribution to peace and stability in Northern Ireland.'

'So what were you doing in the States? The word was you were raising money for the Provos. I take it that's not true?'

Brady chuckled. 'Damn right it's not. The da put that about to explain my disappearance: it was better than admitting he'd fathered a British agent. I think he hoped that sometime I'd be daft enough to go back and he could finish the job.

'But Mammy didn't raise no fools. I knew I could never go back; to be safe I had to disappear for good. So Special

Branch got the FBI to add my name to the list of the dead in a car crash, and that's when Joseph Bailie was born. Twelve years ago. Until you turned up I hadn't heard the name Liam Brady for twelve years.'

'The Provos, Special Branch and now Drugs Squad,' mused Donovan. 'You'd like living on a volcano.'

Brady shrugged. 'You get used to it. To tell the truth, it was being a brickie's labourer I couldn't stick. When I first came to England this was. I was reduced to picking fights with the foreman for a bit of excitement. So I volunteered for this. It's funny. A lot of it's just like being a brickie's labourer, but that's all right because I'm deceiving them. All the time I'm fetching and carrying, and putting grease on rope-burns and living in a dirty caravan with the kind of people the Provos wouldn't meet socially, I'm thinking ''They don't know''. I'm cleverer than them and they don't even know it.'

He seemed to be talking at least half to himself: a man given a rare opportunity to talk freely finding that he couldn't break the habit of communing inwardly because for months at a time that was the only safe way. 'That's what makes it OK. The results too, knowing that when we move on the dealers'll be rounded up with the stuff on them. But what keeps you going from day to day is working with these men who think they're so smart and saying to yourself, ''They don't know.'''

'Is Davey part of it?'

Brady was scathing. 'St Michael the Mouth?—no. He has his faults but actually hypocrisy isn't one of them. Neither him nor the Iron Maiden are involved. Kelso set it up, Danny—the French guy with the beard?—organizes the supply end on the Continent, the rest of them take a cut mostly for keeping their mouths shut. It's money for old rope. Davey even pays them. Actually, they should be paying him.'

Donovan nodded slowly. 'So you let slip about your past

as a hard man and Kelso brought you in as muscle. Which means going round with him and seeing who he's dealing with. You pass that back, and when the circus moves on Drugs Squad moves in.' He sniffed sourly. 'You should have told us what was going on. I wouldn't be sitting here if you had, and you wouldn't be finished as a spy.' He wondered if he should apologize for that.

Brady shrugged. 'I've been with them seven months already, there's a limit to how long you can keep any operation going. We never meant for them to go back to France.' He chuckled ruefully. 'I shan't be on the dole. When I'm ready to go again there'll be another job waiting. You've been a damn nuisance to me, Cal Donovan, but don't flatter yourself you've broken something I can't mend.'

In the early evening Brady said he had to go out again. Long-sufferingly, Donovan put his hands behind him.

'This is the last lap,' Brady promised. 'It'll be over by bedtime. We're meeting Scoutari up at the castle. My lads'll be waiting. When we've rounded them up I'll come back here and cut you free. OK?' Donovan nodded grudgingly. 'OK then.' Brady left. His feet crunched in the cinders for a pace or two, then the silence came surging softly back.

Achingly uncomfortable, Donovan lay in the fading light and listened to the silence pattering down like ashes. The minutes groaned past. To fill them he entertained absurd fancies: like, Suppose Brady's feeding me a line to keep me quiet while he finishes his business with Scoutari and disappears. Suppose I've spent the day in a disused railway wagon recalling old times with a drug smuggler, and not only did I not try to escape, I helped him tie me up. Suppose he never comes back.

If there was no sign of Brady by morning, rather than try to explain to Shapiro how he'd been fooled he thought he'd hobble over to the canal and throw himself in.

The cinders whispered again to the pressure of footsteps. His first thought was that Brady had forgotten something. But it wasn't Brady, who would have come straight in. Someone was searching the line of wagons: looking for him.

He couldn't think what that meant. It was far too soon for it to be finished, for Scoutari and Kelso and as many of their associates as couldn't outsprint a fit policeman to be telling their lawyers they'd been framed and for Brady to have sent someone to free him. It could be someone sent by Kelso to keep an eye on him while Brady was away.

Or perhaps someone at Queen's Street had finally realized he was missing, that the man on the phone was an imposter and his last genuine contact was with Shapiro twenty-four hours ago. If they asked at the hospital they'd be told he had never gone there. They'd get no answer on his phone; someone calling at *Tara* would see a light but find no one aboard. Then they might think to search for him, and they just might come here.

Friend or foe? He couldn't tell. He levered himself half upright against the timber wall, drew a breath to shout with. Then he thought better of it. If it was the police they'd find him and the extra minutes would make no difference. If it was someone else they'd find him too, but an extra few minutes might make all the difference in the world.

FROM THE SHUNTING yard to Broad Wharf was a fifteen-minute walk for a man who was also trying to think. Brady had worked out the details hours ago, and gone through them time and again while the day passed. He thought he was on top of the situation, that he had all the likely eventualities covered. But he'd been doing this job too long to think that likely eventualities were the only possible ones. He spent these last minutes trying to foresee the unforeseeable and planning how to deal with that too.

He didn't have long to wait for the first eventuality he

hadn't foreseen. It came stumping towards him as he reached the wharf: Kelso, his kitbag over one broad shoulder, strong legs bustling his massive body along. There was a grim unease on his granite face that hardly softened when he caught sight of Brady. 'Damn. I hoped I'd catch you before you left.'

Brady's eyes scanned his expression like radar. 'I thought we were going to the castle.'

'Change of plan,' grunted the Geordie. 'Not my idea, Scoutari's. I had to agree, he wouldn't go ahead otherwise.'

'So where are we meeting now?' Brady was afraid he knew.

'Same as last time, an hour from now. Only I wanted to see you first, see what you make of it. Is he taking us for a ride? We could just not show. If he wants the stuff he'll have to play ball sooner or later.'

For a moment Brady was thrown. 'We need to get it wrapped up, then I can—you know.' A thought occurred to him and he sucked in a sharp breath. 'Does Scoutari know about the copper?'

Kelso's gaze shifted defensively. 'I had to tell him. He wanted to know why we were bringing the deal forward: he thought we were in trouble, he was going to pull out. So I told him. He's happy enough now he knows it's under control.'

All his careful planning performed a stately backflip in Brady's head. It was falling apart before him. His people would be at Castle Mount while the action was proceeding at the shunting yard. Nor did he believe he had fifty minutes to sort something out. Scoutari had changed the arrangements at the last minute because he wanted Donovan to himself for a while.

When they reached the yard Scoutari would be waiting. Control of the meeting place gave him an advantage: it didn't mean he intended to cheat them but it would make it easier. As Kelso said, they could just not turn up. But that meant leaving Donovan at the mercy of a man who needed first his information and then his silence. For all Brady knew Donovan was already dead. Nor was there any way of knowing what information he might have parted with first.

'Terrific,' Brady growled softly, looking away because although he could keep the despair out of his voice he didn't want Kelso to see his eyes.

SEVEN

BRIAN GRAHAM got home and found nowhere to park in his drive. From his car he watched in mounting surprise as two detective constables followed by DCI Shapiro followed by his wife emerged from his front door and hurried towards the offending vehicles. None of them saw him until he called out, in equal measures of puzzlement and unease, 'Liz? What's going on? Where are you going?'

She turned at his voice, and for a moment her expression was distracted and irritable, as if a child had come plucking at her sleeve while she was trying to get on with something important. The way she looked at him he thought she was going to slap him down: Not *now*, Brian, I'm *busy*. Just in time she stopped herself and came over. She looked strained. Her eyes were hollow.

'You are not going to *believe* what's been going on here. I've had Lothario on the patio and Lady Macbeth in the shrubbery. I've lost my shoe in the canal. Listen, I have to go. I'll give you the gory details when I get in. All right?'

It was a rhetorical question: no answer was required. He knew that if he said, 'No, stay here, tell me now,' she'd have shaken her head and gone anyway. 'All right,' he said quietly. He was not a man to make a scene but such ready compliance bespoke defeat. 'You'll be back later?'

She gave a harassed shrug. 'It might be a lot later.' Then she hurried to Shapiro's car, the little convoy sped away down the hill and she was gone.

MICHAEL DAVEY drove to Broad Wharf in a passion that was half fury, half desolation. He knew now that what he felt for Liz Graham had never been more than half real, a fever-flower rooted in a heady compost of one part empathy to two parts normal healthy lust. She was an attractive, intelligent woman, the sort of woman he would have chosen for a soulmate; but now the dream was over he couldn't think what had possessed him that he had gambled his future on her and expected her to give up hers for him. Liz Graham didn't love him. There was no reason she should. He wasn't sure he loved her so much as his image of her, a custom-built perfection superimposed on her bones like a hologram. A mannequin. He'd created a mannequin to love, and been wounded to the heart when it failed to love him in return.

Now the dream was over, but he couldn't go back to what he had before because the reality was destroyed as well. He'd been willing to give up his God for Liz Graham: now he'd been rejected how could he ask God to take him back? After all he'd done, all he'd worked for, he was going to end up with nothing.

Then there was Jenny. What had Liz Graham been saying about her, that he'd been too upset and embarrassed to listen to? That she loved him. Not admired him and loved their work together: loved him. Also— No. He'd got that wrong; or Inspector Graham had. It was nonsense, bizarre and in execrable taste. Jennifer Mills was a good woman. He'd be lost without her.

At the wharf people were already crowding into the tent. But Mills wasn't there. He found Kelso handing out hymnsheets and told him to stop. 'There'll be no meeting tonight.'

The ganger didn't remember Davey cancelling before, even once in France when 'flu so thickened his accent that he was totally incomprehensible. 'What am I going to tell all the people?'

'Say that I'm indisposed,' Davey said savagely. 'Say that tonight their salvation is in their own hands. Say that in the

interests of economy the light at the end of the tunnel has
been switched off. I don't care what you say. Get rid of
them.' He heaved himself out of the car and into his chair
and lurched away, bent almost double, the massive shoulders thrusting him forward and the following stares spurring
him on.

He wasn't going anywhere in particular, just getting
away from all the tent represented. If nothing had come to
stop him he would have continued at the same muscle-
cracking speed along the tow-path to Doggett's Lock: the
same route he'd taken, at a more leisurely pace on a happier
day, with Liz Graham. If he had he might have been surprised at what he found.

But he didn't get that far. As he rumbled past the alley
between the timber yard and the garden centre, both not
closed and quiet, someone said his name softly and he
braked, spinning the chair. 'Who's there?'

The sun was low and the narrow place in shadow. He
could just see the bulk of the skips, the pile of timbers. No
one moved towards him but the voice said again, 'Michael,'
softly, and this time he recognized it.

'Jenny?' He wheeled himself into the shadows, towards
the sound.

THERE WAS NO NEED for introductions. Donovan had never
had the satisfaction of arresting Jimmy Scoutari—though
Shapiro had—but they'd moved too long in the same circles for there to be any point trying to bluff it out. 'Good
evening, sir—I am a police officer in pursuit of my duty—
how fortunate I am that you happened this way while taking
your daily constitutional...' instead he sniffed dourly and
nodded.

Scoutari nodded too. 'Sergeant.' His face was expressionless, his voice flat. Whatever his antecedents Scoutari
was born two miles from here in the maternity wing of
Castle General: his accent was the local accent. But there

was a slight distinctive thickness to it that was not part of the local argot. 'Aren't you going to ask what I'm doing here?' he said, almost but not quite deadpan.

Without looking up Donovan gave a humourless little snort. 'I know what you're doing here.'

Scoutari shook his head in ill-feigned dismay. 'You're doing this all wrong. You're supposed to say I'm the last person you expected to see, and how relieved you are I came along to save you from the wicked men who tied you up.' He squatted, lithe and muscular as a cat, his face level with Donovan's. His voice dropped a tone. 'Because if I thought you suspected me of being here about, for instance, a supply of stuff'—like most people to whom drugs are part of daily life Scoutari rarely used the word—'I mightn't want you going round saying so.'

It would have taken a simpler man than Donovan to think Scoutari was doing anything more than amusing himself. It wasn't a genuine offer: Scoutari couldn't afford to negotiate. He'd known Donovan was here, and what it meant, and had already decided what to do about it. He might leave town. He might kill Donovan and brazen it out. There were advantages and drawbacks either way, but whichever Scoutari had settled on he wouldn't be swayed by pleading now. Donovan preserved his silence and his dignity.

Scoutari was disappointed. He'd had his share of aggravation from Castlemere CID over the years, had fantasized about having a detective at his mercy. The problem was, Donovan knew he didn't have any. He could be scared, he could be hurt, but he couldn't be teased. With a sigh Scoutari straightened up. 'Don't go away.' He headed for the door of the wagon.

Before he got there a thought occurred to him and he turned back as if there were something he'd forgotten to do. Without explanation, without even catching Donovan's eye, he wheeled like a footballer and kicked him in the face.

Donovan's head cannoned off the wooden wall and he crashed along the floor. Pain richocheted between his jaw and his brain; a filigree of fire radiated at the speed of thought along his facial nerves. Blood and mucus ran from his nose. He moaned in his throat.

Scoutari watched him; only a moment, then he continued to the door. The track was rusty, it only opened a couple of feet. He stood in the gap and spoke to someone outside.

Donovan could hear the words, was too dazed to make sense of them. He knew they concerned him—probably arrangements for the rest of his life—but all he could do was wait: for his brain to stop reeling or someone to cut his heart out, whichever came first.

BRADY RAN, leaving Kelso breathless in his wake. If he'd still had Donovan's mobile he'd have stopped it there and then, calling in all the help he could reach and never mind who heard him. He already had enough to put those involved behind bars. On the debit side he'd blow his cover wide open, this might have to be his last round-up; but that was a small enough price for a man's life.

If he'd still had the mobile. But apart from having to fight Donovan off it he'd been afraid of being compromised: if Scoutari was nervous enough to frisk him, the last thing he wanted found in his possession was a police-issue mobile phone.

He'd already discovered how far you could go looking for a call-box. He believed that if he took the time to summon help it would come too late. He wasn't sure what he could do alone and unarmed, but he'd promised Donovan he'd keep him safe. Liam Brady was a man who'd broken his word more often than he'd broken wind, but it mattered to him not to break this one.

Scoutari had come to the first meet with only his driver for company. That was what they'd agreed: two men each side plus look-outs at the tow-path and Brick Lane. The same rules were to have govenered the exchange at Castle Mount, but the rules went by the board when Kelso let slip that they'd snatched a police officer. Scoutari might have brought a football team complete with substitutes. In one way it hardly mattered. Whether they were three or thirteen, Brady's only hope of controlling the situation was to take a gun off someone else. That wasn't as tall an order for Liam Brady as it would have been for most people, but it would still take some doing.

BY THE TIME the police reached Broad Wharf Kelso had left—and been glad to, happier to deal with Castlemere's new drug baron than with a hoard filled with missionary zeal and deprived of their missionary.

For a while they had waited patiently for Davey to return. They'd seen him wheel away down the wharf, didn't expect he would be long, didn't believe the granite-faced Geordie who told them the meeting was cancelled. But after fifteen minutes patience was giving way to yawns of boredom and rumblings of discontent. These were not, after all, natural churchgoers. They were here not because of God but because of Michael Davey. Their expectations had invested him with a kind of divinity, but not enough that they would forgive him for wasting their time. Stirred to passion three nights before some of these same people had helped burn a man alive. There was an ugly side to their devotion.

So the first task confronting the police when they arrived and were told by a nervous young roadie that Miss Mills hadn't showed up and Mr Davey had been and gone, and the people in the tent had been waiting anything up to fifty minutes and wouldn't go home, and periodically someone struck up a threateningly cadenced 'Why Are We Waiting?' to the tune of 'Come All Ye Faithful', was to disperse the crowd peacefully.

They succeeded but it took a little time. It was dark before the wharf was cleared: searching all the walkways and alleys and derelict buildings backing on to the canal would be a major undertaking. Davey's chair mightn't prove hard to find, there were so many places it couldn't go. But if they found it occupied by the corpse of Michael Davey, his throat slashed ear to ear by the single stroke at a rising angle that was diagnostic of her handiwork, finding Jennifer Mills among the shatter of crumbling brickwork would be quite another matter. It would take lights and manpower, and in the time needed to set it up she might give them the slip again.

But there was no alternative to trying. Shapiro called Queen's Street from his car. As luck—and it was no more than that—would have it, Superintendent Taylor was in his office. 'I need every man you can spare at Broad Wharf, as soon as they can get here. Mills may try to slip away with the departing faithful.'

When he put the phone down there was a momentary hiatus in all the activity that swallowed up the scene in an almost eerie silence. It just so happened that for an instant nobody was talking, clattering over the uneven cobbles or slamming car-doors, and the quiet breathed like a living thing, touching them, daring them to break it.

In another moment someone would have said something—probably Shapiro, issuing instructions—or DC Scobie would have tripped over something with a curse, or DC Morgan would have trotted heavily up the cobbles to investigate the shadow of a stray cat, and the magic silence would have broken up as if it had never been.

But before that a sound as slight and sinister as any they could remember reached out to them from the darkness, a tiny inhuman whine, repeated and repeated, echoing off the rotting brick so that no one could be sure where it was coming from. They looked uneasily at one another, peered into the gloom, failed to see anything, failed to reach any conclusion except that it was coming closer; slowly, that tiny wail like an anguished metronome ground out at each hesitant step.

It was Liz who finally recognized it, though recognition did nothing to reduce the tension building under her breast-bone. She had to force herself to speak aloud. 'The wheel-chair.' The unoiled bearing squeaked with every slow revolution as the thing came towards the lights.

EIGHT

SHE STAYED where she was, silent, ambivalent, cloaked in a shadow that was more than just the setting of the sun. He peered for her as if through fog. 'Jenny? That is you, isn't it?'

Finally she spoke. 'It's me.' Her voice was as strange as her manner, seeming to reach him over a distance.

He kept wheeling towards her, as if it were a distance he could reduce. 'What's the matter, Jenny? Why are you hiding?'

It was a figure of speech, he didn't mean it literally, but she answered as if he did. 'I'm waiting.'

He was puzzled. 'For what?'

'For you.'

He thought then that she must have heard his outburst at the tent, had come to remonstrate with him. It was typical of their relationship that he still thought of her only as an adjunct to himself. 'I'm not going back, Jenny. I'm not talking to anybody tonight. I don't know about the future yet. I don't know if I want to go on doing this or not. Tell them to go to the pub. Tell them to go to the cinema. You can tell them to go to hell for all I care. This time I'm putting me first.'

There were a lot of things she could have said to that. By accident or design she picked the most hurtful. '*This* time?'

Like most things said in argument, it was neither wholly fair nor quite unjustified. Most of all it was unexpected. Davey flinched as from a blow. His voice was a plaint. 'Jenny! That's not— You can't think that.'

'Michael,' she said, and a hushed power was in her

voice, 'I've been with you for five years. I've done everything you needed, everything you wanted, everything you asked of me. But don't presume to tell me what to think.'

'I'm not, I only meant—' But of course that was exactly what he meant. One hand made an irritable, dismissive gesture. 'What's got into you, Jenny? You're not usually this—'

She supplied the word he was groping for. 'Sensitive?' He nodded. Even knowing him, seeing him clearly at last, she was amazed at his selfishness. 'Michael, you have no idea how sensitive I am. You've never wondered.'

He was puzzled by her rancour. He couldn't know what she hadn't told him, and they'd never talked about her feelings. It didn't occur to him that in five years they should have done. Then his face cleared. 'I know what this is about. Liz Graham, and the fact that I was prepared to ditch the crusade for the love of a woman. Well, you'll be glad to know it isn't going to happen. She turned me down.'

'I know,' Jennifer Mills said softly.

'She acted as if the whole damn thing was a figment of my imagination. As if I was a schoolboy who'd mistaken ordinary kindness for affection. But it was more than that, Jenny,' he went on, warming. 'I saw her eyes. She wanted me. But she wasn't prepared to give up for me a fraction of what I'd have given up for her. It was easier—safer—to pretend I'd made the whole thing up.' A bitter laugh reverberated in his throat. 'She told me—'

'I know,' Mills said again.

'No, just there now,' he explained, thinking she'd misunderstood. 'She told me—'

'I know what she said, Michael. I was there.'

Unseen in the growing dark, his expression slowly crumbled and fell apart. 'At Liz's house?' She nodded, the movement visible though her face was not. 'You followed me?'

'You made a fool of yourself, Michael.' There was a

grain of something like satisfaction in her voice. 'She never loved you. She was being polite: a nice woman being kind to a cripple. There was never any question of love. You made a mistake. Understandable, of course: you wouldn't know love if it bit you in the leg.'

He stared at her across the gulf of darkness. 'She also said—'

'She was right about that, too,' the woman said calmly. 'That was my mistake: loving someone with the emotional capacity of a shark. You devour people, Michael. You don't give, you only take.' Her voice hardened. 'This image you project: the man of God ministering to the frightened masses. It's an illusion. Anything they get out of your meetings they bring there themselves: their own strengths, their own decency. All you supply is ego. It's quite a turn-on, isn't it, rows of avid upturned faces hanging on your every word. You're a power junkie.

'It's a little like being a god yourself, isn't it? People don't go to a missionary for logic, they go for diatribe. They don't need to be convinced: the suspension of disbelief is their willing sacrifice. Hit them with the old charisma and they'll roll over and die for you. But don't mistake that for the real thing, Michael. It's a trick, that's all. Like a dog walking on its hind legs.'

From amazement Davey grew quickly to anger. He never could deal with criticism in an adult way. He thought Mills was mocking his achievements because her own life lacked fulfillment. A man of real moral worth would have been gentle with her because of that. Davey went for her heart.

'Five years you've been with me. Why, if you thought it was all a charade? Because you loved me? I wonder you'd waste your precious feelings on a crippled egomaniac! Or was that the point? Maybe you think a cripple's man enough for you. You're probably right: a whole man probably wants more than an old maid has to offer.'

She gave a low animal cry and lunged at him; he repelled

her with a swing of his forearm. His cheek stung and he felt the cool of blood on his skin. 'Use your claws on me, would you, you cat? You don't want to be so touchy. After all, you saw through the mask, didn't you, you know exactly what I am. A trickster, an illusionist.

'Well, you're entitled to your opinion, Jennifer Mills, but there's thousands of people all across Europe who wouldn't agree with you. They think I have something to say. They think it's more than a cheap trick. They come to me in despair and they leave with hope. Now, you can make fun of me and you can make fun of them, but the fact is they get something they need, something they're looking for, or they wouldn't come. And they do come, and keep coming. Hundreds of them. Thousands.'

'They come,' she cried, shrill with exasperation, 'because they're scared shitless about the horror stalking them and willing to try anything, even a bucket-mouthed Welsh prophet, for a promise of better things to come. Give you your due, Michael, you're good at meaningless promises. I should know.'

'It's not meaningless,' he shouted. 'What I teach makes a difference. You know that. Whenever we go back—'

'Things have settled down,' she agreed. 'No more killings. No more tarts with their throats cut. You still don't see, do you? The killings stop because they've served their purpose.'

Davey went cold. 'What purpose?'

'Frightened people turn to men like you. I thought that was a good thing. I thought, Does it matter if some little tart who's going to die soon—of Aids or drugs or at the hands of a dissatisfied customer—goes now, if it brings a whole town to its senses? I thought, It's probably the only chance this little whore will get to make a worthwhile contribution to society. If you're a surgeon or a teacher'—she smiled thinly—'or a preacher, your whole life's a contribution. But how many whores get a chance to change a community for the better? It wasn't hard to convince myself I was doing the right thing, even for them.'

Davey stared at her, and though he was deeply appalled it didn't occur to him to doubt. It fitted with what Liz Graham had said. It fitted in other ways too. 'You killed them? Those young girls? For Christ's sake, woman, are you mad?'

She considered that open-mindedly, then nodded. 'Perhaps I am. It can't be normal, can it, to do something like that? And take pleasure in it.'

'*Pleasure?*'

'Satisfaction then.' Her tone was conciliatory. 'It was at least that. They owed me that much. You did.'

'Me?' The echo was fainter this time.

'Of course you. I did it for you. Because you needed my help, and I've always given you what you needed. Even when I hated it. Even when I hated every shameful, sordid minute. I've prowled backstreets any decent woman would run a mile from, for you. I've dealt with the scum of the earth for you: pimps and madams and girls who make a cesspit of their insides for pay. And I've had to haggle with them, and tell them what you wanted for your money. I've had them in my car, bringing them to you, and an hour later with the stink of you still on them I've taken them back where I found them. Did you never wonder what that was doing to me?'

'I'm a man,' he mumbled, avoiding her gaze, 'and a cripple. I have normal needs but I can't take care of them the usual way. You said you'd help. You said you didn't mind.'

'I gave up everything for you,' she cried. 'I could have had anything I wanted: a husband, children, a nice house. Friends. I don't have any friends, do you know that? And I don't see my family any more because it upsets my mother to see what you've done to me.'

'Me?' he repeated, astonished. 'What have I done? I've done nothing to you.'

'You've squandered my life, Michael.' The bitterness in her voice sank to a quiet accusation that pierced deeper. 'I gave you everything I had—my time and my heart and my soul—and you used them and gave nothing in return. You let me waste my life on you. You said you needed me. I thought it was no distance from need to love, that if I served you faithfully you would love me. I could be patient. I didn't mind waiting.

'In the mean time there was so much to do, so many ways I could help. When you talked about your vision for the crusade I could see what you were capable of but it wasn't going to happen the way you were going about it. That was my mission: to make your dream come true. I thought that, by doing that, working with you and being with you and earning your gratitude, I'd make my dream reality too.

'And do you know, I really thought it was working? I ran myself into the ground for you, but it was worth it because I could see you, feel you, changing towards me. There was a warmth there that was more than the mere friendship we started with. I thought it was, at least, affection. I thought all my investment was finally paying off.

'I don't suppose you remember Hastings, do you?' There was no more light on his face but she knew from his silence that he did not. She gave an odd steely sigh that was half resignation and half indictment. 'No, why would you? It was nothing very special to you. But I thought—God, what a fool!—I thought you were proposing marriage.

'You came to my room in the hotel. You asked me to sit down, there was something you had to say. You apologized in advance for how clumsy it was going to sound but you were used to talking Grand Design, found it hard to discuss personal matters. And of course, being in that chair complicated the issue: it meant there were things you wanted but had no right to ask for... And you were talking slower and slower, and your eyes were glued to your knees.

'I came so close to making an idiot of myself that night. I could see how embarrassed you were. I thought I could put you out of your misery by accepting your proposal before you even got it out. I actually had my mouth open to say Yes—yes, Michael, I'll marry you, yes, please— when? Only what you actually said was, "So could you round me up a hooker?"'

'I loved you, Michael,' she cried in bitter anguish. 'I'd have done anything for you. But you shouldn't have asked that. If it was comfort you wanted I'd have given it. Comfort, companionship, whatever. I'd have done that for you, gladly. But it wasn't me you wanted, it was tarts—little tarts with their dirty minds and their dirty laughs. And always so young. Why, were you afraid a grown woman would despise your frailty? Do you think anyone seeing you in that chair would expect a perfect lover? Don't you think that a woman who loved you might not care about the bits that don't work?'

She was throwing too much at him all at once. He didn't know how to react. He stumbled, 'You said you understood—'

'I lied,' she said quietly. 'I did that for you too.'

Since she first dropped this bombshell—and bombshell it was, he had genuinely never suspected—there had been something he'd needed to know but dared not ask. Now he forced himself. 'You said, killings. How many?'

More than anything she'd said, the fact that she had to work it out, that it wasn't branded in the forefront of her mind in letters of fire, impressed on him how utterly divorced from reality she had become. 'Si-ix,' she said slowly, thinking. 'No, five—the one in Caen was a coincidence. I *was* going to do one of them—who knows, I might have picked her—but someone else had the same idea. I went to the cinema instead.'

'Five,' whispered Davey. 'Does that include—?'

'The two here,' she supplied helpfully, 'yes.'

'One was a hooker. One was a schoolgirl on a pony.' His voice cracked. 'What did you think killing her would achieve?'

Her voice was barred with irritation, as if he wasn't paying attention during lessons. 'You *saw* what it achieved. It filled the tent, night after night.'

'She was a *child*,' he whined. 'What possible quarrel could you have with her?'

'None at all,' she freely admitted. 'She paid the price of this bloody town's indifference, that's all.

'I knew Castlemere was going to be uphill work when I got here. The people I talked to had no interest in moral revival. I didn't want you preaching to an empty tent so I needed something to fire them up. I can still do that for you, Michael. I can bring people to you when you can't bring them yourself.

'I can drive into some town where I've maybe only been once before, late at night, and within half an hour I'll have found where the whores hang out. I look for the same sort of girl as when I'm looking for you.' Ice cracked in her voice. 'How does that feel, knowing that there are girls dead only because they were Your Type? Taller girls, older girls, thinner girls were all quite safe. They'd do just as well to put the fear of God into a town but they wouldn't satisfy me the same. Because what I did I did for you, but the manner of doing it was for me. My reward.

'I hated them for being Your Type. I should have hated you, only then I'd have had to leave. But you and your crusade were all that was left of my life: if I walked away I'd have nothing. So I continued to believe that, even if your feet were clay to the hips, your work was still important. Important enough to demand sacrifices. Instead of hating you I hated the girls, and when a sacrifice was needed they served.' She smiled tightly. 'It was after Hastings that

I saw what I had to do. It was a while before I could make myself do it, but now it doesn't cost me a moment's grief.

'When I came here last week and realized the trouble you were going to have, I searched the papers for some fresh horror you could stir these people with. But there was nothing. So I found a little whore and slit her throat.

'And do you know what happened? Nothing. It was as if she was a stray cat run down in the road. They didn't find her for two days and then she was in the canal. I left her on the wharf but someone tipped her in the canal rather than call the police! I couldn't believe it. What kind of people behave like that? There was a paragraph on page two of the local rag; the police asked some questions, didn't make much progress; then everything went quiet.

'It was as if the little slut had never lived. I mean, that's why I did it: so that her death would make more sense than her life. And these people didn't give a damn. Charisma had died for them, and I'd killed for them, and they didn't even care. Too busy, you see. This is a prosperous little town and everyone's busy grabbing a share. Charisma wasn't their business. They weren't interested.

'I had to get their attention somehow. If they weren't bothered by a tart dying in a dark alley, I thought, let's see what they make of a bit of butchery in their park in broad daylight. The girl on the pony was perfect: as soon as I saw her I knew her death would make the shop-keepers and bank clerks and factory undermanagers sit up and take notice. And by God I was right! Do you remember the tent that night? I thought we'd never squeeze them all in. I thought the canvas would split with their clamour.'

Her voice warmed as she relived it. 'Oh, Michael, do you remember how it was?—the excitement passing between them like electricity? Most of them had never been to a gospel meeting before, never would have done, and it was a revelation to them. The sense of involvement. The way a congregation feeds on itself, concentrating all that faith and commitment until those there are no longer individuals but combine in a great seething mass of energy, ready to move mountains.

'And you, Michael: I thought you were so fine that night. Incandescent. I thought, and I knew it was blasphemous but I thought, It must have been like this watching Jesus preach.'

Davey was stunned. 'A man damn near died because of what I started that night.'

She shrugged that off. 'Sacrifice is part of the process. I believed that what we were doing was more important than any one life.' Her tone altered abruptly then, all the fanatic joy going out of it. It grated like cinders. 'That was before you decided it maybe wasn't as important as getting into bed with another man's wife. The things I'd done for you, that I'd justified by the importance of your mission! But if the mission wasn't so important after all, I wasn't justified in doing whatever was necessary to make it succeed.

'That was when I looked at you afresh. You weren't the man I believed you to be. You weren't worth killing for. You were a man in love with the sound of his own voice. Not me, I knew not me, and not the little tarts you had me buy for you, and not even this woman who was supposed to be the great love in your life. Yourself: your own ego. The rest of us, even the people in the tent who were supposed to be the reason for it all, were just—props. It's all an act. I've spilt blood for you, some of it innocent blood, and you aren't even real. It's all been a terrible mistake. I mistook the charisma for the man.'

He didn't know what to say to her. She seemed to expect an apology. But he hadn't asked her to kill for him, was appalled by what she'd done. Even when he searched his heart he found no impulse of guilt. 'What are you going to do now?'

Her voice was edged with annoyance. 'I'm not going to run, if that's what you think.'

'I'm sure that's wise. The police know. If you want,' he offered, meaning it kindly, 'we could go to them together.'

He caught the movement in the dark as she nodded. 'Yes, we'll go together. But not to the police.' The gleam in her hands as she moved towards him was his first intimation that it was not one of her fingernails that had cut his cheek.

As THE CHAIR came slowly towards them, for long seconds Liz could make no sense of the shape coalescing from the dark. She could not tell if it were one person or two, male or female, in the chair or pushing it. It remained amorphous almost until it reached the little knot of people waiting on the wharf.

Then she saw that it was Davey in the chair, pushing himself awkwardly, the thrust of his arms hampered by the woman's body lying across his legs. Jennifer Mills' head hung limp, moving too readily with the sway of the chair on the uneven ground, and her eyes were open and glazed.

'I broke her neck,' Davey said by way of greeting. 'She tried to stab me and I broke her neck.' His voice was hollow.

But even allowing for the shock there was an absence of feeling, of any real awareness of what had happened, that made Liz wince. For five years he'd used a woman who loved him as a tool, a gadget he'd acquired to make his life easier, like his chair and his adapted car. It was perhaps inevitable that when she finally came to threaten him he'd put her down with no more regret than he'd destroy a dog that turned vicious.

Shapiro recovered his composure first. He shone his torch on the woman's face and put his fingers to the artery behind her jaw. There was no doubt in his mind that she was dead, but he waited for the absence of a pulse to confirm it. Then he looked at Davey. 'Where's the knife?'

The big man waved an unsteady hand back at the alley.

'In there somewhere. I didn't touch it. I didn't want to confuse the fingerprint man.'

Liz stared in disbelief. A woman who'd loved him madly had come at him with a knife; to save himself he'd used those great hands powered by the kind of muscles only men in wheelchairs develop. He'd broken her neck while her mad face panted in his: they were close enough to kiss when he killed her instead. And with her body warm and heavy on his knees he had enough command of himself, enough awareness of his own interests, to know better than to put his fingerprints on the weapon.

Liz cleared her throat. So softly that only Davey and Shapiro could hear she said, 'Because we wouldn't want people thinking any of this was your fault, would we?'

NINE

By the time Brady reached Cornmarket the darkness was complete. But he hardly slowed, and as he neared the shunting yard he was rewarded by a glint of moonlight on metal: a car tucked behind the last wagon. That removed any doubts he'd had. Scoutari had got to Donovan. What he'd got out of him would become apparent soon enough.

Sooner than expected, in fact: they'd left the wagon and moved down to the canal. Scoutari must have needed elbow-room. But he'd yet to get the answers he wanted because he was still asking the questions. His was the voice, low and with the characteristic rasp, that was doing most of the talking. Soon Brady could make out the words.

'Do you think I'm bluffing? Trying to scare you? Do you suppose that if you keep your nerve and don't say anything, pretty soon I'm going to throw my hands in the air and give up with a good grace? Be your age, Sergeant. There are things I need to know. Who you were watching: me or the mission. What's going down and how it affects me. Once I know that I can protect myself; what happens to you then is of no more interest to me. But if you don't tell me I swear to God, Donovan, I'll kill you an inch at a time.'

The huddle of figures resolved as Brady drew near into the shapes of men posed rather theatrically on the tow-path: one standing, one bending, one kneeling in the dirt. He assumed the man on his knees was Donovan: Scoutari was the man bent over him, talking into his face in that oddly flat, insistent tone. The third man was the minder but he was too interested in what was happening to do his job.

Brady came among them out of the dark as if he'd been there all along. 'How's about ye?'

Scoutari straightened like the crack coming out of a whip. 'Jesus! Who—?' Then he recognized the voice. 'You? You're too soon. I told the big man—'

'I know. And he believed you.'

Grudging respect put a degree of warmth into Scoutari's tone. 'But you didn't?'

Brady shrugged. 'You did what I'd have done in your place. Did it get you anywhere? Was it you or us he was watching, has he said?'

'Not yet.'

At the Glencurran accent Donovan's heart gave a cautious lift. Brady coming back had to be good news: how good depended on things he had no way of knowing. Whether he was armed. Whether he had back-up. How long he could keep Scoutari thinking they were on the same side.

'I keep telling you,' he growled, 'I wasn't watching anyone. I live on the canal. I saw people heading this way and wondered what was going on. For all I knew it could have been a card school, a dog fight or the annual outing of Castlemere Morris Men.'

Brady tried not to sound relieved. 'That's what he told me too.'

Scoutari grunted. 'Perhaps he didn't understand how much you wanted the truth.'

They'd hauled Donovan out of the wagon still tied as Brady had left him, his hands behind his back, his ankles lashed with the same short rope. He was on his knees because he could neither sit nor stand.

Brady sighed. 'Well, see if you can do any better.' Donovan's startled glance vanished as Scoutari moved between them.

Jimmy Scoutari had made his name as muscle to a previous generation of gangsters. Violence was his speciality and he'd chosen not to delegate it as he moved up the ranks.

It helped keep him in shape. So he could have continued much longer, except that after a minute or two Brady interrupted again. 'I don't know, maybe it's the truth.'

Scoutari stopped, staring as if the possibility hadn't occurred to him. 'What?'

'That he wasn't watching us officially, just being nosy. He does live on the dock—one of those houseboats, I've seen it. Seems to me, if this was official someone would have come looking—for him or for us—before now.'

'Kelso said you called in sick for him.'

'So I did. But they'd hardly shelve an operation because one of their sergeants wasn't feeling well. Don't let me put you off,' he added generously, 'thump him a bit more by all means, but I think maybe the reason he keeps saying that is that, pathetic as it sounds, it's true.'

Momentarily Scoutari was nonplussed. He straightened up, letting Donovan fall, and stood scowling at him. 'So what now?'

Brady shrugged again. 'Do what we came here for. Kelso's got the stuff. If you've got the money, let's deal and get the hell out of here.'

'What about him?' He poked Donovan with his foot. Then he did it again, harder, in case he hadn't noticed.

'I said I'd deal with him and I will. There'll be nothing to trace to you.'

Scoutari considered, then shook his head. 'I don't want to leave here with him still alive.'

Brady nodded understanding. 'And I don't want to kill him in front of witnesses. No offence, Mr Scoutari, just being practical. If the worst comes to the worst one day and you've got your back against the wall, saying you think I killed him is one thing. Saying you saw me do it is another.'

They were both valid arguments, neither man was being unreasonable. But one of them would have to give way. Finally Scoutari sighed. 'It's too important. He knows me, where I live. You can hit the road and disappear but if he leaves here I'm going down. I want him dead, now. If you won't do it with me watching, I'll do it with you watching. The law won't make much distinction between us if we're caught so you won't go round blabbing about it.'

Brady thought about that, then put out his hand. 'If you feel that strongly about it I'll do it now. But I'm not carrying. Do you have a piece?'

'I thought you were going to drown him.'

Brady eyed him askance. 'That was before you beat the crap out of him. I think we might have trouble persuading an inquest that he slipped crossing the dock when there's footprints all over him.'

Scoutari nodded and the third man reached inside his coat.

Brady knew about guns and he didn't think much of this one: it was more for ease of concealment than either accuracy or stopping power. But it represented at worst half, at best all the fire-power in the immediate area and he was glad to have it.

Donovan lifted his head, dirt caking the blood on his face, and watched him take it, and still didn't know if it meant he was going to live or die. He thought Brady was on the side of the angels but he had no proof, only Brady's word. In one way it hardly mattered: he couldn't resist even if he needed to. All he could do if Brady pointed the gun at him was roll into the canal, in which case he'd die just as surely but slower. He didn't know the depth of water here but it had to be enough to drown a man who couldn't sit up.

When he had the gun Brady looked round but there was no one in sight. Kelso must have decided against joining them. So far as he knew there was no one closer than Broad Wharf almost a mile away. The time of reckoning was come. 'I haven't been entirely frank with you, Jimmy. There was a police surveillance—a proper one, Drugs

Squad. But Donovan didn't know about it. It was luck and guesswork put him on to us, nothing more.'

Scoutari frowned. 'What are you talking about?'

'A police operation to track illegal substances from their sources in Europe to point-of-sale in England, netting those involved at every stage. He wasn't part of it. I was.'

For ten or fifteen seconds, which is a long time when anything could happen and still, second after second, nothing does, the silence stretched out thin and vibrant.

Scoutari was an unpleasant man, vicious and unprincipled, but he wasn't stupid. He knew the truth when he finally heard it. He knew where it left him: in over his head. There was no longer any question of salvaging the situation. Mere survival, evading arrest long enough to disappear, was the best he could hope for now. If he hadn't parted with the only gun he'd have shot his way out. But he didn't mean to wait meekly until the net closed and people turned up with handcuffs. He was thinking too intently to talk.

Brady also had too much on his mind for conversation. This thing had worked out less well than he'd hoped, perhaps better than he'd the right to expect. He had Scoutari and his people, and Kelso and his. He'd hauled Donovan's butt out of the fire. On the debit side, the thing ended here. Brady had hoped to finish the season, rounding up Kelso's contacts in all the towns they visited. He'd envisaged a kind of grand finale on the way back to Dover, looked forward to seeing in Kelso's face the realization that he wasn't going to get there. He could still have that pleasure but he couldn't pull if off long enough to pull in the dealers all round the circuit. Still, there was more to celebrate than to mourn. Brady made no move because he was counting his blessings.

Scoutari's driver was a large young man who took pride in his work. He spent time in the gymnasium and on the shooting range of an otherwise respectable club that turned a deaf ear to the rumours, partly because he won trophies for them and partly because if the rumours were true they didn't want to antagonize him. While he was good at his job he had no desire for upward mobility. He didn't move because Scoutari hadn't told him to, and he was busy wondering if any of this could be blamed on him. He was more afraid of Scoutari than of going to jail.

Donovan didn't move because he was trussed up like a turkey and he didn't say anything because he hadn't breathed for a while. For the first time he was aware of the blood cooling on his face, the sweat on his body. A cautious elation began bubbling in his veins. He thought his troubles were over.

But Scoutari hadn't got where he was today—well, where he was yesterday—without knowing a chance when he saw one. In a flash of inspiration he saw a way out. Not a complete solution, it wasn't going to get his business back for him, but it would leave him free to start again somewhere else. He wasted no time. As soon as the idea came into his head he acted on it.

Donovan was still lying at his feet. Scoutari planted a boot against his hip and pushed hard, and with a yell of alarm the policeman rolled over the edge into the canal. He hit the water with enough of a splash to suggest real depth.

'Now you have three choices.' Scoutari's voice was fast and harsh. 'You can shoot me in the back, unarmed, as I walk to my car, in which case you'll be able to get in there and get his head above water before he drowns. You can try and hold me by force, but that'll take more time than he's got and since you're outnumbered you probably won't even succeed. Or you can forget about me and save him. You can look for me later. There's nothing you can do for him later if you don't get in there now.'

Scoutari wasn't stupid and he wasn't a coward either. He had to walk past the gun levelled at his chest in order to reach his car. He did it without hesitation, without a backward glance, without breaking into a run. After a moment his minder found the courage to jog after him.

'Hold it right there,' shouted Liam Brady. 'I'll shoot you if I have to.'

'Then do it,' said Jimmy Scoutari, opening the door of his car. 'But you'd better do it quickly.'

TEN

WAITING FOR an ambulance to take away the body of Jennifer Mills and a suitable vehicle to transport a man in a wheelchair Liz was swept by a sudden fierce nausea. The blood drained from her face and behind her knees; for a moment she thought she was going to faint. She put out a hand to steady herself.

Shapiro appeared at her elbow. 'Are you all right?'

Embarrassed, she shook her head. 'I don't know. I suddenly felt—shaky.' She couldn't remember anything like this before. She supposed it was the personal nature of the thing: she'd been directly involved with these people. 'Can you spare me for a couple of minutes? I'll take a walk up the canal, clear my head. I won't be long.'

Shapiro understood, perhaps better than she did. 'Been a busy old day, hasn't it? Look, there's nothing to hurry back to. Mr Davey isn't going to give me any problems. Why don't you call it a night, go home? Brian'll want to know what's been going on.'

Liz gave a shiver that was only partly the night turning cool. 'I feel I owe Brian an explanation. But I'm not sure what the explanation is, or even what it is I have to explain.'

Shapiro chuckled, not unkindly. 'I think your first idea was the best. Have a walk, clear your head. Then go home. Tell Brian everything you can think of and work it out together. You've nothing to be ashamed of, Liz. None of what's happened is your fault.'

Grateful for that, she touched his arm. 'Thanks.'

The vehicles stopped in Brick Lane. The ambulance men removed the body on a stretcher, Shapiro helped manoeuvre

the wheelchair between the bollards. No one gave Liz a
backward glance as she turned away.

Walking alone, the canal free now of the terror that had
infected Castlemere's dark places for a week, she felt the
nausea pass, then the tiredness, then by degrees the confusion that had prevented her judging fairly her own role
in these events. The plain truth was both simpler and more
palatable than she had feared. Shapiro was right: she had
done nothing improper. She had acted in a friendly but
professional way towards a man who, whatever his short-
comings, was no criminal. She had not compromised herself either professionally or personally: that Davey had
thought otherwise was his mistake, not hers. Nothing she
had said or done, or omitted to say or do, had threatened
the investigation: if Donovan thought differently that was
his problem.

Or was she being a little too smug—complacent to the
point of naïve? Nothing had happened between her and
Michael Davey. Nothing had nearly happened. But she had
been attracted to him. If it had gone on longer, if he'd had
the wit not to confront her with it, could she be sure that
attraction would not have turned to temptation and temptation in its turn to betrayal? She couldn't.

Of course she couldn't. If circumstances had been other
than they were she would have behaved differently: if
Davey had been a better man, or Brian a worse one, or she
a different woman. It didn't matter. There was no need for
her to cover every conceivable eventuality. Leading one life
free of major disasters was enough of a challenge for most
people. There had been a potential problem; it never turned
into an actual problem; there was nothing she would have
difficulty telling Brian. It sufficed. Her heart lightened as
she walked by the canal.

Because it was too soon for the town to know there
would be no more killings she expected to have the tow-
path to herself. So she was surprised to hear hurried foot-

steps and see a burly man with a knapsack come at her out of the dark. His shape was distinctive; the accent when he returned, somewhat distractedly, her cordial 'Good evening' was conclusive.

'Mr Kelso? I'd never have taken you for a backpacker.'

If he'd made some similar pleasantry in reply she'd have thought no more of it. But he peered at her, jolted in recognition, then thrust her away in one direction and the knapsack in another. It was clearly meant to reach the canal but he misjudged the distance and it came to rest with a soft, solid thump on the edge.

He'd misjudged Liz as well. His reaction startled her but she rolled with it and when he was at full stretch grabbed his arm, tugging him off balance. He lurched across the path and into the wall; by the time he turned back Liz was blocking his escape. She was no match for him physically but she was as tall as he, she was trained and she was angry. She shoved her face at his and snarled, 'I don't know what you're up to but whatever it is I'm nicking you for it.'

Kelso could have pushed past her and run. But he must have known he couldn't outstrip a police officer both younger and fitter than he. He could have turned his strength on her, gone for her with his fists; but it was too late to take her by surprise so probably she would evade any attack he made. Even if he disabled her he won only a brief respite. He wasn't going to walk away from this.

For a time he'd thought he might. After the man he knew as Bailie left him standing unhappily on the tow-path, with enough proscribed substances slung over his shoulder to ensure that if caught he'd come out of prison to a pension, he'd thought again about what they were doing and whether the risk had come to outweigh the gain. The risks had grown hugely when they found themselves in possession of a police officer. Whether they freed him, or killed him, or left it to a man they hardly knew to kill him, the stakes were suddenly a lot higher than he'd bargained for.

Like the proverbial donkey starving between two bales of hay, Kelso hovered undecided on the tow-path for some minutes. Then he made up his mind to put what distance he could, actual and metaphorical, between himself and activities at the shunting yard. He was on his way back to the trucks, to return the contents of his kitbag to their place of concealment, when like the angel Nemesis the woman detective materialized out of the gloom as if there were no more natural time or place to take a stroll and bid him good-evening.

Betrayed utterly by his moment of panic, now his only real choice lay between co-operating with her and making matters worse. He knew he was facing prison. But if he could preserve that distance between himself and Bailie he could still hope to avoid a life sentence. He slumped back against the wall with his hands apart and let the breath run out of him in a sibilant paeon of defeat. He said, 'It wasn't my idea. Topping him. That wasn't my idea.'

Liz had no idea what he was talking about but her blood ran chill. 'Who?'

'The mick detective. I just wanted him out of the way till we made some arrangements. It was Joe Bailie wanted him dead. And Scoutari. Not me.' It wasn't true but he thought it might serve. It was important on these occasions to get one's own version in first.

Liz made herself breathe, searched for a voice. 'Are you telling me Detective Sergeant Donovan is dead? When— where?'

Kelso waved an arm towards Cornmarket. 'The shunting yard. Or maybe the canal—Bailie was going to drown him. I don't know, I came away. I don't need any part of killing a copper.'

Liz stared at him. 'What—just now?' Kelso nodded. Hope sent a surge of adrenalin through her veins. Anger throbbed in her breast. 'You stupid bloody man! He may not be dead yet. There may be time to stop it.' She took off at a run, as fast as she could and faster than was safe on the dark tow-path.

FOR JUST A SECOND Liam Brady thought there was a choice. But of course there wasn't and he knew it soon enough. Quietly, without obvious rancour, he promised Scoutari, 'I'll find you. Wherever you go I'll find you.' Then he dropped over the edge into the canal.

It was deeper than he expected, chest-high cold black water stinking of rot. He stumbled for a footing. There was no current, only the spreading ripples of his own entry, but the bottom was foul with mud and rubbish—broken prams, bicycle wheels, the skeletons of drowned dogs. When he lost his balance and went in over his head the water tasted of stagnation, a century of it, thick and sour and overly biological.

When he clawed the weed from his eyes there was someone above him, a woman on the tow-path who bent and offered her hand. He shook his head, rank water shaking off him. 'Help me. There's someone in here.'

'Donovan?' Recognizing her voice Brady blessed the fates that had sent him a professional. 'Dead? Alive?'

'He was alive when he went in. That's got to be a minute now. Help me find him.'

She threw off her jacket, then she was down in the water with him. Its cold grip on her chest drove a startled gasp from her, the stench she breathed in made her gag. 'Where is he?'

Brady circled his hands above the surface. 'About here. He's tied, he won't be able to get up. And I can't find him.'

They quartered the canal bed, searching with their feet. Even in daylight they couldn't have seen through more than a metre of stagnant water and a veil of green scum. The seconds ticked resolutely by, measuring off the time a man could live without air.

Liz tried to work faster, cover more ground; but she

knew that if she moved too quickly she could pass him by and never know it. If that happened he'd die. There simply wasn't time to cover the same ground twice.

Something snagged her foot so that she almost fell. Cursing she kicked free. But as she moved on there was a soft hurried popping as a string of bubbles exploded under her nose, glinting briefly silver as the moon caught their dying. 'Donovan?' Feeling her stumble over him he'd gambled the rest of his breath to gain her attention. If she'd already turned away, if she'd fallen or otherwise disturbed the water's surface, he'd have died at her feet and the best she could hope was that she'd never know how close she'd come to saving him.

'Over here!' She didn't wait for Brady but snatched a breath and plunged, groping for where her toes had been. Her feet came off the bottom but it didn't matter, she already had contact with his clothes, billowed out by the water, nudging the backs of her hands like soft blind fish. She found the line of his arm and hooked her hand through it, got her feet back under her and heaved.

For a moment, breaking the surface herself, she thought she had him. His body shifted against her legs, seemed to be lifting. Then the movement stopped and however hard she tugged she couldn't get his head above water. She pulled till her feet slid from under her again.

Brady reached them as she went under. But there was no more time. No time to explain the problem—that Donovan was entangled with something immovable on the canal bottom. No time to find out what and free him. He was an engine that had been running on the smell of petrol for two minutes and now even the smell was used up. The engine was going to stop.

But perhaps she could buy him some extra time—a couple of minutes, something. The idea was forming in her mind even as she was falling and she sucked in as much breath as she could hold before letting his tethered weight drag her under.

She made no effort to extricate him. Instead she groped along his body until she felt his hair—too long as always, but if he survived for Shapiro to complain again he could say with absolute truth that he owed his life to his dislike of barbers—stroking the backs of her fingers. Fisting her hand in his collar, letting her legs float away because she didn't need them now, she found his face and his mouth. She kissed him.

Whatever he'd been expecting it wasn't that. His body convulsed with shock and his head jerked back so that most of the air was lost in a silent explosion between them. Damning him roundly she turned for the surface.

Brady was waiting. While she took on air she gasped an explanation. 'He's down here, at my feet. He's caught somehow, I can't get him free. But I can breathe for him while you get him free.'

She went down again. It took her a moment to find Donovan, another to find his face. This time he knew what she was doing. He let her fit her mouth over his and took greedily the air she fed him. When her lungs were empty she left him.

Brady surfaced a second later. 'There's something big down there, a fridge or a cooker or something, the rope's fast in it. Do you have a knife? If I could cut it I could pull him out.'

Liz shook her head. Detectives, least of all women detectives, are not encouraged to carry concealed weapons. Brady started to say something else but she couldn't wait to hear it. 'I have to get back to him. Find something.' She dived, carrying Donovan's life in her lungs.

When next she surfaced there was no sign of Brady, nor did he appear in the time it took her to catch her breath. 'You *bastard!*' She thought he'd despaired of success and quit while he could, leaving her alone to decide when she was too exhausted to keep her sergeant alive any longer. That time would come: she couldn't breathe for both of them *ad infinitum.*

But it hadn't come yet. Stoking the fury that helped blot out her fear, she went down again.

Looking for Brady she'd lost her bearings, wasted seconds finding Donovan again. By then he was desperate, thrusting his head at her face. She gave him what she had left, returned for more. By now her chest was going like a bellows, cramps sliding knifelike under her ribs.

Brady landed with a splash beside her, glass glinting in his hand. 'If you can cut a man's throat with a broken bottle you can sure as hell cut a bit of flex.'

It took longer than cutting a man's throat. The glass edge sliced through the plastic sleeve but he had to break the wire filaments almost one by one. He tried to finish the job on one breath and couldn't, had to go up again for fresh air, wasted more time finding where on the flex he'd been working. Soon he needed to breathe again.

To start with he could feel Donovan moving under him, twisting as he offered his face to Liz, his hands to Brady. But as the seconds ticked by first he felt the tension in the long body mount, its movements becoming spastic with urgency, then seep away till there seemed to be no movement at all.

He thought, It's taken too long. We gave it our best shot but it took too damn long. But though he thought he was attending to a dead man his fingers kept working at the same frantic rate, his brain too numb with disappointment to tell them to stop. His fingertips stung as the effort opened little cuts to the putrid water.

When at last the flex parted Brady hooked his arm through Donovan's, planted one foot against the thing anchoring him and hauled with all his strength, and the flex pulled free. Brady shot to the surface, Donovan shot to the surface and Liz surfaced immediately behind them.

'Help me get him out,' gasped Brady.

'No time.' Liz tipped Donovan's head back until only his face, fishbelly white, was above the water. 'Support his back.' She tore his shirt open, put her ear to his chest. Then she hit him with the heel of her hand. Brady held him while Liz continued compressing his chest, counting as she did. Then she bent her face over his and blew two long breaths into him. His chest rose under her hand. Then she did it again; and again.

A hand touched her wrist gently. Angrily she shook it off. 'Not yet. It's too soon to say he's dead. As long as there's air in his lungs and I can keep his heart going he has a chance. Continue till exhaustion: that's what the book says, that's what I'm going to do.'

The hand found her again, rising from the water. It was very cold and its grip was weak. But she still thought it was Brady's until Donovan turned his head aside, choking up bitter water, gasping down foul air.

ELEVEN

THE FOLLOWING morning they gathered in Shapiro's office: Shapiro, Liz, Donovan and Liam Brady.

Donovan left hospital after a night under observation, a reflection less of his powers of recovery than of the fact that he was a stupendously bad patient, ill-tempered and grudging of care. Castle General put up with him until they were sure he was out of danger, then they threw him out.

Shapiro spent the night shuttling between his office, Superintendent Taylor's office and the interview room where Michael Davey was making his statement. He sat down at five o'clock to catch his breath and woke at eight with a stiff neck and creases in his suit.

Liz spent the first half of the night at the hospital being inoculated against water-borne diseases, and the second half explaining to Brian how she came to be French-kissing her sergeant in the murky depths of Doggett's Canal.

Brady collected the same cocktail of vaccines, reported to his controller, then retired to Donovan's boat for a good night's sleep.

Now they were trading accounts. Donovan had heard most of it from Brady, and Shapiro from Brady's controller, but Liz had missed much of the detail. She came straight to the point which concerned her. 'Your decision not to inform us that you were operating in Castlemere. Had that anything to do with my association with Michael Davey?'

Brady looked blank. 'Association? It's news to me. Anyway, nothing Davey got up to was of any interest to us. I'd been with the crew seven months, I joined up when they came back from France last October. I knew who was behind the drugs operation, who was involved on the edges and who had no idea what was going on. Davey wasn't involved.'

'Then why didn't you tell us what you were doing?'

'Because secrecy is what keeps you alive in this business, Inspector. If we'd tipped you off, the minute that girl turned up dead in the canal you'd have assumed it was something to do with us. Either you'd have turned us upside down, or for fear of compromising my activities you'd have left us strictly alone. Either would have made Kelso suspicious. The guy's cleverer than he looks, he'd never have made this work for so long if he wasn't.

'So we did what we always do: said nothing while it was going down. My chief would've been in touch once we'd moved on. You'd have got the arrests here,' he added generously. 'It suits us for people to think their local force got lucky, it stops them looking any further. But we didn't want Kelso touching until the summer tour was over. You can clean up a lot of towns in three months.'

'So you've been with them seven months,' Shapiro said thoughtfully. 'Long enough to know what Davey was and wasn't involved in. What about Mills? Had you any suspicions about her?'

'Neither of them was involved with the drugs,' said Brady. 'I was sure of that.'

'That's not what I meant. According to Davey, Jennifer Mills killed five young girls, three of them—our two and the one in Le Havre—in the time you were with the mission. Had you no idea that was going on?'

There was the briefest pause, then Brady shook his head. 'I wasn't watching her. Once I knew the drugs were Kelso's province I stuck with him. That was my job, Chief Inspector. I didn't need another one.'

Shapiro had a habit of nodding gently, sympathetically, all the time he was listening to someone answer questions; right up to the moment that the answer was finished and the interviewee sat back, modestly satisfied with his performance, when he went for the jugular. 'So why did you put Charlene Pierce in the canal?'

It was hard to know who was the most startled. Liz had heard nothing of this from Shapiro, Donovan had heard nothing from Brady.

Brady was startled too: it was the last thing he expected. He waited too long to deny it. 'How did you know?'

'I didn't, for sure,' admitted Shapiro. 'Till now.'

'No one saw me and I told no one. I don't understand.'

Shapiro didn't smile. 'The timing, mostly. She died in the early hours, she should have been found when people started moving on the wharf. Since she wasn't she must have been out of sight before then. Mills didn't hide her, she couldn't serve her purpose until she was found. So she was covered up by whoever discovered the body, before anyone else was about. Around the time you people arrived.'

'That's some lucky guess!' exclaimed Brady.

'Not really. Whoever hid her returned that night to put her in the canal. You'd had a long day, you had supper in the caravan then went to bed. The only one with the opportunity to move the body was the man who went to the chip shop. The same man who knew she'd been knifed.'

Brady didn't know Shapiro very well. Slowly he smiled and held his wrists out. 'OK, governor, it's a fair cop.'

Remembering the hours they'd puzzled over that sequence of events, trying to make sense of it, Liz gritted her teeth to avoid saying what she thought. 'In God's name, why?'

'To protect my cover.' He seemed surprised it needed saying. 'The girl had been dead for hours, she was way past any help I could give her. But she could still help me: she could get herself found someplace else. I couldn't call you—people like Joe Bailie don't call the police even when they've done nothing. And if someone else had found her you'd have been all over us and ruined everything.

'Whoever killed her was long gone—and remember, I didn't know who it was, had no idea it was anything to do with me. I thought it was more important to protect an operation that was steadily netting suppliers on the Continent and dealers in England, and would go on doing as long as it continued. So I covered her up—I'd have been seen dragging her over to the canal—and when the day passed without her being found I went back and put her in the water. I hoped she'd float far enough that you'd never know where she'd come from.'

Liz stared at him in astonishment and outrage. 'She was a sixteen-year-old girl and she was *murdered!* And you hoped no one would notice because it was inconvenient?'

Brady was swift in his own defence. 'Inspector, she wasn't my job. My job was infiltrating drug networks. To do it I risk my life on a daily basis for months at a time. I can't take on any more responsibilities. I'm sorry about the girl, but I still don't see her death as any reason to trash an important operation.

'I don't have to tell you all the different ways people die from drugs. They die of addiction. They die of accidents while under the influence of drugs. They die in fights over drugs. They kill to get money to buy drugs. They die of overdoses, of bad stuff and of failure to pay their supplier. It's a plague in every sense of the word.

'What are you saying?—that if I'd called you first thing on Saturday you'd have looked at the body then arrested the Iron Maiden? I don't think so. It was detective work, not forensic pathology, that found her and that was always going to take time. You'd have gained nothing if I'd called, and I'd have wasted seven months' work. OK, it wasn't an ideal solution, but let's keep a sense of proportion. Charisma was a tom, and she'd been dead for hours by the time I found her, and all you can do for the dead is bury them.'

'And Alice Elton?' Shapiro asked softly.

'The kid on the pony?' Brady frowned, failing to make the connection. 'What about her?'

Shapiro spelled it out. 'Alice Elton died because of the time it took us to discover who killed Charlene Pierce. If we'd started thirty hours earlier, and had the information the body could then have yielded, and hadn't been misled into thinking the killer hid her for twenty-four hours before putting her in the canal, we might have got to Jennifer Mills while Alice Elton was still alive.'

Brady tried to shrug that off but the words lacked conviction. 'Cal, who does your governor think he is?—Inspector Morse? No one was going to unravel that mess in three days, however fresh the body.'

Appealed to directly, Donovan made his first contribution to the debate. He said quietly, 'I think maybe you should shut up now.'

Genuinely confused by criticism he had not anticipated, Brady rounded on him. 'Watch your mouth, boy. I'll justify myself to your chief if I have to, but I won't be judged by a man who'd be dead meat but for me. I risked my life for you, Cal Donovan, I'll ask you to remember that.'

Liz said with a kind of restrained fierceness, 'You risked his life for your reputation, Mr Brady. The rest of us will remember that.'

'I don't believe this,' spat Brady, indignant and exasperated. 'I'm getting stick from one copper who can't even look after himself, and another who thinks it matters to Drugs Squad if she's playing away with a travelling preacher. What next—the Talmudic view?'

Shapiro had suffered enough serious, vicious, deeply meant insults from fully-paid-up anti-Semites not to ruffle a feather at this one. He said mildly, 'I'm not an authority, but I think the Talmudic view would be that none of the lives you claim to have saved, including Sergeant Donovan's, balances the death of that child. People who take drugs and those who deal in them choose to do so despite the dangers. They don't deserve your sympathy. And Donovan took his job, as you took yours, in the knowledge that there'd be times when he'd have to risk his neck to do it.

'But Alice Elton was a thirteen-year-old girl riding her pony in a public park in broad daylight, and I can't think of anything you could offer in mitigation if your actions stopped us getting to Mills before Mills got to her.'

Something his oldest friends wouldn't have believed befell Liam Brady. He coloured, the flush working up slowly from the neck of his sweatshirt. He said tautly, 'You can't know that.'

'No,' agreed Shapiro. 'But it's a distinct possibility. I don't know you well enough to know if it'll cost you sleep, but it should do.'

Brady stumbled to his feet. 'I don't think we're achieving anything. If you have a complaint, make it to my chief. As for your homilies, those you can keep.' He left, groping for the door as if he'd momentarily lost his bearings, and Shapiro made no effort to detain him.

Donovan came to his feet like a cat uncurling. 'Excuse me, sir.' He too was gone before anyone could call him back; had anyone wanted to.

He overtook Brady quickly enough that his superiors could eavesdrop without the indignity of putting their ears to the keyhole. 'We're not finished yet. There's still some stuff I want to know.'

Brady eyed him warily. 'Like?'

'Your chief—did he know I was your prisoner?'

'Yeah. He agreed the prize was worth the gamble.'

'Did he know about Charisma?'

Brady's eyes flared. 'Hell, no. He'd only have worried about it. I hoped no one would know. I was unlucky. Only for running down the Iron Maiden when he did Shapiro wouldn't have known either.'

'Jesus God,' exclaimed Donovan in a soft explosion of anger and despair, 'she killed five young girls. What are you saying?—you wish she'd been allowed to continue her career till a less awkward time?'

Brady began reasonably, 'I only meant—'

'I know what you mean. It's the same damn attitude we get from you people all the time: that drugs is the only real game in town, everything else is kids' play. You know something, Brady? I preferred you as a Provo. At least you didn't pretend to be anything other than a ruthless bastard.'

'Back in your pram, sonny,' growled Brady. 'You're a long streak of grief, Cal Donovan, but you're not so big I can't slap you down if I have to.'

'Sure you can,' Donovan snapped back. 'When I'm asleep and don't even know you're there. When you've got a gun in my back. You want a fair fight sometime, Brady, I'll give you one—just the two of us, no witnesses, no come-back. Maybe you'll still beat the crap out of me. But it won't solve your problem either way.'

Brady said, soft as a tiger's purr, 'I'd really welcome your opinion, Cal, as to what that is.'

'That you've become as big a bastard as the bastards you set out to stop. That in order to pass among them you've acquired the same sort of values. You haven't beaten them, you've become one of them. You're a whore, Brady. You sell yourself for money and a few cheap thrills.'

In Shapiro's office they heard the crack of flesh on flesh and exchanged a startled glance. Still they refrained from throwing open the door.

Donovan took the blow with more dignity than Brady delivered it. His cheek flamed but he looked down with only a cold smile. 'What does that change?'

'You don't know what you're talking about.' Brady's voice was rough with anger.

Donovan's was a sneer. 'You and the preacher, you're both addicts. For him it's the adulation, for you the deceit. "They don't know"—remember? Davey's habit blinded him to what he was being used to cover up, and you tell yourself that you do this for the public good when a man on a galloping horse could see you do it for kicks. And that's the story of your life.

'You weren't in the Provos from conviction, you did it for kicks. Then you spied on them for kicks. Now you infiltrate drug operations, and the reason's not all those lives you reckon you're saving, it's still the same one. There's nothing like it to get the adrenalin going, is there? You're hooked. You crossed the line between pretending to be a thug and being one when you stopped seeing the difference between risking your own life and risking other people's.'

Brady dug his clenched fists against his sides because he wanted to strike out again and was ashamed to. Fury left him helpless. He had no words, nothing left to fight with.

'I think you'd better go now.' With masterly disdain Donovan walked away.

In the office Shapiro turned to Liz with satisfaction in his eyes. He murmured, 'Sometimes I see reason to hope that young man will make a police officer.'

Liz smiled. 'So are you going to tell him what Brady's chief said?'

'About whether Donovan might be interested in a transfer? I don't see that I have any choice,' Shapiro said solemnly. 'A young copper's entitled to take advancement when it's offered.'

'Do me a favour,' begged Liz. 'Make sure I'm there when you tell him. I really, really want to see his face.'

A Taste FOR Burning

First Time in Paperback

A pyromaniac is on the loose!

The Castlemere police force is on a case that has become more personal and devastating than any other. As Chief Inspector Frank Shapiro is suspended—pending an inquiry into an eight-year-old arson investigation he'd led—it's up to Inspector Liz Graham and Sergeant Cal Donovan to put an end to the fires that have turned Castlemere into a hot zone.

Then Shapiro's son becomes a suspect and the investigators, including an unofficial Shapiro, must probe the dark side of parental love—and the desperate lengths one will go to protect one's own....

Jo Bannister

A CASTLEMERE MYSTERY

"Excellent" *–Poisoned Pen*

Available in December 1997 at your favorite retail outlet.

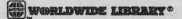

CAMILLA LÄCKBERG

THE
STONECUTTER

A NOVEL

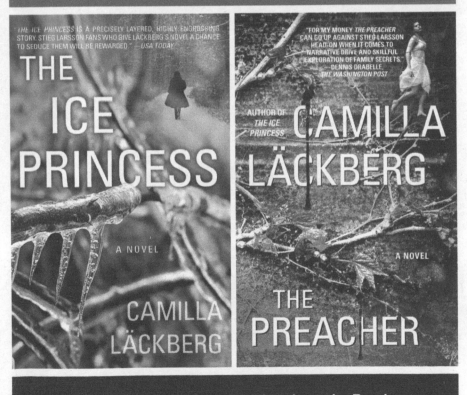

9 781451 621860

"An immersive thriller, spread thick with autumnal chill, and an astute exploration of a fragile small-town community. . . . Läckberg proves here that she can deliver grim drama with a keen eye for personal detail—perfect for those who like their summer reading dark, but human."

—*The Newark Star-Ledger*

"Intense, midnight-sun level of mystery . . . an entertaining read."

—*Bookgasm*

"*The Stonecutter* is one of those rare books that you will be unable to read fast enough, yet you also will want to savor slowly so you can delay the ending."

—*Book Reporter*

Praise for *The Preacher*

"For my money *The Preacher* can go up against the Larsson books head-on when it comes to narrative drive and skillful exploration of family secrets."

—*The Washington Post*

"A master of suspense and plotting, this Swedish crime writer shouldn't be overshadowed by her countrymen Stieg Larsson and Henning Mankell. Her new novel . . . is as good—and then some."

—*Entertainment Weekly*

"Läckberg weaves a solid thriller. . . . This fast-paced tale ensures Läckberg's place on the A-list of Scandinavian crime writers."

—*Booklist*

"Läckberg's many-layered story features plot twists and turns galore. . . . Stieg Larsson fans seeking more Nordic crime fiction may want to try Sweden's top-selling crime writer."

—*Library Journal*

"Läckberg's worthy second thriller show[s] a Ross Macdonald-esque love of twisted family relationships, while Läckberg's colorful, diverse police force . . . recalls the humanist touch of Dutch author Janwillem van de Wetering."

—*Publishers Weekly*

Praise for *The Ice Princess*

"*The Ice Princess* is a precisely layered, highly engrossing story. Stieg Larsson fans who give Läckberg's novel a chance to seduce them will be rewarded."

—*USA Today*

"Läckberg skillfully details how horrific secrets are never completely buried and how silence can kill the soul."

—*Publishers Weekly* (starred review)

"Excellent. . . . Off-season quiet in this small village creates a chilling atmosphere in which silence drives suspense. . . . A must-read for fans of Scandinavian crime literature."

—*Booklist* (starred review)

"Insanely popular. . . . A highly-touted, moody tale. . . . A monstrous bestseller in Europe."

—*The Washington Post*

"Chilly, deceptive and lucid, just like the icy environment it describes."

—*The Literary Review*

"Masterful suspense. . . . Läckberg combines her gift for intriguingly complicated plots and her keen understanding of even the 'grotesques' who live among us. Both erotic and terrifying. I couldn't sift the killer(s) from the suspects although I read obsessively. An absolute must for mystery lovers!"

—Ann Rule, author of *In the Still of the Night*

"Heart-stopping and heartwarming. A master class in Scandinavian crime writing."

—Val McDermid, award-winning,
bestselling author of *Fever of the Bone*

"Camilla Läckberg has a sharp eye for emotional nuances and psychological insight."

—Peter Robinson,
New York Times bestselling author of *Bad Boy*